JUNGLE IN THE SKY

By
MILTON LESSER

I0541533

ARMCHAIR FICTION
PO Box 4369, Medford, Oregon   97501-0168

*For more information about Armchair Books and products, visit our
website at...*

www.armchairfiction.com

Or email us at...

armchairfiction@yahoo.com

HUNTING BIG GAME ON GANYMEDE

They were big game deep space hunters, and their job was to bring back the rarest and most exotic creatures the distant planets had to offer up. They searched for their elusive prey from one end of the solar system to the other. Their adventures took them from the molten surface of Mercury to the frozen wastelands of Uranus.

However, the prize catch of these sought-after alien creatures were the wild anthrovacs, who roamed freely on the surface of Jupiter's distant satellite, Ganymede. These were the creatures the hunters coveted the most—though not as badly as the anthrovacs coveted the hunters!

FOR A COMPLETE SECOND NOVEL, TURN TO PAGE 81

CAST OF CHARACTERS

STEVE STEDMAN
He was hired on as an extra-terrestrial zoologist, but his real purpose was to find out how his brother had died in deep space.

T. J. MOORE
This tough, seasoned space captain was all woman—and more of a man than any one of her crew.

KEVIN McGANN
The Gordat's exec officer. At 200-plus pounds and over six feet in height, he was the one man aboard you didn't mess with.

LeCLARC
It was common knowledge that he would give up his life in defense of his captain. His loyalty was unflinching…or was it?

SCHUYLER BARLING
He specialized in bringing back exotic interplanetary animals to Earth—and he didn't care if he stepped on a few toes doing it.

BRODY CARMICAL
Barling's main competitor. His deep-space hunters knew they had to be the first to reach Ganymede—or there'd be hell to pay.

STEINER
Just an average, hard-working spaceman. All that he and his fellow crewmen wanted to know was…who was leading them?

CHAPTER ONE

THE BIG MAN looked at home among his trophies. Somehow his scowl seemed as fierce as the head of the Venusian swamp-tiger mounted on the wall behind him, and there was something about his quick-darting eyes that reminded Steve of a Callistan fire-lizard. The big man might have been all of them wrapped into one, Steve thought wryly, and there were a lot of trophies.

He was the famous Brody Carmical, and rumor had it he was worth a million credits for each of the many richly mounted heads.

"So you're fresh out of school with a degree in Extra-terrestrial zoology," Carmical grumbled. "Am I supposed to turn cartwheels?"

Steve cleared his throat. "The Placement Service thought you might have a job—"

"I do, I do. That doesn't mean any young pup who comes along can fill it. Ever been off the Earth, Mr. Stedman?"

"No."

"Ever been off the North American continent?"

"No."

"But you want to go galavanting around the Solar System in search of big game. Tell me—do you think they have a Harvard club on every stinking satellite you'll visit? Do you think you can eat beefsteak and drink martinis in every frontier-world dive? Let me tell you, Mr. Stedman, the answer is no."

"Try me, sir. That's all I ask—try me."

"We're not running a school, Mr. Stedman. Either a man's got it or he hasn't. You haven't. Come back in ten years. Ship out around the Solar System the hard way, and maybe we can use you then—*if* you still remember what you learned about Extra-terrestrial zoology. What in space ever made you study extra-zoo, anyway?"

"I found it interesting," Steve said lamely.

"Interesting? As a hobby, it's interesting. But as business, it's hard work, a lot of sweat, a lot of danger, squirming around on your soft belly in the muck and mud of a dozen worlds, that's what it is. Just how do you think Carmical Enterprises got where they

5

The big man looked at home among his trophies.

are? Sweat and grief, Mr. Stedman." Carmical yawned hugely and popped a glob of chocolate into his mouth. His fat lips worked for a moment, then his Adam's apple bobbed up and down.

The hunters wanted animals that lived on far Ganymede—though not as badly as the animals wanted the hunters.

Jungle in the Sky

By Milton Lesser

Steve got up, paced back and forth in front of the desk. "I won't take no for an answer, Mr. Carmical."

"Eh? What's that? I could have you thrown out of here."

"You won't," Steve told him calmly. "Maybe I'm just what the doctor ordered, but you'll never know until you try me. So—"

"So nothing! I said this isn't a school."

"They tell me the *Gordak* leaves on a ten-world junket tomorrow. All I'm asking is to let me ship along as the zoology man. Then, if you're not satisfied, you can leave me at your first port-of-call—without pay."

Carmical smiled triumphantly. "You know where we space out for first, Mr. Stedman? Mercury, that's where. I'd love to see a sassy young pup like you set loose on Mercury in one of the Twilight Cities."

"Is it a deal?"

"It sure is, Stedman. It sure is! But I warn you…we'll expect perfection. You'll not have a chance to profit from your own mistakes. You won't have a chance to make mistakes. One slip and you've had it, is that understood?"

"Yes."

"I'm not going, of course," Carmical said, patting his great paunch and saying with the action that he was too old and too fat for space. "But I'll hear all about the way you were stranded on Mercury, among a lot of Merkies and—"

Steve smiled grimly, said: "No you won't. Next time you see me will be after the ten-world junket. Whom do I ask for on the *Gordak?*"

Carmical dialed for a bromo, watched it fizz in the glass, drank it, belched. "T. J. Moore's in charge," he told Steve. "Old T. J.'s a mighty rough taskmaster, Stedman. Don't say you weren't warned."

"Thanks."

"Well, I'll hear about how you were stranded on Mercury," Carmical predicted.

"You'll see me after the ten-world junket," said Steve, and closed the door softly behind him.

PIT-MONKEYS scurried about the great jet-slagged underside of the *Gordak*, spraying fresh zircalloy in the aft tubes. Spaceport officers were everywhere in their crisp white uniforms, checking cargo, giving terse directives to the crew of the *Gordak*, lounging importantly at the foot of the gangplank.

"Name?" one of them snapped at Steve.

"Stedman."

The man flipped through a list of the expedition's members. "Stedman, huh? I don't see—oh, here it is, in pencil at the bottom. Last minute addition, huh Stedman?"

"Something like that," Steve admitted.

"Well, climb aboard."

And then Steve was walking up the gangplank and into the cool metal interior of the *Gordak*. His palms were clammy, and he wondered if any of the crewmen within the ship noticed the sweat beading his forehead. He'd managed to come this far with a surprising degree of objectivity, and only now did reaction set in, causing his heart to beat fiercely and his limbs to grow weak. *That T. J. Moore must have been spawned in hell,* Charlie had said—and now Charlie was dead. Because of T. J. Moore? Indirectly, perhaps, but T. J. Moore was responsible. Or, if you looked at it on a different level, the cutthroat competition between *Carmical Enterprises* and *Barling Brothers Interplanetary* was to blame. It didn't matter, not really. Charlie was dead. That alone mattered.

A big man with incredibly broad shoulders, hair the color of flame and a florid face to match it, came stalking down the companionway. Steve said, "I wonder if you know where I can find T. J. Moore."

The giant smiled. "You crew or expedition?"

"Expedition," said Steve, extending his hand. "Steve Stedman's my name."

The hand that gripped his was hard and callused. "I'm Kevin McGann, boy. Sort of a liaison man between the crew and the expedition, only they call me the Exec to make everything official. Better take some advice—don't look for T. J. now. T. J.'s busy doing last minute things, and T. J. hates to be disturbed. Why don't you wait until after *Brennschluss*, when we're out in space?"

"It can't wait. I've got to see that Moore knows I'm aboard and under what conditions, because I don't want to be thrown off this ship at the space station. If Moore doesn't like the conditions, Mr. Carmical can be called. But after we blast off it'll be too late."

Kevin McGann shrugged. "It's only advice I gave you, boy. You'll find T. J. down on the third level looking over the cargo holds. Good luck." And McGann took a pipe from his pocket, tamping it full, lighting it and staring with frank, speculative curiosity at Steve. "Stedman, eh?" he mused. "The name's familiar."

"You think about it," said Steve, and made his way toward the third level. Perhaps some of them aboard the *Gordak* had known Charlie, and McGann, being the Exec, must have been around a long time.

The third was the lowest level of the *Gordak*, or that part of the ship nearest the tubes with the exception of the fission-room itself. Here on the third level were the cages that in the months to follow would hold the big game brought within the *Gordak*. But the word cage, Steve realized, could be misleading. A rectangular enclosure, its wall composed of evenly spaced bars—that's a cage. But the bubble-cages of the *Gordak* were something else again. Precisely as the name implied, they were huge bubbles of plastic, complete with remote-controlled airlocks. You could pump in any kind of atmosphere, from Jupiter's lethal methane-ammonia mixture to the thin, oxygen-starved air of Mars, and under any desired pressure, too.

And now, on the third level, a battery of experts was busy checking the bubble-cages for defects, since a leak *after* some noxious gas had been pumped into one of the bubbles could mean death for everyone aboard the *Gordak*. Steve stood there nervously for what seemed a long while. He let his gaze rove up and down the third level, but he only saw the coverall-clad technicians checking the bubble-cages. Kevin McGann had said he could find Moore here, but unless Moore zipped on a pair of coveralls himself and joined in the work—which certainly seemed unlikely—then Moore wasn't around.

SOMEONE TAPPED Steve's shoulder. Startled, he whirled around. A woman stood there, just behind him, staring at him insolently. She was tall, as tall as Steve himself, with her close-cropped blond hair peeking out around the edges of a black cap. She wore what looked to Steve like a glossy black Martian sand-cape, which she let fall straight down behind her so that it almost brushed the floor. Under it, she wore a brief pair of shorts, also black, and a halter. She was muscular in that lithe, feminine way which had grown so popular in the twenty-second century—the century that had finally seen women come abreast of men in all sporting activities and surpass them in some that required special grace and lithe-limbed skill.

"I hope you found whatever you're looking for," she said. She spoke with a complete lack of warmth, which startled Steve for the second time in the past several seconds.

She was a beautiful woman, he realized, but she looked so completely incongruous among the coveralled men that Steve found himself whistling softly. "I never expected to find a girl here," he admitted. "Not on this expedition."

"What's the matter, are you old fashioned? This is the twenty-second century, the enlightened century, remember? There's nothing a girl can't do if she sets her mind to it. A recent survey shows that forty-percent of the homemakers in the U.S.N.A. are men, sixty percent women. Okay, it's only logical that some of the remaining forty percent of females have some tough jobs, too."

"I read the books of the feminist movement," Steve assured her. "But it's going to take a lot to convince me of that. Me and a lot of other people, I suspect."

"Is that so, Mr. Smart-guy? Are you a member of the expedition?"

"Yes."

"Well, anytime you want to hustle down to the gym with me and go a few rounds, let me know."

"Are you serious?"

"Of course I'm serious."

"Well," Steve said, deciding to change the subject and feeling utterly ridiculous about the whole conversation, "let's forget it. I was looking for T. J. Moore."

The woman smiled coldly. "That's me. I'm T. J. What do you want?"

"I—uh—*what?* You're T. J? You—a girl?"

"Will you please hurry with whatever you want to tell me? I haven't got all day."

"My name's Stedman." Steve felt his composure returning. The fact that T. J. Moore was a woman didn't make any difference. But unconsciously, Steve regarded her as a member of the weaker sex, and a large chunk of her fearsome reputation vanished because of it. "I wonder if Mr. Carmical contacted you—"

"He sure did, Stedman."

"Good, then we can—"

"Maybe you think it's good. I think it stinks. Listen, Stedman, maybe you think you can pull the wool over my eyes like you did over Brody Carmical—but you can't. He didn't recognize your name, I did. No kid brother of Charlie Stedman's going to make trouble for me because he thinks I was responsible for his brother's death."

"I didn't say—"

"You didn't have to say. I can see it in your face. But get this straight, Stedman. Your brother died on Ganymede three years ago—of natural causes, that is, if you can call some of the local fauna 'natural causes'. He worked for *Barling Brothers Interplanetary*, so I guess the rivalry between them and us didn't help. But no one killed him."

"I didn't say—"

"Is that all you can say, 'you didn't say?' Try to tell me why you came aboard the *Gordak*; go ahead, try."

"I'm an expert in Extra-terrestrial zoology, and you needed one. Mr. Carmical hired me."

"I know that. But I guess I also know a thing or two that Brody Carmical doesn't. All right, Stedman. You come as far as Mercury. But one slip, just one slip—"

"Okay, T. J.," Steve said, almost jauntily. "I'll watch my step."

"I'm the *Gordak's* captain. You'll call me that. Captain—is it clear?"

"No," said Steve, and laughed. The ten-world junket would be a hard, driving, grueling ordeal come what might, and he wouldn't kowtow to T.J. Moore, male or female, here at the beginning. "No," he said again, forcing the laughter out. "This isn't a military ship, so you won't impose any arbitrary discipline on me."

The woman laughed too, but it was more effective. "I won't, won't I? Once we leave Earth, Stedman, everything we do is dangerous. Everything. I've got to have full authority, every order obeyed at the drop of a hat. Understand?"

"No."

The woman removed the black cap from her head, and Steve noticed, not without surprise, that her pale blond hair wasn't close-cropped after all. It had been piled up inside the cap, and now it spilled down loosely about her shoulders. Smiling, she dropped the cap to the floor. "Pick it up," she said.

"Are you kidding? I'm an expert on Extra-terrestrial zoology. That's what Mr. Carmical hired me for. If you want that hat picked up, better do it yourself." Vaguely, Steve wondered if Charlie had met this woman during those final days on far Ganymede, had fought with her tooth and nail for some priceless specimen—and lost, with no witness but the bleak, desolate topography of the Jovian moon.

The woman turned away from him, called: "LeClarc! LeClarc come here."

ONE OF THE coveralled figures approached them—a thick-thewed man whose muscular strength couldn't be hidden by the baggy clothing. Not as tall as Steve or the woman, he was broad of shoulder and thick through the chest. He had a dark face and deep-set black eyes, and a thin scar ran the length of his right cheek, from eye to chin. "Yes Captain?"

"Stedman here is new. He questions my authority. I wondered if you'd like to work him over some—"

"A pleasure," growled the stocky, gnarled Frenchman, and swung his right fist up in a quick, blurring motion.

Steve didn't have time to parry it. The blow caught him flush on the mouth and jarred his teeth, sent him crashing back against the wall where he slid down slowly until he was sitting on the floor. Groggily, he got to his feet, wiping his bloody lips with the fingers of one hand. LeClarc, chuckling, hit him once more before he could quite pull himself together. The right hand slammed against his stomach this time, driving the wind from his lungs.

He started to fall, but he clawed at LeClarc's middle as he went down, and held on. Still chuckling, LeClarc cuffed him about the ears almost playfully, but the open palmed blows stung him and sent wild rage coursing through his blood. Clearly, that was the idea. LeClarc was enjoying himself—but LeClarc wanted him to fight back.

Steve got a hand up in front of his body, palm up, and drove it against the Frenchman's chin. He felt the neck snap back sharply, heard the sudden click as LeClarc's teeth met with savage force. Bellowing, the Frenchman came at him again, fighting southpaw and bringing a roundhouse left from back behind his body.

But Steve's wind had returned and now he sobbed air in great gulps. He ducked the wild swing and found the Frenchman wide open, pounding lefts and rights to the man's midsection. LeClarc, stunned now, brought his guard down. Steve was in no hurry. He chased the dazed LeClarc around an ever-widening circle, was dimly aware that the other technicians had stopped their work to watch. He jabbed with his left hand, covering the olive face with purple welts. He held the right cocked but did not throw it. Soon, though, he could hear the other technicians who probably liked a good brawl—muttering. The idea, as they saw it, wasn't to cut LeClarc up completely, but to instead win swiftly.

Shrugging, Steve realized that the anger he felt for the woman had blinded him, and after that, he unleashed his right hand, felt the searing contact with LeClarc's jaw, saw a couple of teeth clatter off the wall as the Frenchman's mouth flew open. Sagging first at the knees, then the waist, LeClarc fell to the floor and huddled there inertly.

Steve turned to the woman, spoke out of fast-swelling lips. "You're the Captain and I only work here, Teejay," he made the initials sound like a name. "So I'll take your orders—provided they make sense. That one about the cap didn't. If you want it picked up, you'd better stoop for it yourself."

Not looking back, he climbed the stairs toward the second level, wiping his bloody lips with a handkerchief.

CHAPTER TWO

IT WAS Kevin McGann who showed him around the *Gordak* after *Brennschluss*. Newton's second law of motion carried the ship forward through the near-vacuum of space now, and it would continue that way, plowing ahead at seven miles per second until it was caught and slowed by the space station's gravity. There the bunkers would be reloaded with slow-fission plutonium for the long dash sunward to Mercury.

"...and through there you'll find the fission-room," Kevin was saying. "That's about the size of it, boy. But I warn you to keep away from the fission-room long as that red light is blinking. Everything inside gets pretty hot, and there's enough radiation to kill an army unless the shields are up. Even then, I'd recommend a vacsuit."

"I'll remember that," Steve said, lighting a cigarette.

"Word gets around a ship like the *Gordak* pretty fast. I didn't see your fight with LeClarc, but I sure heard enough about it. There's only one man aboard ship who can beat the Frenchman in a fair fight, and—"

"You?" Steve wanted to know. But it was hardly a question. It looked to him like Kevin could take on two LeClarcs with no trouble at all.

"Yes, boy. Me. But now there are two of us, and you've made yourself an enemy. LeClarc doesn't forget easy, so you'd better be on your guard."

"I'll remember that, too," said Steve, laughing. "But it looks like you keep warning me about something all the time, Kevin. Why?"

"You're Charlie Stedman's kid brother, aren't you?"

"Yeah. Yeah, but how did—"

"How did I know, boy? It's written all over your face, and Charlie may have been with *Barling Interplanetary*, but a lot of us knew him. Charlie was the best, boy."

"Thanks. Kevin, how did Charlie die?"

The giant shrugged eloquently. "I don't know. It was T. J. who found him out on Ganymede. She was out tracking an anthrovac, and you don't track anthrovacs in crowds. Well, it seems Charlie had landed for Barling, and had the same idea."

"He never told me Teejay was a woman, but he said once she must have been reared in hell."

Again, Kevin shrugged. "It's open to question, boy. I don't like T. J., but I like working for her. You take a man like LeClarc, he'll die for T. J. All she'd have to do is ask him, and he'd die. You see, boy, big game hunters don't come any smarter. Trouble is, T. J. knows it and flaunts it. Also, she's a woman but she's strong as a man and knows it, too. She dares you to fight her every step of the way, and it takes a big man to—"

"I thought you said Charlie was the best!"

"And I still do. But a man's got to have some flaws. Maybe he couldn't take T. J. and had to let her know. The same thing happened to you after only five minutes. The gals have won their spurs in every field that was strictly masculine a hundred years ago. Men tend to resent that, especially when a talented woman like T. J. let's them know it, and no bones about it. So…that's T. J."

"Yeah," said Steve, frowning. "That's Teejay."

"What's the trouble, boy?"

"I've got to find out what happened to Charlie, that's all. But Teejay's going to be a problem."

"The grandmother of all problems, you mean. With all of that, though, she can still be all female when she wants to be. Maybe Charlie fell for her—"

"Charlie falling for that cheap, no good—"

"Careful, boy. She's my Captain, and a good one. I wouldn't ship out on the *Gordak* if I didn't think so. Careful. You'll learn in time." Then Kevin smiled. "You know, Charlie was a good-looker and attractive to the girl's. He was romantic—so maybe T. J. fell for him, too. Then they had a parting of the ways and—"

"Sure…" Steve was simmering. "Sure, they fell in love or something—only Charlie forgot to mention in any of his letters that she was a woman. You're barking up the wrong tree, Kevin."

"Maybe…maybe not. I'm only talking off the top of my head, boy. But it's worth considering." Kevin jabbed a thick finger against his callused palm. "What I'm getting at is this, whether they made love or not, I don't think T. J. would kill anyone out of cold blood."

"I'll think about it," said Steve.

A whistle then shrilled through the length of the ship. They were nearing the space station, half as far from Earth as Luna, and deceleration came upon them gradually and would continue to increase until they all had to bed down in the accel-hammocks for landing.

Unexpectedly, Teejay herself was checking in the members of the expedition as their two-hour stop over at the station drew to an end. As he approached her along the gangplank, Steve looked down and saw the station-men wheeling the small but tremendously heavy plutonium bunkers under the ship, each compact unit weighing a couple of tons with its concrete shielding.

"Well, Stedman," said the woman, the broad black sand-cape wrapped around her completely now, as if only the members of her crew had the right to see what lay beneath it, "I see you've never watched a ship getting ready for blast off."

"That's right," Steve admitted. "First trip out."

"You want some pretty sound advice? I'd suggest you stay here at the station and wait for the first Earthbound ship."

"Thanks," said Steve. "But Mr. Carmical hired me at least as far as Mercury, so that's where I'm going."

Teejay grinned. "You're a plucky kid, Stedman. All right, Mercury it is—but LeClarc can do the honors when it's time to see you off the *Gordak* for good. He doesn't exactly like you, Stedman."

"I've been told that."

"All right, move along. There's a whole line of men I've got to check in behind you."

A plucky kid, Steve thought, and laughed. She'd called him that, although he knew she'd probably have a hard time matching his twenty-five years. Well, she'd spent her life in space and on the frontier worlds. Maybe that did make a difference.

Five minutes later, they blasted clear of the space station on an orbit that would intersect the Mercurian ellipse at perihelion. From there, the *Gordak* would visit Venus, Mars, the planetoid Ceres, the four large Jovian moons. Titan and Uranus. Ten worlds in all the hunters would touch on—and each world would offer up its native fauna for the *Brody Carmical Circus*. Steve wondered if there'd be trouble with *Barling Brothers Interplanetary*. There generally was. But then he smiled without mirth, for the chances were he'd never get beyond the first landing on Mercury, anyway.

THERE WERE fifty men in the *Gordak's* crew and another thirty-odd in the expedition, and a spaceship being the complicated, labyrinthine device that it is, it wasn't too strange that Steve failed to encounter LeClarc until immediately before landing on Mercury. The *Gordak's* deceleration tubes had cut in and Steve found the most readily available accel-hammock in the general lounge. The Frenchman was stretched out on the cushions three feet from him.

LeClarc said, "This will be a terrible, hot place."

"I know. At perihelion, Mercury's not much more than thirty million miles from the sun." If the Frenchman wanted to bury the hatchet, fine.

LeClarc then strained to raise himself on his elbows against the increasing deceleration. "Sure," he said, "a hot place. After you foul up, Stedman, my vote will be to leave you on the hot side instead of giving you passage to the twilight zone."

The Frenchman was being illogical and pointlessly childish. "I didn't ask you to fight with me," Steve told him. "Why don't we forget all about it?"

"If you want to, forget, fine. But I, LeClarc, never forget."

"By all in space, LeClarc—" the voice came from the other side of the lounge "—you're a spoiled little child." It was the big Exec officer who spoke, Kevin McGann.

LeClarc did not answer. Kevin winked at Steve, then set his face grimly against the bone-crushing deceleration. Fifteen minutes later, they landed at Furnacetown. The names of the new frontier settlements, Steve thought with a grin, were as picturesque as the names of the old Wild West towns.

There was a huge, priceless matrix of ruby far below the surface near Furnacetown, and the frontier settlement existed to mine from it. But the place was named aptly, for here on the hot side of Mercury, the temperature was hot enough to melt tin and lead. A community of half a thousand hearty souls, Furnacetown shielded itself from the swollen, never-setting sun with a vacuum-insulated dome and a hundred million credits worth of cooling equipment. Even so, the atmosphere within the dome was a lot like New Orleans on a sultry summer day.

The mayor of the town, a man named Powlaski, met them at the landing field. "It's hot," said Teejay, offering her hand and shaking with the plump official, man-fashion.

"It's always hot, Captain Moore. At any rate, be happy that you've beaten Barling here this time."

"Oh, did we? Good. We'll need three asbestos suits, Powlaski. I never did trust plain vacsuits on the sunward side of this boiling mess of a planet. Say, has anyone got a cool drink? I'm roasting."

Someone wheeled out a portable refrigerator and the synthetic gin-and-orange stored therein tasted to Steve's thirsty lips almost like the real thing. Then LeClarc, who had ventured into one of the squat buildings with Powlaski's lieutenant, a middle-aged woman, returned with three heavy asbestos suits draped ponderously over his arm. Their combined weight was perhaps two hundred pounds, but it became negligible under Mercury's weak gravity.

"We're ready," he said, extending one of the suits to Teejay and helping her slip it on over her shorts and halter. This was the first time that Steve had ever seen her without the black cape, which seemed a sort of affected trademark.

"Three suits?" Steve demanded. "What for?"

"The third one's for you, Stedman," the woman told him. "I know your job is to see that the game stays alive in our bubble-cages, but I don't think it would hurt if you had a look-see at the stone worm in its own environment."

"That's not what I meant," Steve told her. "Why LeClarc?"

Teejay shrugged, zipping up the suit. "Because I said so, that's why. Also, LeClarc's something of an expert on the inner planets and he goes wherever I do, anyway."

"Sort of a bodyguard," the Frenchman purred, strapping a neutron gun to the belt of his asbestos suit. "Hey, who's got those helmets?"

And then Steve felt them slipping the thick, clumsy helmet over his head. Kevin stood nearby and the Exec looked like he wanted to say something, but Steve's helmet had snapped into place and from that point he could only talk by radio—and over the crackling interference of the swollen sun, at that.

Moments later, he'd stepped through an airlock at the side of the Furnacetown dome and plodded out on the surface of Mercury.

ON VENUS there was the thick, soupy atmosphere and the verdant tropical jungles. On Mars, the rusty desert and the ruins of an eon-old civilization. But on Mercury you knew at once that you trod upon an alien world. At perihelion, the sun swelled to almost four times its size as seen from Earth, and because Mercury's tenuous atmosphere had boiled off into space half a billion years ago, the sky was black. The sun had lost its spherical shape, too. Great solar prominences licked out at the blackness, and the visible corona seemed to swell and pulse.

Underfoot, Steve could feel the crunchy ground powdering beneath his asbestos boots with every step. And far off toward the horizon, a jagged ridge of blood-red mountains bit at the black sky like festering, toothless gums.

Before long, Teejay's voice sang in Steve's earphones. "Over here, you boys." And Steve could see her crouching, shapeless in the loose asbestos suit, off to his left. The sun's heat had parched a long, snaking crack in the surface and Steve lumbered over to it clumsily, letting his shadow fall across the crevice. "Those stone worms are umbra-tropic," he called, and waited.

"I don't wonder," said Teejay, looking up at the sun through the smoked goggles of her helmet.

The stone worms, Steve knew, were attracted by darkness— hence they generally dwelled in the deepest crevices, although a man's shadow might bring them to the surface. He'd never seen a stone worm, but he'd read about them and seen their pictures.

"You'll see something very unlovely," Teejay predicated. "The stone worm isn't a carbon-basic animal, but a silicate creature with a sodium-silicon-nitrogen economy. It's about four feet long and kind of like some ghastly white slug. It—hey, Stedman, get on your toes!"

The worm was coming.

It poked its head up out of the crevice first, and then the sluglike body followed, curling quite instinctively until the whole thing lay in Steve's shadow. Four feet long and a foot across at the middle, it looked like the product of nightmare. The head was one huge, lidless, glassy eye—with a purple-lipped mouth where the pupil should have been! The mouth opened and shut like a fish, but when Steve lifted the monster by its middle and brought it into the sun, the lips puckered fully shut and the white slug began to thrash dangerously.

But under the influence of the sun's heat it soon subsided. Trouble was, Steve thought vaguely as they made their way back toward Furnacetown with the quiescent monster, the sun's heat did not subside. Probably, it was his imagination, but the sun had seemed to become, if anything, stronger. He looked at the others, but they merely walked forward, unconcerned. Maybe he'd tired himself subduing the stone worm, for he knew that might seem to intensify the heat.

Inside his asbestos suit, Steve began to sweat. It did not start slowly, but all at once the perspiration streamed down his face and body.

It was then that his left leg began to burn. Down below the knee it was, a knife-edged burning sensation, which became worse with each passing second. Someone had heated a knife white-hot, had applied its sharp point to the nerve endings of his leg—and then twisted. It felt like that.

Screaming hoarsely, Steve fell and watched through burning eyes as the stone worm commenced crawling slowly away. It was LeClarc who went after the worm and retrieved it, but Teejay knelt at Steve's side and, surprisingly, real concern was in her voice when it came over the radio.

"What's the trouble, Stedman?"

"I don't know," Steve gritted.

"I'm hot all over—and my leg feels like it's on fire. Yeah, right there. Ow! Go easy!"

Teejay frowned or at least Steve guessed she frowned by the way she spoke. "There's nothing much we can do about it, Stedman. Seems to be a hole—just a pinprick, but still a hole—in the asbestos. It's a wonder you weren't screaming bloody murder before this. How's the air?"

It *was* getting hard to breathe, Steve realized, but dimly, for his senses were receding into a fog of half-consciousness. Something hissed in his ears and he knew Teejay had turned the outside dial of his air pump all the way over. It made him feel momentarily better, but the pain still cut into his leg.

"I've got the worm," said LeClarc. "But what happened to him?" He asked the question innocently—too innocently.

Teejay didn't answer. Instead: "Can you walk, Stedman?"

"I—I don't think so."

"Then I'll carry you. But remember this: if we get you back all right, you can thank the twenty-second century feminist movement. Can you picture an old-fashioned gal slinging a man over her shoulder and toting him away like a sack of grain? Here we go."

She got her arms under Steve's shoulder, tugging him upright and swinging him across her back in a fireman's carry. He felt in no mood to question her motive, but he could sense the triumph in her as if she had said, "See, I'm as strong as a man, and don't you forget it."

Steve couldn't help responding to the unspoken challenge. "Sure," he said, "I can thank the feminist movement, but more than that I can thank Mercury's light gravity, Teejay. We're lucky I don't weigh more than fifty pounds here."

An hour later they arrived back at Furnacetown, but by then Steve was unconscious from the pain.

CHAPTER THREE

"HOW ARE YOU feeling, boy?" It was Kevin McGann, the battered, unlit pipe clamped tightly between his teeth as he spoke.

Steve sat propped up in a bed in the *Gordak's* infirmary, his left leg wrapped in bandages from knee to ankle. "Pretty good, I guess. Kind of weak, but there's no pain."

"You're lucky the Captain got you back here in time. Four inches of your calf was cooked third degree, but she carried you back here soon enough to cut it away and spray on syntheplasm before deep decomposition set in. You'll be as good as new in a week, and no scar, either. Thanks to the Captain, boy."

"Yeah," Steve admitted. "Sure. But what I want to know is, how did it happen?"

Kevin shrugged his massive shoulders. "I won't make any accusations, boy, not without positive proof. But I took the liberty to examine your suit, and it looked to me like someone had punctured a small hole almost all the way through. The heat did the rest."

"You mean LeClarc?"

"I never said that. But LeClarc was the one who got the suits, so he—more than anyone—was in a position to do something like that. Further than that I won't carry it. This is not an accusation."

"Suits me," Steve told him. "And thanks, Kevin. But after this, Frenchie had better watch his step. Are we out in space again?"

"Yes. Passed *Brennschluss* forty-eight hours ago."

"What?"

"Sure. They had you doped up for two days, till the syntheplasm had a chance to set."

"How soon can I get out of bed?"

"Depends. If you don't mind hobbling around on crutches, today probably. If you want to wait till you can walk, four or five days. What's your hurry, boy?"

"I've got to take care of that stone worm, remember?"

"Say, that's right! No one knew what to do, so they suspended it in a deep freeze until you could go to work. A hideous brute, I might add."

"Will you ask the doctor to give me some crutches?"

McGann nodded.

"Swell. First, though, I'd like a good meal. And listen, Kevin— I guess Teejay saved my life, at that. Want to tell her I'd like to see her?"

"Of course," said Kevin, who left the white-walled infirmary, grinning from ear to ear.

By the time Teejay arrived, Steve was eating his first solid meal in two days. "Hello," he said. He almost found himself adding, "Captain"—but he checked the impulse just in time.

"McGann tells me you're ready to get to work today."

"That's right."

"Good. That stone worm won't stay in ice indefinitely—not when it lives on the sun-side of Mercury."

"Teejay, I want to—well, I want to thank you for saving my life."

The woman opened her cape, reached inside, took a pack of cigarettes from an inside pocket and puffed on one until it glowed. "Don't thank me," she said coolly. "It really isn't necessary. You're the only extra-zoo man aboard, Stedman, so we needed you. I'd have saved a valuable machine under the same circumstances."

"Well, thanks anyway."

"There's one thing more, Stedman. As far as I'm concerned, you haven't proven yourself yet. So the same conditions apply to our next landing point."

"Where's that?"

"Venus, of course. Do you think I want to play hopscotch all over the Solar System? Well, you finish your meal and give that stone worm a nice comfortable bubble to live in."

Teejay then departed.

LATER, Steve evacuated the air from one of the bubble-cages and increased the temperature to seven hundred degrees Fahrenheit. After he'd supervised a slow warming process for the worm and seen it deposited—still drowsy—in the bubble with sufficient quantities of silicon-compounds to keep it well fed, Steve hobbled with his crutches to the general lounge. Teejay sat there with half a dozen of the Venusian experts, for the hunt would be much more protracted on that teeming jungle-world. The woman stood up at once and crossed the floor to Steve. "How's the worm?"

"Fine." He always felt a little edgy and on his guard when she spoke to him.

"And how's the extra-zoo expert's bum leg."

"Coming along, I think."

Teejay turned to the six men seated around the lounge and said, "This is Steve Stedman, our extra-zoo man—at least temporarily. Stedman, Phillips knows more about amphibians than any man alive, Ianello is our arboreal expert, Smith ferrets out the cave-dwelling mammals—we hope, Waneki goes floundering around after sea-monsters, St. Clair is—"

Teejay was abruptly cut off by something buzzing shrilly on the adjacent wall. She flipped a toggle switch and spoke.

"Captain here."

"Radio from Earth, Captain. Mr. Brody Carmical himself."

"Is that so?" said Teejay, her eyebrows lifting. "Give me a circuit." And, a moment later, "What's the trouble, Brody?"

The big man's voice came through faint and metallic over more than fifty million miles of space. "Plenty, T. J., Barling has decided to start in the middle this year. Some of our...er...contacts told us his ship's rocketing for Ganymede, and fast. You'll have to get there first if you can, naturally."

"We'll get there," said Teejay, quite grim, and cut the connection.

Steve had time for only one thought before he was swept along in the general rush, crutches and all, after Teejay galvanized the room into activity. She might take orders from Brody Carmical, but she even had a way with the big man, making him cow to her—perhaps unconsciously.

Teejay was yelling and pointing, it seemed, in all directions at once. "Hey you, Ianello, shake a leg down to the fission-room and tell 'em to start straining. Smith, get me Kevin McGann on the intercom. Waneki, you can forget all about those Venusian sea-monsters and tell the docs to be ready for plenty of acceleration cases. You better bed down right now, Phillips. You're not as strong as the rest of us, not with sixty years of junketing behind you. Hello, McGann? Listen, Mac, I want the entire crew assembled in General inside of ten minutes. Yeah, expedition too. Everyone but those boys down in fission. And tell your orbit man to figure a way to get us off this trajectory and on a quick ellipse from here to the Jovian moons. Yes, that's what I said—the Jovian moons."

She paused long enough to take a breath and turn to Steve. "Well, Stedman, we'll be dropping down over your brother's grave on Ganymede before you know it. Maybe then you'll be able to remove that chip from your shoulder."

"Me? From *my* shoulder? Sister, you've got things backwards."

But the woman pivoted away, and Kevin's voice bleated over the intercom: "Crew and expedition—all to the general lounge on the double! You boys in fission stay put, Captain's orders. This is urgent."

Almost before Kevin's voice had stopped echoing through the corridors, LeClarc popped into the lounge. "You wanted me, Captain? You need help?"

"I wanted everyone. Everyone can help. Just sit still till the rest of 'em get here."

LeClarc looked a bit miffed, but he took a seat in glum silence. In twos and threes the members of the crew began to drift in, wild rumors circulating among them in whispers. Finally, LeClarc counted noses and told his Captain that everyone except the fission crew was present.

Teejay nodded and stepped to the center of the floor. She removed her cape and dropped it, discarding it so suddenly and yet with such a polished flourish that a complete silence fell upon the large room almost at once.

She paced back and forth, her bare, lithe limbs flashing under the green-glowing wall panels. "You've all come to know that cape," she said, her voice strident and alive. "It's a sort of affectation I have. But it's not necessary. Like everything that's not necessary, it must be discarded, at least temporarily. Men…we're in serious trouble."

Just like that, inside of a few seconds, she had them eating out of the palm of her hand. She went on to say that Barling's ship had already blasted off from the Earth for Ganymede, how, unless their efforts here on the *Gordak* were Herculean and then some, Barling's ship would reach Ganymede first. "And you all know what that would mean," she continued. "Like the elephant of two centuries ago, the Ganymeden anthrovac is the one solid necessity for any circus sideshow. But the anthrovacs have a way of going into hiding when they're disturbed. So, if Barling gets to Ganymede first, we've had it. We can all start looking for jobs after that. Do you understand? I want full acceleration from here to Ganymede, as soon as we can get the new orbit plotted. Nothing but the immediate problem—to reach the Jovian moons before Barling—nothing else matters. If I tell you to work two shifts and go without sleep one night, you will do that. If I decide that a man must go beyond the shieldings in fission, he'll climb into a vacsuit and hope for the best. It's going to be like that, men, and I can't help it. I crack the whip and you jump. Any questions?"

She stood dramatically, hands on hips, somehow poised on tiptoes without straining, a tall, impressive and quite beautiful figure.

"Yes," said one of the orbiteers. "I have a question. Can I get to work on the new orbit at once?"

There were hoarse shouts of approval, some applause and a scattering of deep-throated laughter. Steve watched Teejay walk off her improvised stage, complete master of the situation. If it were humanly possible for the *Gordak* to reach Ganymede before Barling, they'd do it.

IN THE WEEKS that followed, Steve learned something of what the big Exec officer had meant that first day he had spoken about Teejay. She drove her men relentlessly and some of them may have resented it. But she drove herself as well, and once when a crewman had gone beyond the shieldings to repair the mechanical arms which regulated the flow of powdered plutonium fuel from the bunkers and had emerged with a serious case of radiation sickness, Teejay donned a vacsuit and went in herself to finish the job.

Most of the men liked her. Some, frankly, did not. But all of them knew they served under a captain as good as any.

Two days before landing on Ganymede, Teejay gathered her chief lieutenants for a final planning session. Kevin was there, and LeClarc, and a tall, wraith-thin man with a bushy head of white hair named Simonson, and Steve. Teejay spread a chart out and peered down at it intently. "This is Ganymede Northeast," she said, indicating the circled, central area of the map. "It is here that, for some reason, the anthrovacs gather. And here inside the circle is an area of one thousand square miles that Mr. Simonson has marked off—yes, Stedman, the red square. We'll be operating there. If the Barling ship has landed ahead of us, we can assume the same for them."

Teejay paused to light a cigarette, then crushed it out after her first puff. "The darn smoke gets in my way when I try to think," she smiled, and went on, "Anyway, here's the square. We'll be using the crew and the expedition—everyone aboard ship— because we're in a hurry. Simply put, we'll be a bunch of beaters to drive the anthrovacs together at the center of the square. Then, well, then it's up to Mr. Simonson and Stedman. Any questions?"

"Yes, Captain," said LeClarc. "Just how do we get the anthrovacs aboard ship?"

"Don't ask me. But you might ask Mr. Simonson."

The bushy-haired man named Simonson grunted. "Ummmm. There are several ways. We could set up elaborate traps, such as Thorndyke employed two years ago, and—"

"Can't," Teejay objected. "No time."

"Why don't we just clobber them?" LeClarc suggested. "A few might die, but we'll get the specimens we want."

Steve shook his head. "You don't know your anthrovacs. Chase them and they'll try to run away. But hurt them—just hurt one of them so the rest of them can see—and they'll swarm all over you until either all the men or all the anthrovacs are dead, or both. No, there's another way."

"What's that?" Teejay leaned forward, chin cupped in hands, definitely interested.

"Anthrovacs are non-breathers. Most gasses won't hurt them, but you can give them a good, old-fashioned oxygen jag with the slightest whiff of pure oxygen."

"I've heard of that," Simonson said.

"Sort of like getting them drunk, isn't it, boy?" Kevin wanted to know.

But LeClarc wasn't satisfied. "I still say we ought to clobber them. We can't waste time experimenting with any crazy jags."

"It's no experiment," Steve told him coldly. "It works."

"I still say we ought to—"

"Clobber them, I know," Teejay finished for him. "If there's any clobbering to be done, LeClarc, I'll let you know. Meanwhile, we're trying Stedman's plan. Any further questions?"

No one spoke.

"Good. Mac, I want you to let Mr. Simonson and Stedman pick three men to help them. You're to divide the rest of us into groups of half a dozen each, with each group serving under a leader. I'll give each leader a designated area in that square, so there won't be a lot of bumbling around when we land on Ganymede. LeClarc..."

"Yes, Captain?"

"Take yourself a group of three idle technicians and check all the vacsuits. If there's any trouble, make sure it's repaired before we land. What are you gawking at me like that for?"

"I only thought—"

"What? What did you think? Speak up, man..."

"I thought you would have a job of more importance for me. Had you, for example, decided that we ought to clobber—"

"Clobber, clobber, clobber! Will you shut up and get to work?"

"Yes, Captain." And then more than a little stooped of shoulder, LeClarc left the lounge.

Teejay didn't pause for breath. "You...Stedman...what's so funny? What are you laughing about?"

"Nothing. It's just the way LeClarc—"

"Forget it, before you get clobbered."

CHAPTER FOUR

GANYMEDE. After the landing, an unreasoning fear gripped Steve tightly. It wasn't anything he could put his finger on, but he felt it gnawing at the fringes of his mind, probing, seeking, thrusting for a way in. There was nothing to be afraid of, and Steve smoked one cigarette after another while the six-man parties disembarked to take up their beater-stations on the edges of the square.

Ganymede, he recited to himself, is the largest satellite in the Solar System. 664,200 miles from Jupiter, it has a diameter of thirty two hundred and six miles, or bigger than the planet Mercury and almost as large as Pluto. It swings around Jupiter in a little over seven Earth days and in appearance its moonscape was enough like Luna to be a twin-brother, except for fat, bloated Jupiter hanging in the sky.

What was there to be afraid of? Steve didn't know. His brother had died on Ganymede—and the circumstances of Charlie's death still bordered on the mysterious. Well, he'd see for himself about that. Did the fear crawl around the edges of his brain because he thought Teejay was responsible? But that didn't make sense, for to a certain degree he'd thought that all along. Unless the appalling thought of having to fight Teejay and her whole loyal crew had taken hold of him unconsciously.

"What are you moping about, boy?"

"Huh? Oh…Kevin. Nothing much, I guess. I—"

"You look to me like you've seen a ghost. What is it, scared?"

"Yeah. Yeah, I guess so."

"So what? Buck up, boy."

"I don't want to be scared."

"Who does?"

"That's not what I mean. It's one thing to say that if you aren't—"

"Who isn't? Don't look at me, boy. And didn't you watch all the men trooping outside with the blood drained from their faces, and their eyes sort of big and too bright behind the faceplates? We're all scared."

"But why?"

"Mean to say you spent too much time on zoology and forgot about other things? Like, for instance, Ganymede-fear?"

"Huh? How's that?"

"Everyone is afraid, Steve. Everyone. Whenever a man gets near Ganymede, he suddenly becomes afraid. It's some sort of a psychological or maybe para-psychological phenomenon and none of the medicos could ever figure it out. It isn't the kind of fear that paralyzes, boy, but still, it holds on all the time a man's on Ganymede and it doesn't leave until he blasts off again. Didn't you ever hear about that?"

"No. That is, I knew it happened somewhere, but I forgot where."

"Well, that's all there is to it, boy."

"All? Don't you think it's enough? Something lurks out there, something makes people afraid, and we've never been able to find out why, but you say—"

Teejay came up and smiled at them, but there was something grim about her smile. "You can always tell when someone comes to Ganymede for the first time. He's jumpier. Just relax, Stedman. By the time they start beating the anthrovacs in toward the *Gordak* you'll be feeling better—and raring to go to work with that oxygen-jag stunt of yours, too." And she added, "Say, have you been watching your stone worm?"

"He sure has," Kevin told her. "He took me down there yesterday and that worm's been growing fat on all the sand he's fed it. Sand for food...that's what that worm eats. Imagine how that would settle the over-population problems on Earth if people, too, could eat sand."

"Yes, and then..." Teejay was speaking again, but her words were lost to Steve as he stopped listening. It occurred to him all at once that they were engrossed in their meaningless conversation for one reason only—to keep the fear from their minds. If you thought about something else, the fear would retreat at least in part, and if you could hold a conversation about everything and nothing, that was even better.

Steve almost jumped off the floor when a metallic voice blared forth from the loudspeaker, echoing and re-echoing in the near-empty room.

"Captain! Captain, this is Moretti, Group Seven."

"Go ahead, Moretti," Teejay said into the mike. "I'm listening."

"Who the devil's on radar, Captain?"

"Why—no one! We forgot."

"There's a ship coming down. We can see it plain as day out here."

"What ship?" Teejay asked softly, but they all knew the question was totally unnecessary.

Moretti's voice dropped almost to a whisper as he uttered, "It's Barling..."

WITHIN TEN minutes, all the beaters had been called in. Barling's big ship, the *Frank Buck*, snorted back and forth angrily on its landing jets.

"Are they gonna land or ain't they gonna land?" someone said as Kevin broke out the neutron guns and saw that every third man had one.

"Depends on their boss," said Kevin. "If he figures we can be scared off, he'll land. Otherwise, maybe he'll go away."

"Not that little stinker," Teejay told him. "Not Schuyler Barling. He won't go away. Will the fact that we're here first matter? It will not, for Schuyler knows we can't prove it. You ought to know better than to hope for that, Kevin. No, we can figure that Schuyler will move in on us."

"What happens then?" Steve demanded.

Teejay shrugged her bare, beautiful shoulders. "That I don't know. Schuyler may be a stinker and may be predictable, but he's not *that* predictable. Hey, it looks like the *Frank Buck* is coming down."

The big ship, Steve saw, was doing precisely that. Its jets had been cut, and the ship fell like a stone. Twice its length separated it from the rubble-strewn pumice when the pilot kicked his jets over again, and something seemed to slap the *Frank Buck* back up toward the starry sky. The result was a first-rate landing.

"That would be Schuyler showing off," said Teejay wearily. He must have been born in a tube and weaned on jet-slag, and he sure lets you know it."

Fifteen minutes later, Schuyler Barling and three of his officers entered the *Gordak*.

Barling got out of his vacsuit first, a tall, handsome man of about thirty, with short-cropped blond hair, pale blue eyes and petulant lips. "Captain Moore," he said, bowing slightly from the waist. Making fun of Teejay.

"Mr. Barling…" As ever, the woman seemed cool and unruffled.

"With us," said Schuyler Barling, "it's in the family. I work for my father. Obviously, it means something to me whether he succeeds or not. But you, Captain Moore, you're a hired hand. You work for Brody Carmical, on a paycheck. Therefore, your loyalty could not possibly be as strong as mine, and—"

"Get to the point!"

"We arrived here on Ganymede almost simultaneously. One of us will have to leave."

"It didn't look simultaneous to me."

Barling ignored her. "Yes, one will have to leave, because the anthrovac is frightened off easily and unless a hunt is carried on with the utmost precision and timing, no one will catch any anthrovacs."

"Go on," said Teejay. She spoke quietly, but Steve knew the woman well enough to realize her temper was coming to a boil, inside.

"My *Frank Buck* got here first," Barling told her blandly. "Therefore, you will leave."

"That's a stinking lie!" Teejay cried. "We were here first and you know it."

"Who can prove it? The *Frank Buck* landed first." Barling's hand flashed down to his waist and came up gripping a neutron gun. "If we have to, we'll force you to leave."

Teejay stood with hands on hips, facing him. "I know I'm not conducting myself like a lady, but then, this is the twenty-second century," she said, smiling—and struck out with her balled right fist. It bounced off Barling's jaw with savage force and the man stumbled back against the wall and crashed to the floor, his neutron gun clattering away. Barling shook himself, tried to rise. He got to hands and knees, then fell forward on his face.

Teejay whirled on his officers.

"All right, get him out of here! Come on, move."

THE THREE men looked at each other. None of them did anything.

"You see, boy?" said Kevin, grinning. "That's our Captain and we'll fight for her. She won the beauty pageant five years ago in Cerestown, and she can fight like a man. She's a woman for the stars, and we're proud to—"

"Shut up," said Teejay. "That won't get us anywhere."

By now, Barling had stirred, had come up, dazed, into a sitting position. He rubbed his jaw, winced. "Assuming we return to our ship, we still won't leave Ganymede. Not without our anthrovac."

"Nor will we."

"But you had to hit me! You had to flaunt your—"

"No one told you to draw your gun."

"—flaunt your Amazonian prowess."

"Stop sniveling, Schuyler. I think we'll have to reach some sort of a compromise, but I'll dictate terms, not you."

"Yes?" Barling growled up at her. "Who says we'll obey?"

"Get up off the floor! You look so silly, sitting there and rubbing your chin.

Barling stood up, retrieving his gun but holstering it. Kevin watched him, toying with his own weapon—not pointing it at anyone in particular, but tossing it back and forth idly from hand to hand.

"Give us twenty four hours," said Teejay. "We'll look for our anthrovac. In that time, none of your men are to leave the *Frank Buck*. After that, you get twenty-four hours, and we're confined to the *Gordak*. Then us, then you. And so on, till one of us gets his anthrovac. Then he pulls out and the other is left here. Is it a deal?"

Barling considered, said: "Well, yes—with one change. *We* get the first twenty four hours."

"No."

"Then you can forget your deal, Captain Moore."

"Well, then let's toss for it." Teejay reached into a pocket of her cape, flipped a coin to Steve. "Here, Stedman. You toss it."

"Who gets to call?" Barling demanded.

"Do you want to?"

"Well—"

"Good. Then I will. Ladies first, you know. Go ahead, Stedman."

Steve tossed the coin, and Teejay cried: "Heads!"

Palming the coin, Steve flipped it over on the back of his left hand, peered at it. Staring up at him was the metallic likeness of Angus MacNamara, first man to reach the planet Mars. "Heads," said Steve, and one of Barling's officers came over to verify it.

Barling shook his head stubbornly. "How do I know it isn't a phony, a two-headed coin?"

Teejay glared at him. "That's insulting, Schuyler."

"Well, I'd like to look at it. How do I know—"

"You don't. But I said it's insulting. So, if you want to see the coin, you'll have to fight me!"

"Never mind," said Barling, climbing into his vacsuit. "You get first try." And all of them garbed in their vacsuits once more, the men of the *Frank Buck* departed.

"Get those beaters out again!" Teejay was calling into her microphone.

Kevin grasped Steve's arm and said, "Go ahead, boy. Look at the coin."

Steve did. It had two heads. And later, Teejay said to him, "Listen, Stedman. All the beaters are out now, but frankly, I don't trust Schuyler."

Steve said he didn't blame her and Kevin was there to nod his red head.

"So, Stedman, the beaters have their jobs to do. That's almost everyone. But temporarily at least. It leaves you and Mac here with nothing to do."

"That's true," said Kevin.

"But not for long, Mac. Schuyler may try something, I don't know what. You two are probably the strongest men on this ship. I know what you can do, Mac—and I saw a sample of Stedman at work when he had that little run-in with LeClarc. All right...you two hop into a couple of vacsuits. That is, if Stedman's ready to fight for us if he has to—"

Steve chuckled. "I don't go around carrying two-headed coins Teejay, but I know a rat when I see one. I'll go...and your friend Schuyler better not try anything." He was almost surprised at his own words. Teejay had a way of garnering respect, and if he didn't watch himself, he'd be talking like Kevin soon. Well, perhaps the woman merited it. His thoughts took him that far, and then he remembered Charlie. "I'll go," he said again, almost growling.

"But you still have a chip on your shoulder—well, never mind. I'll expect quarter-hourly reports from you two."

"You'll get them," said Kevin, climbing into his vacsuit.

INCREDIBLY, Steve found himself out on the bleak, desolate surface of Ganymede, walking with Kevin past the long, silent length of the *Frank Buck*. And here outside the confining walls of their spaceship, the Ganymede-fear seemed stronger. Steve felt it as something palpable, clutching at his heart and constricting it, bringing sweat to his forehead and clouding the inside of his helmet with moisture.

Fear—of what?

Not of the frontier world itself surely. Not of some unknown menace lurking out among the craterlets and ringwalls. No, for while Ganymede was not yet as familiar as Mars or Venus, mankind had still explored it extensively. There were the strange anthrovacs animals that looked like over-sized and less brutish gorillas but which were not protoplasm creatures and which took their energy directly from sunlight and cosmic radiation. But that was all—no other life existed on Ganymede, and the anthrovacs on their frigid, airless world were something of an oddity.

Then what caused the fear? And was the fear responsible in any way for what had happened to Charlie?

"Hey, Steve…snap, out of it," Kevin's voice floated in thinly on the intercom.

"Huh? Oh, yeah, Kevin…sure. It's that fear. Sort of gets you out here. You can't help it."

"I know. A ship seems to cut it off to some extent, boy. But it's around, lurking, waiting to get you."

"What do you mean, waiting to get you?"

"Well, not directly. But it makes you make mistakes. Men have died that way—paying so much attention to the fear that they didn't pay enough attention to whatever was happening."

"Kevin, do you know anything about how Charlie died you haven't told me?"

"Maybe. Maybe not. It's kind of vague, boy. Teejay went out alone and when she came back…well…she looked scared. That's common enough on Ganymede—everyone looks scared. But Teejay looked puzzled and confused also, and that's not like her. She wouldn't talk much for a time, and when she did she just said she'd found Charlie Stedman, your brother, dead."

"Where?"

"What do you mean, where? Out here on Ganymede, naturally."

"No, I mean exactly where. What was done with the body?"

"That I don't know," said Kevin, and Steve could picture him frowning inside his helmet.

"Well, I guess…" Steve started to reply, but he suddenly paused a moment. Then, almost whispering, he said, "Kevin…listen closely…do you hear something?"

"Hear something? How can you hear anything on Ganymede with no air to carry it? Except on the radio, of course—I hear you. Get a grip on yourself, boy."

"No...no I hear something... *There* it is, louder. My God, Kevin! My God—" Then, clumsily in his vacsuit, Steve Stedman began running away across the frozen pumice of Ganymede.

"Hey, come back! Back here, you crazy fool—" Kevin charged after him, taking long, ungainly strides in the light gravity. But Steve was quicker and soon the distance between them increased and Kevin realized he wouldn't be able to overtake Steve at all.

"Come back! What do you hear, boy? At least tell me that."

Steve muttered something over the raido and ran on.

Amazed, Kevin lumbered back toward the *Gordak*.

"But what made him do it?" Teejay demanded a short while later.

"I told you all I know, Captain. He said he heard something and then he started running. I chased after him, but I just couldn't catch him. He...he told me what he heard."

"What? Well...what was it?"

"Uh...you won't like this...'cause it doesn't make any sense. But he said he heard his...his *brother* calling him. His brother, Charlie Stedman. Calling from somewhere out there on Ganymede."

"Charlie Stedman is dead." Suddenly Teejay was curt and pre-emptory.

"That's what I thought, too."

"Forget it. It's the Ganymede-fear, Mac. Somehow it got to Stedman stronger than it got to most people. Maybe his brother was hit that way, too. Maybe, right now, Stedman is off his rocker, running out across the pumice somewhere, shouting his brother's name into the soundless void of space."

"We'll have to find him," said Kevin.

"How can we, Mac? He's got air for five or six hours, and Ganymede is big."

"I'm going to take a set of shoulder-jets and go looking for him, Captain. I hope you won't try to stop me. I'm going either way."

Shrugging, Teejay went to a cabinet, handed Kevin a pair of shoulder-jets, which he strapped at once to his vacsuit. The

37

woman took another suit and another pair of jets. "Once I heard voices out here on Ganymede, too," she said. "So did Charlie Stedman. They killed Charlie and they almost killed me. Enough's enough, Mac. I'm going with you."

CHAPTER FIVE

THE RINGWALL was not very large. Slowed by his vacsuit, a man might cover its diameter in half an hour. But Steve did not traverse the circular area. Instead, he climbed the ringwall laboriously and then made his way down, tumbling and sliding, to the rocky floor of the shallow crater.

The voice came from within it—from within the crater. It couldn't be! He told himself that more than once. The rock of Ganymede itself might carry sound, but you'd feel it only as a throbbing through the soles of your boots, for the vacuum of space that encroached on all sides could not transmit sound-waves.

That was science. That was elementary. But the voice whispered in his ears, ebbing and flowing, first loud, then soft— and science be damned.

Charlie was calling. *I am Charlie Stedman. I am Charlie Stedman.* That was all, but it was enough. Charlie's name, and Charlie's voice.

"It can't be happening," Steve said, aloud, and heard his own voice roaring inside the helmet. It drove the other voice, the impossible voice, out for a moment, but it returned. Around the inner circumference of the ringwall Steve ran, seeking a source for the impossible. Sobbing, stumbling, he plunged ahead. It was only when he returned to his starting point—a needle-like pinnacle of rock—that he realized his supply of air would be exhausted in three hours.

"He couldn't have gone much farther than this, Mac."

"We've got plenty of air, Captain. I'm not giving up—"

The two figures soared on spurting jets a hundred feet above the surface of Ganymede. When Teejay went higher every few moments, she could barely make out the two spaceships, far away to the left. Occasionally she saw the beaters working in teams of six, their cumbersome tanks of oxygen strapped to their backs.

"Did you hear the voice, Mac?"

"No."

"Had Stedman been drinking?"

"That's ridiculous. The boy was with us, and you saw for yourself."

"True. And I've said that the voices of Ganymede are no strangers to me, anyway. Maybe I was trying to rationalize."

"We'll see when we find Steve."

"*If* we find him. The fear can make you do crazy things out here, Mac. Like going for too long without sufficient oxygen."

"That's what I'm worrying about."

A phonograph needle caught in one groove, spinning out its brief message over and over again—that was the voice. *I am Charlie Stedman.* And the ringwall might have been the record, Steve thought bitterly, except that it was utterly deserted. He hadn't covered its entire rock-strewn area; an army of searchers would be necessary to do that. But he had seen enough to convince him that—

The thought fled.

Coming toward him over the floor of the ringwall was a huge anthrovac, walking erect with a shuffling gait. Charlie's voice grew louder...

"It's no good, Mac. We can't find him."

"As soon as we turn back he's as good as dead."

"Our air won't last forever," said Teejay.

"He's got even less."

"Ten more minutes?"

"All right, ten. But why did you come out here with me if you're ready to give up so easy?"

"Who said I am? I'm trying to be practical. Listen, I saved Stedman's life once already—and stayed out on the hot side of Mercury longer than a person should, too. I like Stedman, but if we find him, better not tell him or I'll break your neck...hear? So I want to find him, but I don't want to sacrifice your life or mine in the attempt. Is that clear?"

Kevin said that it was.

A moment later, Teejay climbed higher. Half a thousand feet above the surface of Ganymede she circled. Abruptly, she leveled off at a hundred feet again, said:

"There's something over there, Mac. In that ringwall."

"What?"

"I don't know. Movement. A big figure and a little one. The big one seems too large for a man, but the smaller—well, let's go."

The anthrovac paused a dozen yards from Steve. There had been nothing hostile in its movements to begin with, and now it might have been a statue for all the activity it displayed. From crown of head to small, hand-like feet, it stood almost a yard taller than Steve, but it did not have the great-muscled girth of a gorilla. Instead, it looked quite manlike, except for the incredibly broad shoulders, the thick, matted hair covering its entire body, the too-long arms, the nine feet of height.

Did the voice emanate from it?

Now that the creature had approached him, Steve wasn't sure. The voice continued, pulsing and throbbing in his ears like the Ganymede-fear itself—*but in his ears*. Not from the bleak terrain around him, and certainly not from the anthrovac.

"I'm going crazy," he said, aloud, driving the voice away temporarily. "No. No, I'm not, because I realize it too soon. A crazy man doesn't realize it and doesn't warn himself about it— certainly not at the outset." But did that mean the voice had any real existence? How could it?

I am Charlie Stedman...

Smiling bleakly, Steve picked up a loose chunk of rock, tossed it at the anthrovac. The creature merely swung its huge body gracefully at the hips, avoiding the missile. Then it stooped, found a stone for itself and hurled it at Steve. He ducked, feeling completely and tremendously foolish. He should have been pre- pared, for the anthrovacs are playful and can mime almost any hu- man action.

He did not duck in time. He felt the stone *thunk* against his helmet, peered with horror at the glassite inches from his face until he saw that it hadn't cracked. Grinning now, he shook his fist at the creature, watched it duplicate the motion with its great hairy hand. It was a game, Steve told himself, a lot like the meaningless conversation Teejay and Kevin had had to dispel the Ganymede-fear.

But if the anthrovac could mime human actions, perhaps the anthrovac could also mime voices! That would necessitate telepathic powers, naturally. But the anthrovac, like many denizens of terrestrial forests and tundras, changed its habits immensely in captivity. A captured anthrovac, one that had been reared with one of the circus troupes, could never tell you what a wild anthrovac was like. And a wild anthrovac, somehow living on airless Ganymede and taking its energy directly from cosmic and solar radiation, might be able to do anything.

I am Charlie Stedman...

Steve carried the thought to its logical conclusion. Suppose an anthrovac—this anthrovac that faced him now—had somehow heard Charlie speaking. Charlie might have been introducing himself to someone: "I am Charlie Stedman."

But the hypothesis wasn't much more than a bubble, and it burst completely when Steve remembered he was the only one who could hear the voice.

"Hey, Stedman! You trying to kill yourself?"

Steve whirled, looked up. Two figures, no more than vaguely human in their cumbersome vacsuits, hovered over him, jetting around in circles. The anthrovac had seen them too—and now, apparently alarmed by the twin forms floating just out of reach, the creature turned and bounded away over the uneven terrain.

"What gave you that idea?" Steve called into his intercom. "The anthrovac wasn't looking for trouble."

"I don't mean that, stupid." Teejay had a way of jarring him back to reality with a few words. "I mean, how much air have you got left?"

Steve looked at the gauge. "Enough to return to the *Gordak*, provided I get on my horse."

"We'll walk with you, then," said Teejay, and dropped to the ground at his side. "I think I'll hold onto your arm, too. You're liable to go wandering again, and we might not be able to find you."

Kevin alighted, switched off his jets. "How about the voice, boy? Do you still hear it?"

"Why—no! But I did a minute ago, until the anthrovac ran away."

"That's peculiar."

"There's a lot that's peculiar out here on Ganymede, Kevin. I think—"

"Stop thinking and start walking," Teejay told him.

Less than two hours later, they reached the *Gordak*. A vacsuited man met them at the airlock, and Steve saw LeClarc's face through the glassite helmet.

"I'll bet you were worried," said Teejay.

"Sure," LeClarc answered, drawing a neutron gun from his belt. "See, my Captain, I'm so worried I can hardly think straight. Will the three of you please turn around and march over to the *Frank Buck?*"

They were too stunned to do anything else.

"DON'T MIND ME," Kevin said, within the *Frank Buck*. "If I'm confused it's merely because I can't believe this. Not you, LeClarc, not you."

They'd been ushered into the main lounge of the *Frank Buck*, a ship of about the *Gordak's* dimensions, but two or three years older. LeClarc stood there with his neutron gun, watching them carefully. In a few moments, Schuyler Barling joined them, a greasy salve covering the discoloration on his jaw. The jaw looked painfully swollen too, and Barling rubbed it speculatively. "I won't forget this," he growled briefly to Teejay, then turned to LeClarc. "Kevin McGann I know, but what about this man?"

"Stedman?" said LeClarc. "You'll want him, because he's the extra-zoo man on the *Gordak*. If you took McGann and the woman alone, they still might be able to do their work on Carmical's ship. But with Stedman our prisoner as well, their hands are tied over there."

"What is this?" Teejay demanded defiantly. "What's the meaning of—"

"Will you be quiet and let me do the talking?" Barling interrupted her. "It was LeClarc who radioed and told me your coin had two heads. If you wanted to play the game that way, I wasn't going to stand by and let you. So—"

"So," LeClarc took up the thread for him, "we got together, Mr. Barling and I."

"But you, LeClarc," said Kevin. "You'd jump through a fire-hoop into a pit of acid if Captain Moore told you to."

"Would I?" LeClarc chuckled softly.

"Yes. Yes, you would."

"Perhaps there was a time I'd have done that, McGann. Perhaps. But then I thought the Captain needed me, and wanted me to help her, too. Now, with you and Stedman—well, LeClarc isn't so important, is he?"

"So that's it!" Kevin roared. "You're jealous. Not jealous the way a man should be, when he loves a woman, but jealous because you believed Captain Moore had discarded you—had decided you weren't such an essential cog in the *Gordak* machine."

"Shut up." LeClarc took a quick step toward Kevin and hit him, hooking his left fist at the bigger man's jaw. Kevin staggered but did not go down. Bellowing, he charged at LeClarc, but the Frenchman waved him off with the neutron gun.

"Stop it, LeClarc!" Barling snarled. "I didn't have you bring them here to make a shambles of the lounge. Just stand off in the corner and watch them. I'll do the talking."

"You realize, of course," Teejay told him calmly, "that this is kidnapping."

"Is it? Who's to say? You never entered the *Gordak*; LeClarc met you within the airlock. For all your crew knows, the three of you are out on Ganymede somewhere without much air left. After a time, they'll have to give you up as dead. With the Captain gone, and the Exec, and the expert on Extra-terrestrial zoology—their expedition won't amount to much. It looks to me like old man Carmical will be without a circus this year, unless he resorts to a strictly terrestrial shindig."

"What happens then?" Teejay wanted to know.

"Well, I'll be frank with you. I haven't decided. I can't simply return you to civilization, of course."

"Of course," Teejay echoed him acidly.

"Then you'd be able to holler 'kidnapper'. It would seem that you give me only one alternative. Ah—excuse me a moment."

A trio of men had entered the lounge and the leader, a stocky man of about thirty-five, was beaming. "We've got three," he said.

"Splendid, splendid. In that case, nothing remains to keep us on Ganymede."

"Chief, I'm sure glad of that. This place can give you the heebies, and you never know why. Those three anthrovacs should be a fine core to build your circus around, though."

"Three anthrovacs?" Teejay cried, her composure fading for the first time. "You've got three anthrovacs?"

Barling nodded. "LeClarc here was good enough to tell us Stedman's plan. A first-rate idea, as you can see, only we were able to carry it out. Frankly, I wasn't so optimistic at first."

"Let's get back to us," Teejay suggested. "You were saying...?"

"Ummmm, yes. There's only one alternative, and much as I regret—"

"What is it? What's the alternative?"

"Please, must I say it? I think you know, and there's no need for me to—"

"No, I want to hear it."

"Suit yourself," said Barling. "The only solution is this...we'll have to eliminate you."

"When?"

"The sooner the better. But Captain Moore, you're making me feel—"

"That's all I wanted to know!" Teejay cried, and hurled herself at Barling. "We might as well try to escape while we still have a chance."

AFTER THAT, things happened almost too fast for Steve to follow. Kevin got the idea at once, charging at LeClarc before the Frenchman had time to gather his wits. The neutron gun hissed violently, searing a three-inch chunk out of the ceiling. But then

LeClarc was struck by two hundred pounds of Kevin McGann, and went down before the onslaught.

Something exploded against Steve's jaw and he did a quick flip and landed on his back. He'd hardly had time to declare himself in the battle, when one of Barling's men had jumped him. Now the man came down atop him, flailing with both fists, but Steve chopped at his face with short, clubbing blows and scrambled to his feet while the man caught his breath.

Steve didn't wait, plunging toward the man with murder in his eyes—and failed to reach him. An arm circled his neck from behind and he was dragged to the floor again, by the second of the three anthrovac hunters. He rolled over, saw Kevin and LeClarc off to his right, standing toe-to-toe and slugging. And beyond them, Teejay was cuffing Barling around the lounge with lusty, man-sized blows. Barling went down under the onslaught, falling at the woman's feet, but then the third hunter had grasped her swirling black cape from behind, throwing it over her head and tripping her. She fought blindly as she went down, taking the hunter with her; and with Barling, they became a tangled melee of thrashing arms and legs.

Steve rolled out from under the second hunter, but the first one met him halfway and pole-axed him down to the floor again with a hard right hand. Sobbing, clutching at the man's legs, Steve began to pull himself upright and got a knee in his face. He went down again, and this time everything in the room receded into a vague, shadowy fog.

When Steve could see again, there was still no order to the chaos. He hadn't lived a violent life like Kevin or Teejay—such things were not part of his background, although he'd boxed in college and won the light-heavyweight championship, too. But there was something different, something elemental about a free-for-all brawl.

LeClarc lay on his back, supine. He looked to be out of it for the duration of the fight, which still set the odds at four to three against the trio from the *Gordak*. Right now Kevin held his own with the two hunters who'd done Steve in, at least temporarily. But that couldn't last, for both were big, muscular men. And Teejay? She was a woman, so perhaps the odds were even worse. Steve smiled grimly as he clambered to his feet to help Kevin. Teejay was a woman, but she was the new twenty-second century woman, and proud of it. The third hunter kicked and thrashed helplessly on the floor as she held him in a head-scissors and at the same time fended off Barling, who was crawling around them and looking for an opening. Teejay, definitely, was an asset.

Steve got to hunter number three quickly, pulling him off Kevin and straightening him with an uppercut. After that, it was a set-up. Steve pounded once and then again with his left hand at the man's midsection, then finished by crossing his right and feeling it crunch against the man's jaw.

"Now I see how you could take care of LeClarc that first day!" Kevin yelled, and promptly polished off the other hunter with a blow that lifted him completely off the floor.

As one, they whirled around to face the other side of the room. Barling and his henchman had finally got the upper hand. Teejay lay on her side, her hands behind her back. Not unconscious, she was completely spent, and an almost equally exhausted Barling was attempting to tie her hands with the black cape. The hunter sat there, dull-eyed, watching them. It was Kevin who lifted the hunter and hurled him away, and when Steve rolled Barling over and pushed him against the wall. The man did not resist.

Teejay climbed to her feet, unsteadily. "I—guess I'm growing—soft," she panted. "Maybe—I don't know—maybe training and muscle-toning from—infancy—aren't the answer. A gal just isn't cut out for rough and tumble fighting." Her hand flashed up to her forehead, the back of it resting against her brow. "Ooo, Steve, catch me—"

She fainted in his arms.

Somehow, they got Teejay into her vacsuit. The walls of the lounge were soundproofed, and the struggle had attracted no one. Silently they made their way out of the lounge and through the corridors of the *Frank Buck*, heading for the airlock. Steve toted Teejay over his shoulder, and remembering Mercury, felt very good about it. He ached all over from the fight and he knew he'd need some mending. But she'd called him Steve, and that—suddenly and ridiculously—was most important.

"What's going on here?" A crewman met them in the corridor and bellowed his challenge.

Kevin raised the neutron gun he had taken from LeClarc.

He never used it.

A fraction of a second later, the *Frank Buck* blasted off from the surface of Ganymede, and sudden acceleration threw them all to the floor. As Steve was to learn later, no hands were at the controls. No *human* hands.

CHAPTER SIX

"THIS, ROUGHLY, is the situation," began Barling, pacing back and forth, speaking out of swollen lips and averting the right side of his face with its puffy cheek and blackened eye. "We are all in this together, and—"

"That's real good coming from you," cried Teejay. "Six hours ago, you wanted to kill us. Now, because something unexpected pops up, you're flowing over with comradery. So as long as it serves your purpose, you'll be chummy...is that it?"

"No. If we can get out of this I'll forget about killing, provided you forget about kidnapping."

"Well..."

"You haven't any other choice, Captain Moore."

"He's right," Kevin admitted. "But what's the trouble we're in, Barling?"

"Six hours ago you three jumped us and almost made your escape. But the *Frank Buck* took off, suddenly, without warning. *None of my men were at the controls.*"

"That doesn't make sense," Steve objected.

"I didn't think so, either. I almost don't know how to explain it, what I've seen with my own eyes after my men held you in detention here in the lounge."

"Why don't you start at the beginning?" Teejay said, and yawned.

"Don't be funny. Somehow, the anthrovacs escaped from their bubbles and—"

"What?" Steve cut in, more than slightly incredulous. "Anthrovacs are mellow creatures and unless they're attacked they won't do anything violent."

"That's what I thought, Stedman. I don't know what to think now. The anthrovacs escaped and freed all the other animals. We've been out longer than the *Gordak*; we have a couple of dozen prize specimens. Lead by the anthrovacs, they've taken over the ship."

"Now you're joking," Teejay told him. "They're all brainless, those creatures, except for the anthrovacs."

"They *were* brainless, Captain Moore. But not now. Now they behave logically, with a purpose, and they've taken over the *Frank Buck* from stem to stern—all except those animals that need a special sort of atmosphere to breathe, and they've remained in their bubbles. Otherwise, the animals took over. And I suppose you can imagine—the crew was too astounded to resist, especially since the anthrovacs had gotten hold of neutron guns and seemed to know how to use them. Result—we've all been disarmed, we're prisoners aboard our own ship, and bound for I don't know where."

"Sounds crazy to me," Teejay said, and stalked toward the door.

Steve took a quick step after her, but Barling held him back. "Let her find out for herself, Stedman. Then maybe we can talk sense."

Teejay opened the door, stepped out into the corridor. Tensely, Steve waited, ready to bolt after her at the first indications of trouble. But what he heard was a yelp of surprise from the woman, who then came running back into the lounge, slamming the door behind her.

"A Martian desert cat!" she cried. It didn't do anything; it just stood there, all ten feet of it, looking at me!"

"Then you believe me?" Barling demanded. "As I see it, we must have been struck by some cosmic radiation which mutated the animals, and—"

"No," Steve told him bluntly. "That's impossible. First place, any such change would have to be selective. All the animals wouldn't be affected. And more important, mutation takes generations to manifest itself. You never see the change at all in the original creature. Look at Earth, way back in the early years of atomics. Genes were mutated at those two cities—Nagasaki and, ummmm, I forget the name of the other. Anyway, genes were mutated, but it took over two hundred years for those mutations to become apparent. See what I mean?"

"I do," said Barling. "And that's precisely why I think we ought to fight this thing together."

"Well," Steve nodded, "we have a real problem on our hands. We can't do anything about it until we know what's going on—only the mystery's a little deeper than you think. First, I heard a voice out on Ganymede. My brother's voice."

"Your brother's?" Barling scratched his head. "Oh, wait a minute...you must mean Charlie Stedman who was killed out here a few years back?"

"Yeah...Charlie. And you can't hear voices on Ganymede, but I heard them, *inside* my head. Also, don't forget the Ganymede-fear. I'd say these three things will somehow fit together when we learn what's going on."

"Provided we can find out," Teejay told him. "You can keep your scientific mysteries for a while, Steve. What I want to know is this...where are we going, and why?"

"Ask your desert cat out there." Kevin's laughter was sour.

"What we need is a good turn-coat," Teejay assured him. "Someone who can go out among the animals and ask questions. I'm joking, of course, but if anyone could do it, it would be that rat, LeClarc."

Steve frowned. "That's not as funny as it sounds. Has anyone seen LeClarc since the fight?"

"No..." Kevin slammed fist against palm.

Steve was about to answer, but quite suddenly the lights blinked out. Somewhere outside, a dozen animals roared their fear. Within the lounge, Kevin commenced cursing lustily and an involuntary moan escaped Barling's lips.

The darkness was the bleak, utter black of deep space. Further, Steve realized, the steady humming of the fission engines had ceased.

Minutes later, impossible pain gripped him and flung him, sobbing to the floor. He'd never felt anything like it, a gripping, grinding, twisting torment that tried to turn him inside out. He heard the others dimly, reeling about the lounge and falling to the floor, and in the darkness someone fell near him.

"Steve? Steve, is that you?" Teejay asked painfully.

"Yeah." The pain seemed to come in waves, and Steve gritted his teeth when the second wave turned out to be worse than the first. He reached out with his hand, found Teejay's and squeezed it. "Hold on. It can't last forever."

"It better not."

When her hand tensed in his, then relaxed, Steve knew she'd fainted. And soon after that, his own senses reeled and deserted him.

Teejay's hand was still tightly clenched in his when he regained consciousness. A dozen feet from them, Kevin sat up, shaking his head slowly back and forth. Schuyler Barling lay stretched out on his stomach.

"Whatever happened," Kevin growled, "I didn't like it."

Teejay extricated her hand, looked at Steve, smiled. "It's still awful quiet outside."

It didn't remain that way for long. As if Teejay's words had been a signal, a voice boomed at them from the wall-microphone. "We have landed. All humans will please file out into the main corridor in an orderly fashion and make their way to the airlock."

Schuyler Barling sat up groggily.

Teejay said, "I could swear I know that voice from somewhere."

"And I," Kevin told them. "It's familiar, though I can't place it."

Steve felt his heart pounding. The voice was Charlie's.

THEY STOOD on a flat, grassy plain that stretched halfway to the horizon and then began to undulate into low hills. And far off, shrouded by purple mists, a range of mountains loomed distantly.

Purple mist; a purplish cast to the sky; a fiercely bright blue sun. "What world is this?" said Kevin.

The crew of the *Frank Buck*—a hundred men—stood in a long, thin file outside the ship. They'd balked at first, but silently, the three anthrovacs had ferreted them out with their neutron guns, never uttering a sound, merely motioning with the weapons. Of the other animals Steve saw nothing, but within the corridors of the *Frank Buck* he'd encountered a sand crawler and a desert cat, both dead.

The seconds fled, became minutes. When half an hour had passed, the crew became restless and some of them ambled off on the grassy plain until one of the anthrovacs herded them back. The *Frank Buck's* Exec, a short, wiry man, strode within the ship and came out a few moments later, scratching his head. "I can't understand it," he said. "None of the instruments work. I thought we could just pile back into the ship and blast off, but apparently someone has other ideas."

Someone did.

Someone came striding across the plain, a small dot of a figure at first. He came closer.

Steve ignored the anthrovacs and ran forward. "Charlie!" he cried. "Charlie!"

The man was shorter than Steve, and stockier. His eyes searched Steve's face briefly, and he said: "Should I know you?"

"Should you! I'm your brother!"

"Interesting...but quite impossible."

The words hardly registered, and Steve babbled on, "We thought you were dead. It was Teejay here who reported back to Earth saying you'd died on Ganymede. Now you're alive and—" Abruptly he whirled, turned to Teejay. "You lied, damn you! Here's Charlie, see? Charlie was never dead. But you said—"

"I said Charlie was dead." The woman met his gaze levelly. "He was. I know a dead man when I see one. He was dead."

"But—"

"But nothing. I don't know who this is. I can't explain it. That has nothing to do with what happened on Ganymede several years ago."

"Yes? Then what *did* happen? Why did Charlie write once that you must have been spawned in hell? You never did want to tell me what happened on Ganymede, did you? Maybe Charlie can."

"That is my name, Charlie Stedman. It is the name this body has always had, although when I do not inhabit it I assure you I am not Charlie Stedman," the stocky man said. "You see, the original inhabitant of the garment—the body—was destroyed. The name applied to the body as well as the inhabiting mind. The language remained engraved in the brain cells, and impersonal parts of the memory, too. In that sense, I am Charlie Stedman. Does it satisfy you?"

"Hell, no," said Steve, bewildered. Mystery had been piled upon mystery, with no solution in sight. And grim confusion turned to grimmer anger as he faced Teejay once more. "All right, start talking. Just how did you find Charlie? And what made him hate you like that? Talk, dammit!"

"Okay, I will. But I don't know why Charlie hated me, and that's the truth. I only met him once or twice and…" A look of realization came over Teejay's face. "…unless it was Schuyler here. Hey, Schuyler…"

Barling moved over to them. "What is it?"

"Answer this question, and answer it truthfully…*please*. Do you make it a practice of poisoning the minds of your men against me and my crew?"

"Well…I don't know exactly what you mean by poi—"

Teejay grabbed a handful of his shirt and twisted, constricting the collar about his throat. "Answer me," she said firmly.

"I—I guess, so. It's only business, Captain Moore. The more they hated you, the more they'd be willing to fight you in the hunt every step of the way."

"How about Charlie Stedman?"

"I don't remember. Probably, it was like that."

Teejay flung him away from her and looked at Steve.

"Does that satisfy you?"

"For that part, yes. But what about the rest of it?"

"Not much to tell. I was out alone on Ganymede, a few miles from the ship. I thought I heard voices, sort of inside my head. I went forward to explore, just like you did, and also like you, I almost didn't have enough air to get back. Especially since I found your brother on the way."

"And he was dead?" As he spoke, Steve looked at his brother, standing right there in front of him, and wondered if anyone ever asked a more impossible question.

"Yes. He was dead. I don't know how he died, but I placed my ear against the chest of his vacsuit. The heartbeat is amplified through it, you know. But there wasn't any. After that, I ran back to the *Gordak*, and I had barely enough air to make it. I reported Charlie's death, of course."

Charlie's death. She sounded sincere. But there was Charlie, standing two paces to her right and apparently listening to an account of his own demise.

CHARLIE CLEARED his throat. Quite evidently, it wasn't Charlie at all, but Steve could think of the man in no other way, for down to the smallest physical detail, he was Charlie. "That will suffice," he said. Again, it was Charlie's voice, but expressionless. "Enough of bickering. You will all march with me toward those hills, and we have a long journey before sunset."

The nine-foot anthrovacs took up their positions one on each side of the column and one behind it, and no one disobeyed. Once Steve looked back over his shoulder and saw the purple mists had almost completely swallowed the *Frank Buck*.

Then the irony of the situation struck Steve and he smiled— almost. He'd come to Ganymede after anthrovacs. But he'd left that pumice-covered satellite under an anthrovac guard! Fine thing. A mighty hunter was he! Clear across the universe to be bagged by his own game!

Obviously, Steve thought as they marched on, the blue daystar was not Earth's sun. Somehow, in a matter of moments, they'd left the Solar System entirely. He knew that theories had been advanced about traveling through something called sub-space, something that could make flight to the farthest stars almost instantaneous, since sub-space existed outside the space-time continuum. And that wrenching from one spatial plane to another might explain the tremendous pain they'd undergone, too. But surely the *Frank Buck* had never been equipped for such flight. The whole concept of sub-space flight was strictly theoretical and hadn't even reached the drawing-board stage.

Then how had it happened?

Kevin had some vague, half-formed ideas on the subject, and he let Steve know about them. "It's a puzzler, boy. They took us a long way, space alone knows how far. I don't pretend to know why; we can't figure that out—not yet. But I know this...they could not have done that without help. Someone had to bring the ship."

"The anthrovacs?" Steve suggested.

"Not the anthrovacs. For all their handling neutron guns and taking the *Frank Buck* over, they're just big apes to me. Maybe they were able to take the ship off Ganymede, but no more than that. They had help, boy, and from the inside."

"Who? Who do you mean?"

"I'm not sure I know. But look at it this way. The *Gordak* wasn't taken, the *Frank Buck* was. Why? I'll tell you why, or at least I'll tell you one possibility. There were scores of men on each ship, but while the *Gordak* had only one animal—the stone worm you got on Mercury—the *Frank Buck* had dozens. All right so far, boy? Well, here's what I think...*whoever took the ship wanted both men and animals.*"

"I still don't understand."

"I'm not sure I do, either. Let's get back a little. The *Frank Buck*, not the *Gordak*, was taken. Strange, isn't it, that just before that happened LeClarc bolted our ranks and joined the enemy! Does that mean LeClarc had to be on the *Frank Buck* before anything happened? And where is he now, anyway? I haven't seen him since the fight; I don't think anyone has. Now, a man spends years idolizing a woman—I've been around, and I think I told you LeClarc would have done anything for Captain Moore. Suddenly, he gets sulky because he's out of favor with her and decides on a double-cross?" Kevin paused and shook his head, then ran a hand through his red hair. "It smells bad, boy. Sure, he was sulky, but the LeClarc I knew would have come crawling to Captain Moore, anyway. This one didn't. Maybe it means he isn't the same man. Maybe it means he's something like that thing that calls itself your brother. That's not Charlie Stedman and you of all people know it. Trouble is, boy, you can't admit it to yourself."

"I won't argue about it," Steve replied. "But you're off the beam there. Charlie doesn't remember me, but LeClarc's memory seemed fine."

"That's true. I can't explain it, except whatever happened to both of them, we don't know a thing about it. Maybe it works in a different way on different people. Maybe because Charlie was dead first, his personal memories were lost, but maybe LeClarc's weren't because he was possessed while alive."

"Possessed?"

"Yes, possessed. Oh, I don't mean by spirits or anything like that. But possessed nevertheless. I won't say the anthrovacs were possessed, for we don't know enough about them to begin with. But look at those other animals now, the ones that died. You won't deny that something took over their brains?"

"Damned right I won't. But I still don't see how it all adds up."

"Nor do I," said Kevin. "Unfortunately, the brutes seemed to have perished in transit from Ganymede to here, wherever here is. It could be that the strain on their brain-tissue, with sentience and intelligence taking over where before only sentience had resided, was simply too great."

Kevin paused, then concluded, "Whatever the reason, whatever the reason for all of it—I think you'll find LeClarc knows all about it."

The blue sun had neared the horizon and the purple mists had become cool and chilling at journey's end. It was then that they saw LeClarc.

CHAPTER SEVEN

THE COLUMN of men had traversed the grassy plain and climbed steadily through the region of undulating hills. Suddenly, hidden until the last moment by a rise in the terrain and spread out at the foot of the higher mountains, they saw a city. Circular, walled, pleasantly pastel-tinted despite the purple gloom, it lay before them, lights that might or might not have been electricity winking on to dispel the gathering darkness.

And there, at the city's gateway, stood LeClarc. LeClarc—and not LeClarc. The man seemed as much LeClarc as the short stocky figure who led the procession seemed Charlie Stedman. "Welcome to Uashalume," he said, and Steve pulled up short at the sound of his voice. There was something of the volatile Frenchman in it, but something else that was alien.

"You will be billeted in temporary quarters for the night," LeClarc continued. "You will of course have no need for such quarters after tomorrow's bazaar."

"Of course, my foot!" Teejay cried petulantly. "See here, LeClarc, we've been getting orders and directives without knowing what they mean or why they were given or—"

"Must you be so impatient?" LeClarc's smile was almost devoid of mirth. "You've come one hundred thousand light years, and surely you can wait until morning."

"Light years?" Steve gasped.

Then Kevin, "One hundred thousand...?"

The academic problem didn't bother Teejay as much as the human one. She said, defiantly, "What he needs is a good swift kick."

LeClarc failed to wait for that, or anything else. Chuckling, he led the first anthrovac through the high-arched stone gateway and the other two creatures herded the humans in after him. Charlie— although obviously, the man was not Charlie—went on ahead with LeClarc, and Steve had to restrain Teejay with a few terse words.

The purple mists cloaked the city completely now, and as they plodded along a wide roadway, Steve half-saw figures watching them from the darkness. He could not make the figures out, however, and he heard nothing but the sounds their feet made on the stone roadway.

Presently, they came to a smaller, divergent path that led back to the base of the wall. Here, in deepest shadow, was their destination—a squat, rectangular building carved from stone. A gate creaked and clanged open before them; they streamed through, weary after hours of forced march; the gate clanged resoundingly behind them. Charlie had not entered with them, nor LeClarc, nor the anthrovacs. It took Steve only a moment to discover the gate had been securely fastened from the outside.

"I guess we bed down here for the night," he said, grinning ruefully.

Teejay shrugged, then wrapped the black cape tightly about her. It was cold and damp in the one large chamber that took up the interior of the building. In the center of the place stood a stone table, and on it a gas lamp that flickered and spluttered and cast grotesque shadows as the men wandered about. There were no beds, no furniture of any sort except for the table. And the two small peephole windows were fifteen or more feet off the ground.

The crew of the *Frank Buck* gathered in small, anxious knots and whispered grimly among themselves. After a time, men circulated between one group and another, and finally one of them, evidently designated as spokesman for the rest, approached Schuyler Barling.

He seemed nervous and frightened—unsure of himself. "Captain Barling, my name's Steiner, and the fellows thought that—well, that I might speak for them. We don't know exactly what's going on, but we don't like it."

"I can't blame you," said Barling matter-of-factly.

"Point is, sir, we want you to do something about it."

"Eh? Me? What in the world can I do?"

"We don't know that, sir. But a spaceman's a peculiar individual. Some say he's got characteristics you won't find elsewhere, and one of them is that he has complete confidence in his captain."

"Well…thank you very much, Steiner."

"Me, I work in fission. I like to have that confidence. And the rest of the men…they like to have it too. When they lose it, they're kind of at a loss. We don't want to think we've lost it here, sir."

"Well…again…what do you want me to do?" Barling was restless, fidgety, twisting his hands together.

"Lead us, sir. Tell us you can get us out of here. Tell us we must be prepared to fight behind you and maybe to die, but lead us."

"But how can you expect me to lead you when I don't know what's happening? How can I plan for escape when I don't know what it is we have to escape from?"

"There's talk among the men, sir," Steiner went on. "Some of them are for you, although I'll be frank. There aren't many, sir. But they need a leader, all of them agree on that. What they want to know is…are you their man?"

Barling squared his thin shoulders arrogantly. "I'm the *Frank Buck's* Captain."

"The *Frank Buck* lies behind us in those purple mists, sir. Could you find it? Finding it, could you make it run again?"

"I don't know."

"Then the fact that you're the captain of the *Frank Buck* doesn't mean much. We've decided that leaves us without a leader, sir. And we need a leader."

Barling smiled coldly. "Are you trying to tell me the men have selected you?"

"No, sir. I'm not. But the majority of the men have made their choice, and…" He paused for a moment, took a deep breath, then nodded slightly in Teejay's direction. "…and it's Captain Moore."

"What?" Barling looked completely dumbfounded.

"Keep in mind sir, those of us who've been with the *Frank Buck* the longest have heard a lot of bad talk about Captain Moore—but only on ship. That always changed whenever we made planetfall. The talk in all the frontier towns always held her in high regard. So with all due respect, sir, when there are decisions to be made, we'd like her to make them."

"A woman? When all your lives may be at stake?"

ONE OF THE three hunters who'd fared so poorly in the lounge fight strode forward, and said, "Look at yourself, sir. You're beaten and battered, and that's Captain Moore's work. Did her sex matter then?"

Barling reddened but said nothing.

"We have a pressing need for a leader," Steiner continued. "Our behavior cannot be chaotic. The leader must plan for us, and we must be prepared to carry out those plans with no hesitation. We must have faith in our leader."

Teejay joined them, the slightest hint of a grin on her face. "Thank you, Mr. Steiner. There was a time not long ago when what you've just finished saying would have meant more to me than anything. Literally, more than anything. But would you think it strange if you hear that I don't think that now?"

"What do you mean?" Steiner asked.

"I'm a twenty-second century female, strong as a man and proud of it. *Too* proud, Mr. Steiner, for I've spent my whole life trying to prove it. Plenty of men have cursed me for it, I'll bet, and

I guess they were right. So I don't want the job you offer. It took a kind of free-for-all brawl to make me realize it, but a woman's still a woman, and that's one thing I had to learn. I fought your Captain Barling and I beat him. I could probably do it again. But I—well, I was fighting with Captain Barling and saying to myself all the time, 'This is stupid. What are you—a girl—doing this for? Don't you know you shouldn't go around fighting like a man?' "

Steve noticed in the dim light that Teejay had begun to blush.

"I hate to bare my life before you like this, Mr. Steiner, but the way it adds up I've suddenly found I've had enough of fighting and galavanting around. So the answer is no…I won't be your captain. The way I feel now, I can't be."

"Where does that leave us?" Steiner asked her sullenly. "We don't think Captain Barling can do the job, whatever the job turns out to be. It's one thing to serve on a largely automatic ship under Captain Barling, but another thing to have to take his orders here—wherever we are."

"May I make a suggestion?" Teejay asked. Steiner nodded and most of the men grumbled their assent.

"There are two men here who can lead us the way we should be led," she continued. "One is Kevin McGann, Exec of the *Gordak*; the other is Steve Stedman."

A stir of surprise passed among the men. It was one thing to offer their allegiance to the Captain of another ship—and an unusual thing at that—but quite another to offer it to a couple of men they hardly knew. The men began heated discussions once more, louder this time, and Teejay drew Steve off into a corner.

"Does that surprise you?"

"It sure does, Teejay. On both counts. But I'll tell you what, I think I could like you a lot better in your new role, and—"

"What?" Her voice was soft and he felt her hand snuggle into his.

"I—I like you plenty right now." He slid his arms around her waist, drew her toward him, one small part of his mind expecting a roundhouse right-handed wallop from the old Teejay. But she merely sighed contentedly and slipped her arms around his neck. He kissed her tentatively at first—then long and deep. Teejay's eyes were all aglow they he finished.

"You lug," she said, "if you didn't do something like that, and soon, I was going to be an Amazon just once more and make you do it."

Steiner stood before them clearing his throat. "Captain Moore?"

"Yes?" Teejay hardly saw him. "The men have decided to accept your recommendation. McGann and Stedman it is, Captain Moore. They bark and we'll jump. And we'll be hoping decisive something comes of it."

"If it's at all possible, they'll get us out of here," Teejay predicted, and squeezed Steve's hand.

"Any orders, sir?" Steiner looked at Steve.

"Ummmm, no. Except that we'd like to have this corner to ourselves for a while."

"Done," said Steiner, smiling and striding away.

"I have one order," Kevin called out loudly, and silence fell on the room quite abruptly. "Let's all get the hell to sleep before we're too tired to do anything when morning comes."

A PURPLE-BLUE dawn crept in through the two small windows, bringing strange bird-sounds with it. Steve was stiff and chilled and he'd slept badly on the hard stone floor. The groans and frowns all around the room showed him he wasn't the only one. Teejay slept like a baby, the cape wrapped about her, and she didn't arise until one of the men began to bang on the stone and metal door.

"Is it morning?" said Teejay, coming into Steve's arms almost before she was fully awake. "I had the nicest dreams, darling!"

Abruptly, Steve whirled away from her. The door had begun to creak in ponderously on little-used hinges.

An anthrovac bent and came within the chamber, bearing a bath-tub-sized bowl of what looked like hot, steaming cereal. It was deposited near the table, along with a dozen or so stone spoons. Foolishly, one of the men darted for the doorway. Reaching out with a long, hairy arm, the anthrovac scooped him up by the scruff of the neck and flung him back inside. He got to his feet with a nasty gash on his forehead, which Teejay bandaged with a strip of cloth ripped from the hem of her black cape.

The spoons were passed around after that, and the men of the *Frank Buck* dug into the gruel with gusto. It had been fifteen hours since any of them had eaten and surprisingly, the gruel turned out to be quite palatable, with an appealing, nutlike flavor.

The anthrovac waited fifteen minutes, then lifted the huge bowl and departed with it. But the door didn't close fully.

Charlie Stedman came through it.

"Good morning," he said. "We're a little late, and we'll have to hurry if we want to reach the bazaar in time for opening."

"Are you sure we want to?" Kevin demanded sarcastically.

And Steiner suggested: "Maybe you'd like to answer a few questions first."

"Sure," added Teejay. "About a thousand questions."

It was as if the man hadn't heard them at all. "Outside a vehicle awaits you. There is room for all, provided each man occupies one of the squares you will find marked off on the floor. Let's go."

Angry, sullen, but still thoroughly bewildered, the men trooped outside.

The vehicle was a sort of bus, although the noise of a gasoline engine or the purring of a fission engine would have shocked Steve here on the world called Uashalume. As it turned out, the bus started with a whining whistle, which quickly climbed to the supersonic and faded beyond the level human ears could reach. Within the vehicle there were no seats, but the floor had been divided into two-foot squares, a thin white line marking off each box. When each man had occupied his square, the bus slipped away from the squat building and was soon streaking down the roadway at a good clip.

Steve saw other buildings, most of them squat and shapeless. And now, with the coming of daylight, he could see some of the inhabitants of Uashalume. He'd steeled himself for it. He hadn't expected human beings. Any variety of six-legged, multi-tentacled, bug-eyed creatures would have been strictly in order.

He gasped.

He got more than he bargained for. Hardly two of the creatures gazing in at them were alike! The differences were not those you might expect to find among the members of a particular species. The differences were *extreme*.

A furry thing hovered alongside the open-windowed bus on six gauze-like wings.

Multiple eyes stared up at them out of a pool of amorphous protoplasm.

A bony, stick-like creature with four arms and one cyclopean eye covering almost its entire head peered at them.

An ecto-skeletoned monstrosity made clicking noises as they passed.

Big horrors and little horrors. Steve found himself laughing harshly. What did all his knowledge of Extra-terrestrial zoology amount to now? Extra-terrestrial—that meant the Solar System, one tiny, inconsequential corner of a great galaxy. But here, here on Uashalume, denizens of a hundred Solar Systems might have been gathered.

Why?

Such utterly different creatures—each conforming to a particular environmental niche—would not be found together. Unless someone had probed the depths of space for life forms that might all be capable of surviving on Uashalume, as, indeed, humans could survive there! But why? The question returned, taunted him. Again, such a gathering couldn't be out of direct choice. If each of the creatures seemed so completely strange, so horrible, so ludicrous to human eyes—they probably appeared that way to one another as well.

Steve wondered how some of them might describe the obnoxious, featherless, hairless bipeds that walked upright on two limbs and carried two other limbs for more varied purposes than walking. Bipeds that called themselves humans. And that, precisely, was the point. Such a gathering stemmed from no natural cause. Such a gathering had been imposed arbitrarily, but for what purpose? And what, if anything, did the bazaar have to do with it? A bazaar of the worlds, bringing together for trade, creatures of every form and size and color? Steve doubted that somehow, for the bazaar would lack a universal means of exchange, and even if barter were resorted to, how could totally alien life-forms assess the value of completely foreign produce? They couldn't.

This left Steve with nothing but a lot of half-formed questions and no answers at all.

He had a hunch he'd begin to get some answers when the bus reached its destination. As with the inhabitants of Uashalume, he was to get more than he bargained for.

CHAPTER EIGHT

THEY MILLED about in confusion on a large raised platform under the blue sun. A sea of impossible creatures rolled and seethed on all sides of them, shutter-eyes, pin-hole eyes, simple light-sensitive receptors, multiple-tube eyes—hundreds of varieties all intent upon them.

Steve heard voices around him on the platform, confused, alarmed. "What's happening?"

"This place looks like an auction block!"

"Look at those creatures, will you?"

"Are we for sale or something?" The human voices faded into a meaningless babble. Someone else was speaking, but not aloud. It was like Charlie Stedman's voice, that day on Ganymede. Steve heard it inside his head and this time—because they all stood about more bewildered than ever—he knew that the *Frank Buck's* crew heard it too.

"Friends of Uashalume," the voice purred mentally, "here, at opening day of the bazaar, we have a most unusual treat. Most unusual. Two of us, as you know, have already tested the models in question, and we find them entirely satisfactory."

Charlie Stedman and LeClarc stepped forward and bowed.

"For the rest of you, one hundred choice specimens! We set no fixed price, but let this be said about the new garments. They are unspoiled, virgin material; they've not been used before. You'll find them stimulating for that reason alone, I'm sure. As for the vital statistics, they vary in height from three and a half to five *klars;* in weight from fifteen to twenty-nine *jarons;* they are a bisexual lot, although only one female of the species is present; their intellectual capacity is on the seventh level, their better minds can attain to problems of relativity and universal field; emotionally, they have twice the range of any previous garment!"

The voice paused significantly, permitted that point to sink in. "Yes, twice the range. None of us have ever experienced such strong, vital emotions. Can you imagine...twice the emotional range of the *scouradi* of Deneb XIX! It means a new way of life for those among us who select some of these humans for their own.

"Now, the auction-master will please step forward."

"We *are* for sale," Steiner gasped. It was Charlie Stedman who came to the fore, climbing the auction-block and looking around him. After a time, he singled out Steiner and pulled the man forward by an elbow. "The first specimen is typical," he droned in English, and Steve figured he spoke mentally to the assembled throngs, reeling off the height, weight, and other vital statistics for Steiner. Finally: "What am I bid?"

Mental voices sang out, one after another:

"Three *char!*"

"Four."

"Six."

"Ten *char.*"

"Ten?" The man who was Charlie Stedman laughed. "Ten *char* indeed! One hundred is not enough."

The bidding continued, became hot, became a contest between two mental voices. Steiner went for seventy-four *char*, whatever a *char* was.

They took him down and carted him away, struggling. It looked like an ugly scene would develop, for a score of men surged toward the front of the block angrily. But some of the creatures held what looked like strange, possibly lethal weapons, and Kevin growled: "Not now! There's no sense getting all of us killed. Relax, and we'll see."

Grumbling, the men subsided, and Kevin turned to Steve: "If this isn't the damndest cosmic joke of all."

"What do you mean?"

"We're hunters, big game hunters. We go out into space to hunt for specimens, only this time we've become specimens ourselves. This time we weren't the hunters, but the quarry!"

The auction continued, and one by one the men were sold. One of them, a radar technician, bolted and ran. He was cut down quite efficiently by one of the hand weapons and Charlie Stedman asserted it was a pity one of the specimens had been lost. "Keep your tempers," Kevin said grimly as a wave of anger washed over the auction block. "I don't like it any more than you do, but we won't fight until we understand—and then perhaps we'll have a chance."

WHEN HALF the men had been taken, Charlie Stedman reached for Teejay and dragged her forward. "This," he said, "is the female of the species. You will notice the long hair atop her head and the twin out-thrust developments of the upper ventral region; these are the marks of distinction. And for two reasons we will demand a special price for the female.

"First, we are primarily interested in these humans for emotion. Stronger garments we have, and garments that live longer. But none attain to the human emotional level. And, among the humans, the female is capable of stronger surges of emotion, perhaps because in general she is physically weaker and must compensate for it, although, from what I've seen, this particular specimen is a physical match for the others.

"Second, one specific high degree of emotion is possible only when a male and a female are in one another's presence. Therefore, whichever one of you owns the female can be certain of that added stimulus, and, as a consequence, certain of a more satisfactory garment from the emotional point of view. Now, what am I offered?"

Teejay went for three hundred *char*.

Kevin had to circle Steve's body with his huge arms and hold him firm as they took Teejay away. He had found the woman in her quite suddenly, and he loved her all the more for it. His potential worst enemy had become his lover. And now, brief hours later she was taken from him, perhaps forever. "Let go of me! Get your filthy hands off me. That's Teejay they're taking! Teejay!"

"And they'll take you too. But you're going alive, not dead. Stand still and let them get on with this."

"Don't you realize what they've been talking about?" Steve shouted his rage. "They'll *wear* us, like clothing. They'll get inside our brains and share our bodies with us, like they've done with all these other creatures. Did you think these monsters were all native to Uashalume? I wouldn't be surprised if none of them were. They've all been taken, as we have, from their own worlds. They all live here—as clothing. Maybe the masters don't have physical form at all, maybe they're just mental essence.

"And all they want to do is run the gamut of our emotions. They know how to play with emotions, too. Remember the Ganymede-fear, Kevin?"

"I remember, boy." Kevin still held him.

"Well, that was their work. Probably, Ganymede was their base in our Solar System, although it's possible they first got into LeClarc's brain on Mercury. And Kevin, all those theories you had were right!"

"Yes, I know. And sub-space—"

"The hell with that. They're taking Teejay and they may take all of us and spread us out all over the face of this world. We'll never find each other. We'll—I—"

"You're next, Steve Stedman." It was Charlie's voice, and Steve felt Kevin release him with a word of warning, felt himself drawn to the front of the block. Somehow, he found he was incredibly objective as the bidding began. He was claimed for one hundred fifty *char* and led away by a creature with a stilt-like body and six arms. Or rather, he thought, that was the garment. But the real creature—the mental entity within it—had grown tired of last year's cloak, and Steve was to take its place.

Moments later, Steve's buyer whisked him away in a smaller version of the bus that had taken the *Frank Buck's* crew to the bazaar. On the outskirts of the city, the car stopped. Steve climbed out, followed the stilt-figure up a flight of stairs as a round, fat, furry creature bounced up behind him with a weapon.

Inside, the place looked like a laboratory. And at the center of the room squatted a great round tank, large enough to hold a man. A green liquid boiled within it, but somehow Steve got the impression of boiling without much heat. He became absorbed in the idea, reached up over the lip of the tank to verify it on a thoroughly peculiar impulse.

Something struck him from behind. He staggered to his knees and tried to keep his eyes opened. The hard stone floor slammed against his face as he lost consciousness.

HE WAS floating, and when he could see again, a murky green haze surrounded him.

Floating, completely submerged!

He felt no desire to breathe. He did not have to breathe at all. It was as if his life had been suspended completely, as if there was no need for his body to carry out its normal functions. But he wasn't dead. He could open his eyes and stare at the green liquid, and he could think.

And after a time, vague forms appeared outside. He saw the walls of the laboratory and the shining instruments—through green murk. And he saw something else moving about, a shadowy form. The stilt-like creature?

Abruptly, sharp pain lanced from the front of his skull to the back. Briefly. And it did not repeat itself.

A voice whispered, "You are struggling. Do not struggle, for it can only prolong the inevitable. Transfer takes time, of course; but the longer it takes the more unpleasant it will be for you."

"Go to hell."

It was then that the pain came back—stronger. And something almost physical pushed in at his mind, something ugly, unclean, wet with a damp, chilling moisture that brought twinges of fright. *Like the Ganymede-fear, but more intense.*

"To struggle is useless."

The wet feeling, like fingers now, fingers that oozed slime, clung to his brain, probed it, bore inward.

"Why struggle? I think you will make a good fit."

"Go away. Damn you, go away!"

"I see the auction-master was right. Emotionally, you are strong."

The fingers departed, came back again, more insistent. No longer wet, they were digits of fire now, burning, burning.

Steve screamed soundlessly and fainted.

When Steve came to, he was outside the tank. He was tired and did not feel like walking. Nevertheless, he walked. At first he did not understand. He thought: *I will sit down and rest.*

His body failed to obey, continued walking.

"We share this body," the voice whispered to him, within his skull. "You are merely an observer as long as I am awake. I am in control. Henceforth, I dwell in this body."

"I want to sleep."

"You will learn that your mind can sleep while your body does not. And the body interests me, human. The body is capable of strong emotion. I want to feel that emotion."

The place, Steve realized later, was a sort of proving grounds. He felt himself walking, walking. He reached the edge of a cliff, stared down from giddy heights. He felt himself teetering on the edge, saw jagged rocks far below him. He jumped. He did not want to, but he jumped.

"We'll be killed!" he cried, icy fear making his heart pound.

"That is fear," said the voice in his skull. "That is wonderful fear. So strong—"

Something cushioned their fall, slowly. *Their* fall, not his alone. For the creature shared it with him.

He tumbled, but slowly, like a feather…like a wraith of fog. He alighted on the rocks with hardly a jar, cushioned by some advanced application of a force field. A large cube of metal was there to convey them to the top once more.

After that, he became giddy. He did not know why, but the impulse to laugh was too strong to resist. He laughed until it grew painful, laughed until the tears came to his eyes.

"That is joy," said the voice. "I can instill joy in you. But the way you express it…that is unique. More!"

And Steve's laughter bubbled up insanely again. The creature was wrong—not joy. Hysteria, more nearly. Unused to emotions, the creature could not tell them apart.

Something grabbed his arms and held it. A giant vise that could crush and twist. He saw nothing, realized that it was some mental trick—but thoroughly effective. His arm was being wrenched from its socket, slowly, terribly.

He clenched his teeth, groaned. From somewhere far off, the voice laughed calmly. "I like that. Oh yes, I do. I like your reaction to pain."

An intense loathing he had never before experienced took hold of him. At first he thought it was another trick, but he could sense alarm in the creature which shared him. The loathing, then, was his body's reaction to its parasite. Almost, he could feel the creature squirming, and he gave free reign to the emotion.

"Stop!" The voice was strident, alarmed.

I hate you, Steve thought intensely. *I hate you.*

"Stop! I warn you, you will kill us with that, or drive us insane."

Vertigo followed the loathing as the creature fought back. Steve was tired, suddenly more tired than he'd ever been. He sank back into blackness, knew even as his senses fled that his mind alone would sleep, not his body. With two minds, the body would not sleep at all—and in a matter of months it would perish of fatigue. But the creature within him feared his hatred, and that he must remember.

THE DAYS followed each other in a slow, tortuous procession. Nothing seemed to satiate the parasite, for each day it strove for new emotions, and after a time Steve learned he could frustrate it by regarding everything as unreal, imaginative, non-existent.

Sometimes, the guest slept when the host did not. At such times, Steve found, he had freedom of a sort. His field of action was not circumscribed in any way except that violent activity would awaken the parasite. Steve toyed with his freedom, timorously at first, then grew more confident. He played with it, basked in it after steady days of control. He even discovered he could use the telepathic abilities of his uninvited mental guest.

He missed Teejay, wondered about her, longed for her. His astonishment was so extreme when he first heard her voice within his head that he almost awakened the parasite.

"Steve? Steve, is that you?"

"Teejay—"

"I've been trying to reach you. When these creatures sleep, we can use *their* minds."

"Then you're all right?"

"All right as can be expected, but they've been running me through all sorts of emotional mazes. My clothing is torn and they don't care about it. My skin is torn and bruised. They don't care about that, either. They'll run us down. Did you notice all the other creatures here? Some of their bones are broken—if they have bones—and the breaks appear to have never been set. They're bruised and bloody and infected and the parasites don't care! Why should they when they can get new bodies? But Steve—oh, Steve, I've never felt so unclean in all my life and it's just as if I've been defiled and—"

"Take it easy, Teejay. Thinking like that won't help."

"I hate them. Oh, I hate them. I—"

"Listen. I want you to concentrate like that. Hate weakens them. Remember how the animals aboard the *Frank Buck* died? Well, since our emotions are so much stronger than the parasites, maybe, maybe—"

"You mean it could work in reverse?"

"I don't know."

"You want me to try, darling?"

"Yes—no! We can't do it now. If it works, we'd still be leaving a hundred men here. They're doomed, Teejay. We're all doomed unless we can do something about it, and soon. But at night they sleep. Yeah, they sleep at night! If we can contact the others, and make a concentrated effort of it, using the telepathic powers of the parasites—"

"Shhh! That's enough, Steve. My friend here is getting up. I can feel him stirring inside my head. Shhh, later!"

At the end, hope had made Teejay her old spunky self again. But when Steve's own master awakened, that hope seemed mightily slim indeed.

Each night they managed to contact two or three of the others, and the word was supposed to be passed on. Finally, it was arranged. The night for action was decided upon, and for some few of them it would be a gamble, for there was no guarantee that all the parasites would be asleep. Once the attempt was made, however, there would be no turning back. Whoever was left behind—was left behind.

Provided the plan worked at all.

CHAPTER NINE

THE CREATURE was asleep again.

"I hate you," Steve said quietly.

Silence.

"I hate you." He thought it now, thought it with all his being—and somehow he could sense the thought was being reinforced as scores of men concentrated on it around the city. The mind within him stirred sluggishly, but he pushed it under again. Hate, hate, hate.

Hadn't the creature said it could kill them both? A gamble. Everything was a gamble. Naturally the parasite would say that.

Steve began to sweat, physically. He was weak and the muscles of his arms and legs trembled. His mind found the strange telepathic channel of the parasite, traveled inward along it—with hatred. That, at least, was easy. He did hate the creature so thoroughly and so completely that the feeling pushed everything else from his mind.

A concert of hatred, all over the city. And slumbering masters who might or might not awaken.

"Stop!" A clarion command inside his skull. The parasite was fighting back.

Steve tumbled to the floor and lay there, writhing. Two minds fought for control of his body, and he was being pushed back and out of control. He got to his feet stiffly, strode to a cabinet, took out a knife. He stared at the knife, fascinated, pointed it toward his chest.

"One of us must die, human, but it shall not be me!"

He drove the knife inward, slowly, an inch at a time toward his chest. He felt the point sting, saw a thin trickle of blood. For a moment, he fought to possess his arms and the knife with them. That was a mistake—almost, a fatal one.

The parasite wanted that, for in such a battle it would win every time. Perhaps it could not fight his hatred, but it could fight anything else he had to offer.

The knife went in, scraped against a rib.

Steve yelled hoarsely, drenched every atom of his soul in hatred. Slowly, he withdrew the knife, watched bright red blood well up after it.

Something tugged at his mind, slipped away—first scalding, then wet. It oozed out, and pain blurred Steve's vision as he tumbled to the floor again.

When he got up moments later and managed to staunch the flow of blood, he knew the parasite had perished.

BARELY SIXTY of them met near the city gate—grim and weary, most of them with fresh wounds. Steve's joy was an emotion the dead parasite would have loved to share when he saw Teejay among the sixty. Kevin was there too, and Steiner. Surprisingly, Schuyler Barling seemed more sprightly than the rest.

"LeClarc?" Steve demanded.

"He was the first," said Kevin. "Stronger control, perhaps. He's among those who could not make it."

"Maybe they're still alive."

"No," Teejay told him. "I saw three men die, horribly. Most of the others probably did, too."

"Don't you see, boy, we can't chance survival for all of us to seek out one or two who might still be alive! It wouldn't be fair." Kevin shook his head grimly.

Steve knew he was right. He was far too exhausted to argue, anyway. "Then we'll go as we are?"

"Well, there are half a dozen others in the gate-house now, forcing information from some of the hosts."

"What information?"

"About sub-space, boy. A hunter named McSweeney was possessed by a scientist of sorts, and he learned the sub-space gear is a compact little device that a man can carry. They store a few dozen of 'em in the gate-house, and—hello!"

Half a dozen men emerged from the stone structure, and one of them fell as a beam of energy seared out and caught him. A variety of creatures streamed out after them, triggering strange weapons. Soon the fighting became general, and it looked for a time as though the humans—without weapons of any sort—would be slaughtered. But Steve grabbed one of the stilt-creatures, twisted its neck quickly—and heard a sharp cracking sound. The creature fell and Steve plunged down with it, coming up with the hand-weapon and firing into the ranks that bore down upon them.

As others of the aliens fell, men retrieved their weapons, fighting back with ever-increased firepower, although their numbers were decreasing. And battling thus, they broke through the gate and out among the purple-misted hills. Hissing beams of energy emitted sufficient light to see by, and Kevin's voice could be heard roaring above the sounds of fighting:

"Stick together! If a man's lost in this purple fog, he's done for! Stick together!"

It was a nightmare. Steve fought shoulder to shoulder with Teejay. Now that he'd been reunited with her, there'd be no more separation, he vowed silently. Not unless he died here on the purple world.

Energy beams crossed back and forth as the men retreated, stumbling and darting among the little hillocks. Time lost its normally rigid control. Hours might have been minutes, or the other way around. Time became utterly subjective, with each man living in his own particular continuum. For Steve it seemed at least a short version of eternity until they reached the *Frank Buck*. And when they did, dawn was streaking the horizon with pale blue radiance, casting a deep purple shadow from the ship to where they fought.

It was Kevin who reached the airlock first. Kevin who sprung it open. Two by two they filed in, still facing the aliens and firing their weapons. At the last moment—when fully half of those who remained had entered the ship—the three anthrovacs appeared, came loping across the plain toward them.

Steve cut the first one down and drew careful aim on the second. It wasn't necessary. The third anthrovac abruptly turned on its fellow and sent it reeling, senseless, with one blow. In the confusion, its parasite must have been careless, must have relaxed its control. The anthrovac, which made a habit of miming men, whirled and began to wreck havoc among the pursuers.

It helped turn the tide of battle, and with Steve and Teejay, it was the last to enter the ship.

"TWENTY-TWO of us," Kevin said grimly. "There are twenty-two who survived." They all sat about, nursing their wounds. The ship had flung itself back through hyper-space and now hovered a million miles off Ganymede.

"You're wrong. There are twenty-three." It was Charlie Stedman. In the darkness and confusion, he'd managed to fight his way back with them. But why?

"Charlie!" Steve forgot the question. "You're free too."

Charlie lifted a neutron gun. "No. You're wrong. None of us is free. You'll find a ship has followed you here. And you're going to follow it back."

Of course, Steve thought dully. Charlie was dead. Charlie could not return as himself. But they were right back where they started from, for the creature who was Charlie could force their return.

Kevin stood near the viewport, spoke grimly. "He's not lying. There's a ship out there."

Schuyler Barling smiled coldly and took up his position near Charlie. "You all rejected my command once," he said. "You shouldn't have. I had no desire to come back to Earth like that. I've also learned that I can share my body on an equal basis with my master, something none of you would consider. Now we'll take you back."

Almost eighty men had died—for nothing. Steve held Teejay's hand briefly then released it. One life more wouldn't matter, and if there were a chance...

"Charlie, don't you remember anything?"

"What should I remember?"

"I'm your brother."

"That much I knew when I called you on Ganymede. But there are no emotional ties. Keep back!"

Steve took a step toward him. "You're my brother, and you wouldn't kill me. You can't."

It was wild, impossible, and he knew it. The creature was not his brother, had not been his brother for years. Yet if some small vestige of his brother's emotional memories remained—

"Keep back, I warn you!"

Steve could see the finger tightening on the trigger when he dove. His shoulder jarred Charlie's knees, and they went down together, rolling over and over on the floor. The neutron gun hissed once, between them, and Charlie relaxed.

A smile tugged at the corners of his mouth for a moment, and he said, "Steve." He died that way, with the smile still on his lips.

Schuyler Barling was laughing and screaming, froth flecking his chin. The delicate balance between parasite and host had been entangled, possibly beyond repair. Neither could dominate, and the result was a hopeless, gibbering hulk of a man.

"Poor devil," said Kevin. "He'll get psychiatric treatment on Earth, if that will help."

Steve crossed to the airlock, climbed into a spacesuit.

"What the hell do you think you're doing?" Teejay wanted to know.

"You're forgetting about the other ship. We haven't got a blasting cannon on the *Frank Buck*, and there isn't one down on the *Gordak*, either. But with no absorbing medium in space, one of these neutron guns can be a potent weapon." Steve clamped the fishbowl helmet down over his head and activated the airlock.

Soon he stood outside, with nothing but space on three sides of him. On the fourth, his magnetic boots gripped the *Frank Buck's* steeloid hull as he set himself, ready to fire the small handgun.

Energy flared brightly from its muzzle, and the other ship, a slim, sinister shape miles off in the void, flared up with it and dissolved in a shower of sparks and mist. But the neutron gun had a kick that dislodged Steve from the hull and sent him spinning off into space next to the ship.

Through the lock-port, no more than four feet away, he saw Kevin donning a vacsuit. The big Exec reached out to grab him but his arm fell a full foot short. All at once, Kevin was dwarfed by the anthrovac as the big animal joined him, scratching its head as Kevin reached out hopelessly into space. The gap was increasing.

Did the anthrovac understand? No, Steve thought; an anthrovac could no more understand than a parrot could actually talk. But like a parrot, an anthrovac could mimic.

A huge hairy arm reached out into space, the hand locking on Steve's gauntleted fist. He was drawn back into the *Frank Buck* and to safety, firing one more shot at the remains of the alien craft as he was pulled in. It was many minutes before they could stop the anthrovac from probing out experimentally into empty space.

"YOU KNOW," Steve told Teejay and Kevin later, "I think at the last minute my brother understood."

"It looked that way to me, boy," Kevin nodded. "So he died happy. But there's a lot of work for Earth to do. We'll have to clear the System of anything that remains here of Uashalume's power. And then maybe someday we'll have to get up an expedition and clean out that foul place."

"One good thing came from it," Steve told them. "We've got a subspace drive now, and the stars are ours." He lit a cigarette, frowning. "But I think we ought to go easy on our game-hunting, and you can tell that to Brody Carmical or anyone else, Teejay. Those creatures out there were hunters too, you know."

"Forget about the past, will you?" Teejay snapped at him, then grinned when he looked hurt. "I still feel unclean, Steve. I'd love to sit in a hot bath for about twenty-four hours straight."

Steve grinned back. "If we were married, I could scrub around your shoulder-blades for you."

Kevin cleared his throat ominously. "They made me Captain of this ship, didn't they. What are we waiting for?"

The ceremony was brief, and after it, Steve and Teejay hustled back to the recreation rooms and swimming pools with a bar of strong soap, a couple of washcloths, and a lot of pleasant ideas.

THE END

If you've enjoyed this book, you will not want to miss these terrific titles...

ARMCHAIR SCI-FI & HORROR DOUBLE NOVELS, $12.95 each

D-11 **PERIL OF THE STARMEN** by Kris Neville
THE FORGOTTEN PLANET by Murray Leinster

D-12 **THE STAR LORD** by Boyd Ellanby
CAPTIVES OF THE FLAME by Samuel R. Delaney

D-13 **MEN OF THE MORNING STAR** by Edmund Hamilton
PLANET FOR PLUNDER by Hal Clement and Sam Merwin, Jr.

D-14 **ICE CITY OF THE GORGON** by Chester S. Geier and Richard Shaver
WHEN THE WORLD TOTTERED by Lester Del Rey

D-15 **WORLDS WITHOUT END** by Clifford D. Simak
THE LAVENDER VINE OF DEATH by Don Wilcox

D-16 **SHADOW ON THE MOON** by Joe Gibson
ARMAGEDDON EARTH by Geoff St. Reynard

D-17 **THE GIRL WHO LOVED DEATH** by Paul W. Fairman
SLAVE PLANET by Laurence M. Janifer

D-18 **SECOND CHANCE** by J. F. Bone
MISSION TO A DISTANT STAR by Frank Belknap Long

D-19 **THE SYNDIC** by C. M. Kornbluth
FLIGHT TO FOREVER by Poul Anderson

D-20 **SOMEWHERE I'LL FIND YOU** by Milton Lesser
THE TIME ARMADA by Fox B. Holden

ARMCHAIR SCIENCE FICTION CLASSICS, $12.95 each

C-4 **CORPUS EARTHLING**
by Louis Charbonneau

C-5 **THE TIME DISSOLVER**
by Jerry Sohl

C-6 **WEST OF THE SUN**
by Edgar Pangborn

ARMCHAIR SCI-FI & HORROR GEMS SERIES, $12.95 each

G-1 **SCIENCE FICTION GEMS, Vol. One**
Isaac Asimov and others

G-2 **HORROR GEMS, Vol. One**
Carl Jacobi and others

If you've enjoyed this book, you will not want to miss these terrific titles…

ARMCHAIR SCI-FI & HORROR DOUBLE NOVELS, $12.95 each

D-21   **EMPIRE OF EVIL** by Robert Arnette
       THE SIGN OF THE TIGER by Alan E. Nourse & J. A. Meyer

D-22   **OPERATION SQUARE PEG** by Frank Belknap Long
       ENCHANTRESS OF VENUS by Leigh Brackett

D-23   **THE LIFE WATCH** by Lester Del Rey
       CREATURES OF THE ABYSS by Murray Leinster

D-24   **LEGION OF LAZARUS** by Edmond Hamilton
       STAR HUNTER by Andre Norton

D-25   **EMPIRE OF WOMEN** by John Fletcher
       ONE OF OUR CITIES IS MISSING by Irving Cox

D-26   **THE WRONG SIDE OF PARADISE** by Raymond F. Jones
       THE INVOLUNTARY IMMORTALS by Rog Phillips

D-27   **EARTH QUARTER** by Damon Knight
       ENVOY TO NEW WORLDS by Keith Laumer

D-28   **SLAVES TO THE METAL HORDE** by Milton Lesser
       HUNTERS OUT OF TIME by Joseph E. Kelleam

D-29   **RX JUPITER SAVE US** by Ward Moore
       BEWARE THE USURPERS by Geoff St. Reynard

D-30   **SECRET OF THE SERPENT** by Don Wilcox
       CRUSADE ACROSS THE VOID by Dwight V. Swain

ARMCHAIR SCIENCE FICTION CLASSICS, $12.95 each

C-7   **THE SHAVER MYSTERY, pt. 1**
       by Richard S. Shaver

C-8   **THE SHAVER MYSTERY, pt. 2**
       by Richard S. Shaver

C-9   **MURDER IN SPACE** by David V. Reed
       by David V. Reed

ARMCHAIR MASTERS OF SCIENCE FICTION SERIES, $16.95 each

M-3   **MASTERS OF SCIENCE FICTION, Vol. Three**
       Robert Sheckley, "The Perfect Woman" and other tales

M-4   **MASTERS OF SCIENCE FICTION, Vol. Four**
       Mack Reynolds, "Stowaway" and other tales

If you've enjoyed this book, you will not want to miss these terrific titles...

ARMCHAIR SCI-FI & HORROR DOUBLE NOVELS, $12.95 each

D-31   **A HOAX IN TIME** by Keith Laumer
           INSIDE EARTH by Poul Anderson

D-32   **TERROR STATION** by Dwight V. Swain
           THE WEAPON FROM ETERNITY by Dwight V. Swain

D-33   **THE SHIP FROM INFINITY** by Edmond Hamilton
           TAKEOFF by C. M. Kornbluth

D-34   **THE METAL DOOM** by David H. Keller
           TWELVE TIMES ZERO by Howard Browne

D-35   **HUNTERS OUT OF SPACE** by Joseph Kelleam
           INVASION FROM THE DEEP by Paul W. Fairman,

D-36   **THE BEES OF DEATH** by Robert Moore Williams
           A PLAGUE OF PYTHONS by Frederick Pohl

D-37   **THE LORDS OF QUARMALL** by Fritz Leiber and Harry Fischer
           BEACON TO ELSEWHERE by James H. Schmitz

D-38   **BEYOND PLUTO** by John S. Campbell
           ARTERY OF FIRE by Thomas N. Scortia

D-39   **SPECIAL DELIVERY** by Kris Neville
           NO TIME FOR TOFFEE by Charles F. Meyers

D-40   **JUNGLE IN THE SKY** by Milton Lesser
           RECALLED TO LIFE by Robert Silverberg

ARMCHAIR SCIENCE FICTION CLASSICS, $12.95 each

C-10   **MARS IS MY DESTINATION**
           by Frank Belknap Long

C-11   **SPACE PLAGUE**
           by George O. Smith

C-12   **SO SHALL YE REAP**
           by Rog Phillips

ARMCHAIR SCI-FI & HORROR GEMS SERIES, $12.95 each

G-3   **SCIENCE FICTION GEMS, Vol. Two**
           James Blish and others

G-4   **HORROR GEMS, Vol. Two**
           Joseph Payne Brennan and others

BRINGING THE DEAD BACK TO LIFE

It appeared to be the supreme irony. Humanity, apparently, feared being recalled to life even more than it feared death itself.

When Harker joined the little group of scientists, he didn't realize the problems he would be facing. Their amazing discovery made it possible to revive corpses to full, seemingly healthy life. Harker and his scientist comrades felt this amazing discovery would be heralded by humanity as the greatest boon of all time.

But Instead, the world fought them, bitterly and savagely. Bewildered, they could find no way to fight back. The problem was Harker's to solve, and there seemed to be only one answer...
Harker himself had to die!

CAST OF CHARACTERS

JAMES HARKER
They wanted him to act as a public advocate, arguing the case for the reanimation of the dead.

DR. BENEDICT LURIE
He wanted to give the world the science of reanimation. But was mankind ready to accept it?

CAL MITCHISON
This fired, disgruntled ex-employee decided to start a smear campaign against his former employers.

DR. MARTIN RAYMOND
The head of the reanimation project. He took on all the stumbling-blocks and obstacles thrown in his way.

SIMEON BARCHET
Money man for the great project… He sometimes proved to be more of a hindrance than a help.

DR. DAVID KLAUS
Twenty-nine years of age is ancient for an ex-prodigy. Watch him close though, he might put a scalpel in your back—literally!

RECALLED TO
LIFE

By
ROBERT SILVERBERG

ARMCHAIR FICTION
PO Box 4369, Medford, Oregon   97501-0168

*For more information about Armchair Books and products, visit our
website at…*

www.armchairfiction.com

Or email us at…

armchairfiction@yahoo.com

CHAPTER ONE

THAT MORNING James Harker was not expecting anything unusual to happen. He had painstakingly taught himself, these six months since the election, not to expect anything. He had returned to private law practice, and the Governorship and all such things were now bright memories, growing dimmer each month.

Morning of an Ex-Governor. There was plenty to do: the Bryant trust-fund business was due for a hearing next Thursday, and before that time Harker had to get his case in order. A pitiful thing: old Bryant, one of the glorious pioneers of space travel, assailed by greedy heirs in his old age. It was enough to turn a man cynical, Harker thought, unless a man happened to be cynical already.

He reached across his desk for the file-folder labeled BRYANT: Hearing 5/16/33. The sound of the outer-office buzz trickled into the room, and Harker realized he had accidentally switched on the interoffice communicator. He started to switch it off; he stopped when he heard a dry, thin voice say, "Is the Governor in?"

His secretary primly replied, "Do you mean Mr. Harker?"

"That's right."

"Oh. He—he doesn't like to be called the Governor, you know. Do you have an appointment with him?"

"I'm afraid not. Terribly foolish of me—I didn't realize I'd need one. I don't live in New York, you see, and I'm just here for a few days—"

"I'm extremely sorry, sir. I cannot permit you to see Mr. Harker without an appointment. He's *extremely* busy, you see."

"I'm quite aware of that," came the nervous, oddly edgy voice. "But it's something of an emergency, and—"

"Dreadfully sorry, sir. Won't you phone for an appointment?"

To the eavesdropping Harker, the conversation sounded like something left over from his Albany days. But he was no longer Governor of New York and he was no longer the fair-haired boy of the National Liberal Party. He wasn't being groomed for the Presidency now. And, suddenly, he found himself positively yearning to be interrupted.

Illustrated by BILL BOWMAN

recalled to Life

It was the greatest scientific breakthrough

of all time: reanimation after death. The trouble

was, it created more problems than it solved.

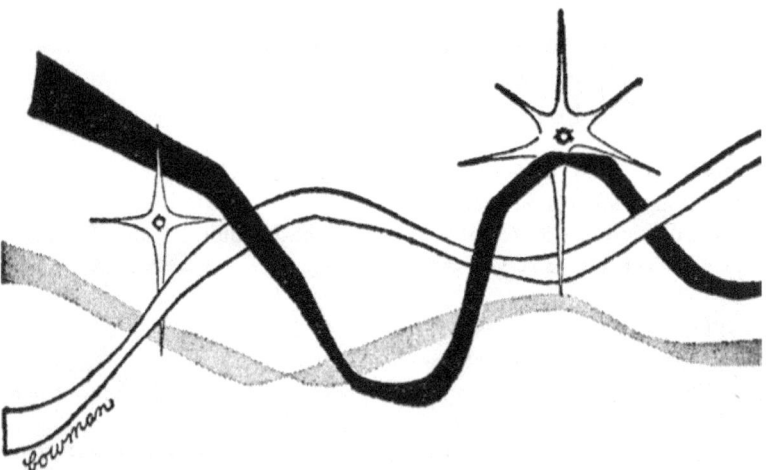

He leaned forward and said, "Joan, I'm not very busy right now. Suppose you send the gentleman in."

"Oh—uh—Mr. Harker. Of course, Mr. Harker." She sounded startled and irritated; perhaps she wanted to scold him for having listened in. Harker cut the audio circuit, slipped the Bryant file out

By ROBERT SILVERBERG

of sight, cleared his desk, and tried to look keenly awake and responsive.

A timid knock sounded at his office door. Harker pressed the open button; the door split laterally, the segments rising into the ceiling and sliding into the floor and a man in short frock coat and white unpressed trousers stepped through, grinning apologetically. A moment later the door snapped shut behind him.

"Mr. Harker?"

"That's right."

The visitor approached Harker's desk awkwardly; he walked as if his body were held together by baling wire, and as if his assembler had done an amateur job of it. His shoulders were extraordinarily wide for his thin frame, and long arms dangled loosely. He had a wide, friendly, toothy grin and much too much unkempt soft-looking brown hair. He handed Harker a card. The lawyer took it, spun it round right-side-up so he could read it, and scanned the neat engraved characters.

It said:

BELLER RESEARCH LABORATORIES
Litchfield, N.J.
Dr. Benedict Lurie

Harker frowned in concentration, shook his head, and said, "I'm sorry, Dr. Lurie. I'm afraid I've never heard of this particular laboratory."

"Understandable. We don't seek publicity. I'd be very surprised if you *had* heard of us." Lurie's head bobbed boyishly as he spoke; he seemed about as ill at ease a person as Harker had ever met.

"Cigarette?" Harker asked.

"Oh, no—never!"

Grinning, Harker took one himself, squeezed the igniting capsule with his index finger's nail, and put the pack away. He leaned back. Lurie's awkwardness seemed to be contagious; Harker felt strangely fidgety.

"I guess you're wondering why I came here to see you, Mr. Harker."

"Yes, I am."

Lurie interspliced his long and slightly quivering fingers, then, as if dissatisfied, separated his hands again, crossed his legs, and gripped his kneecaps. He blinked and swiveled his chair slightly to the left. Sensing that the sun slanting through the window behind the desk was bothering Lurie, Harker pressed the *opaque* button and the room's three windows dimmed.

Lurie said finally, "I'll begin at the beginning, Mr. Harker. The Beller Research Laboratories were established in 2024 by a grant from the late Darwin F. Beller, of whom you may have heard."

"The oil magnate," Harker said. *And a notorious crank*. The lawyer began to regret his impulsive action in inviting the gawky stranger in to see him.

"Yes. Beller of Beller Refineries. Mr. Beller provided our group with virtually unlimited funds, established us in a secluded area in New Jersey, and posed us a scientific problem: could we or could we not develop a certain valuable process? I'll be more specific in a moment. Let me say that many of the men Mr. Beller assembled for the project were openly skeptical of its success, but were willing to try—a triumphant demonstration of the scientific frame of mind."

Or of the willingness to grab a good thing when it comes along, Harker thought. He had had little experience with scientists, but plenty with human beings. Lurie's speech sounded as if it had been carefully rehearsed.

"To come to the point," Lurie said, uncrossing his legs again. "After eight years of research, our project has reached the point of success. In short, we've developed a workable technique for doing what we had hoped to do. Now we need a legal adviser."

Harker became more interested. "This is where I'm to come in, I suppose?"

"Exactly. Our process is, to say the least, a controversial one. We foresee multitudes of legal difficulties and other problems."

"I'm not a patent lawyer, Dr. Lurie. That's a highly specialized field of which I know very little. I can give you the name of a friend of mine—"

"We're not interested in a patent," Lurie said. "We want to give our process to mankind without strings. The problem is, will mankind accept it?"

A little impatiently Harker said, "Suppose you get down to cases, then. It's getting late, and I have a lot of work to do before lunch-time."

A funny little smile flickered at the corners of Lurie's wide mouth. He said, flatly, "All right. We've developed a process for bringing newly-dead people back to life. It works if there's no serious organic damage and the body hasn't been dead more than twenty-four hours."

For a long moment there was silence in Harker's office. Harker sat perfectly still, and it seemed to him he could hear the blood pumping in his own veins and the molecules of room-air crashing against his eardrums. He fought against his original instincts, which were to laugh or to show amazement.

Finally he said, "I'll assume for the sake of discussion that what you tell me is true. If it is, then you know you're holding down dynamite."

"We know that. That's why we came to you. You're the first prominent figure who hasn't thrown me out of his office as soon as I told him why I had come."

Sadly Harker said, "I've learned how to reserve judgment. I've also learned to be tolerant of crackpots or possible crackpots. I learned these things the hard way."

"Do you think I'm a crackpot, Mr. Harker?"

"I have no opinion. Not yet, anyway."

"Does that mean you'll take the case?"

"Did I say that?" Harker stubbed his cigarette out with a tense stiff-wristed gesture. "It violates professional ethics for me to ask you which of my colleagues you approached before you came to me, but I'd like to know how many there were, at least."

"You were fourth on the list," Lurie said.

"Umm. And the others turned you down flat?"

Lurie's open face reddened slightly. "Absolutely. I was called a zombie salesman by one. Another just asked me to leave. The third man advised me to blow up the labs and cut my throat. So we came to you."

Harker nodded slowly. He had a fairly good idea of whom the three others were, judging from the nature of their reactions. He himself had made no reaction yet, either visceral or intellectual. A year ago, perhaps, he might have reacted differently—but a year ago he had been a different person.

He said, "You can expect tremendous opposition to any such invention. I can guess that there'll be theological opposition, and plenty of hysterical public outbursts. And the implications are immense—a new set of medical ethics, for one thing. There'll be a need for legislation covering—ah—resurrection." He drummed on the desk with his fingertips. "Whoever agrees to serve as your adviser is taking on a giant assignment."

"We're aware of that," Lurie said. "The pay is extremely good. We can discuss salary later, if you like."

"I haven't said I'm accepting," Harker reminded him crisply. "For all I know right now this is just a pipe dream, wishful thinking on the part of a bunch of underpaid scientists."

Lurie smiled winningly. "Naturally we would not think of asking you to make a decision until you've seen our lab. If you think you're interested, a visit could be arranged some time this week or next—"

Harker closed his eyes for a moment. He said, "If I accepted, I'd be exposing myself to public abuse. I'd become a storm-center, wouldn't I?"

"You should be used to that, Mr. Harker. As a former national political figure—"

The *former* stung. Harker had a sudden glaring vision of his rise through the Nat-Lib Party ranks, his outstanding triumph in the 2024 mayoralty contest, his natural ascension to the gubernatorial post four years later—and then, the thumping fall, the retirement into private life, the painful packing-away of old aspirations and dreams—

He nodded wearily. "Yes, I know what it's like to be on the spot. I was just wondering whether it's worth-while to get back on the firing line again." He moistened his lips. "Look, Dr. Lurie, I have to think about this whole business some more. Is there someplace I can call you this afternoon?"

"I'm staying at the Hotel Manhattan," Lurie said. He retrieved his calling card and scribbled a phone number on it, then a room number, and handed it back to Harker. "I'll be there most of the afternoon, if you'd like to call."

Harker pocketed the card. "I'll let you know," he said.

Lurie rose and shambled toward the door. Harker pressed the *open* button and the two halves of the door dropped into their slots. Rising from the desk, he accompanied Lurie through the door and into the outer office. The scientist's stringy frame towered five or six inches over Harker's compact, still-lean bulk. Harker glanced up at the strangely soft eyes.

"I'll call you later, Dr. Lurie."

"I hope so. Thank you for listening, Governor."

Harker returned to the office, reflecting that the final *Governor* had either been savagely unkind or else a bit of unconscious absent-mindedness. Either way, he tried to ignore it.

He dumped himself behind his desk, frowning deeply, and dug his thumbs into his eyeballs. After a moment he got up, crossed to the portable bar, and dialed himself a whiskey sour. He sipped thoughtfully.

Resurrection. A crazy, grotesque idea. A frightening one. But science had come up with a method for containing the hundred-million-degree fury of a fusion reaction; why not a method for bringing the recent dead back to life?

No, he thought. He wasn't primarily in doubt of the possibility of the process. It was dangerous to be too skeptical of the potentialities of science.

It was his own part in the enterprise that made him hold back. What Lurie evidently had in mind was for him to act as a sort of public advocate, arguing their case before the courts of law and of human opinion. It was a frighteningly big job, and if the tide swept against him he would be carried away.

Then he smiled. *What have I to lose?*

He eyed the tridims of his wife and sons that occupied one corner of his desk. His political career, he thought, couldn't be any deader than it was now. His own party had cast him loose, refusing to name him for a second term when he indiscreetly defied the state committee in making a few appointments. His law practice did well, though not spectacularly; in any event, he was provided for financially by his investments.

He had nothing to lose but his good name, and he had already lost most of that in the political mess. And he had a whole world to win.

Revival of the dead? *How about a dead career,* Harker wondered. *Could I revive that too?*

Rising from his desk, he paced round the office, pausing to depolarize the windows. Bright morning sunshine poured in. Through his window he could see the playground of the public school across the street. Thin-legged girls of nine or ten were playing a punchball game; he could hear the shrieks of delight or anguish even at this distance.

A sudden sharp image came to him: himself, nine years before, standing spreadlegged on the beach at Riis Park, with Lois staring white-faced at him and three-year-old Chris peeking strangely around her legs. It was a blisteringly hot day; his skin, to which sand had adhered, was red, raw, tender. He heard the booming of the surf, the overhead *zoop* of a Europe-bound rocket, the distant cry of refreshment venders and the nearer laughter of small girls.

He was not laughing. He was holding a small, cold, wet bundle tight, and he was crying for the first time in twenty years. He huddled his drowned five-year-old daughter to him, and tried to pretend it had not happened.

It *had* happened, and Eva was dead—the girl-child who he had planned would be America's darling when he reached the White House, fifteen years or so from now.

That had been nine years ago. Eva would have been nearly fifteen, now, flowering into womanhood. He had no daughter. *But she could have lived,* Harker thought. *Maybe.*

He returned to his desk and sat quietly for a while. After twenty minutes of silent thought he reached for the phone and punched out Lurie's number.

CHAPTER TWO

HARKER HAD an appointment to visit old Richard Bryant at three that afternoon. He was not looking forward to it. Since Bryant was confined to his home by doctor's orders, it meant that Harker would have to visit the old man, and that meant entering a house where death seemed to hang heavy over the threshold, a house filled with graspingly impatient relatives of the venerable hero of space-travel's infancy.

At half past two Harker notified his secretary that he was leaving; he gathered up the portfolio of relevant papers, locked his office, and took the gravshaft down to street level. He emerged on First Avenue, and walked quickly downtown toward 125th Street.

It was a bright, warmish, cloudless May afternoon. A bubble of advertising was the only blot on the otherwise flawless sky. The Manhattan air was clean, tingling, fresh. Harker never breathed it in without thinking of the vast dynamos of the puritron stations every ten blocks apart, gulping in tons and tons of city soot each second. In his second year as Mayor, the entire Brooklyn puritron assembly had "accidentally" conked out for four hours, thanks to some half-forgotten labor squabble. Harker remembered the uproar *that* had caused.

At 125th Street he boarded the cross-town monorail and moments later found himself disembarking at the Riverside Drive exit. He signaled for a cab; while he waited, a blearyeyed old man shuffled over to him, shoved a gaudy pamphlet in his hands, greeted him by name, and shuffled away.

He looked at it. It was one of the many official organs of the Watchtower Society. As he stuffed it in the corner disposal-bin, he smiled in recollection of that organization's motto: MILLIONS NOW LIVING WILL NEVER DIE.

Gravely he proposed a substitute: MILLIONS NOW DEAD WILL LIVE AGAIN.

The attendant images effectively choked off the mood of good humor that had been stealing over him. He remembered that in only two days he would be journeying across the Hudson to see whether the Beller Laboratories people had actually hit on something or not.

The cab drew up. Harker slid into the back seat and said, "Seventy-ninth and West End, driver."

The house was a massive, heavily chromed representative of late twentieth-century architecture, settling now into respectable middle age. Harker had visited it on three separate occasions, and each time his discomfort had increased.

It had no gravshaft; he rode up in a human-operated elevator. The operator said, "I guess you're going to visit Mr. Bryant, eh, Mr. Harker?"

"That's right."

"The old gentleman's been poorish lately, sir. Ah, it'll be a sad thing when he goes, won't it?"

"He's one of our greatest," Harker agreed. "Many people up there today?"

"The usual lot," the operator said, halting the car and opening the door. It opened immediately into the foyer of the huge Bryant apartment. Almost at once, Harker found himself staring at the fishy, cold-eyed face of Jonathan Bryant, the old man's eldest son.

"Good afternoon, Jonathan."

"Hello, Harker." The reply was sullenly brusque. "You're here to see my father?"

"I didn't come for tea," Harker snapped. "Will you invite me in, or should I just push past you?"

Jonathan muttered something and gave ground, allowing Harker to enter. The living room was crowded: half-a-dozen miscellaneous Bryants, plus two or three whom Harker did not know but who bore the familiar Bryant features. A horde of vultures, Harker thought. He nodded to them with professional courtesy and passed on, through the inner rooms, to the old man's sickroom.

The place was lined with trophies—one room, Harker knew, consisted of the cockpit of the *Mars One*, that slender needle of a ship that had borne Rick Bryant to the red planet nearly fifty years ago, an epoch-making flight that still stood large in the annals of space-travel. Trophy-cases in the halls held medals, souvenir watches, testimonial dinner-menus. Old Bryant had been a prodigious collector of souvenirs.

His doctor, a tiny man with the look of an irritated penguin, met him at the door to the sickroom. "I'll have to ask you to limit your stay to thirty minutes, Mr. Harker. He's very low today."

"I'll be as brief as I can," Harker promised. He stepped around the barricade and entered.

Helen Bryant, oldest of the daughters, sat solicitously by her father's bedside, glaring at him with the tender expression of a predatory harpy.

Harker said, "If you'll excuse me, Miss Bryant, your father and I have some important business to discuss."

"I'm his daughter. Can't I—"

"I'm afraid not," Harker said coldly. He waited while she made her proud retreat, then took her seat at the side of the bed.

"Afternoon, Harker," Bryant said in a tomb-like croak. He was not a pretty sight. He was seventy-three, and could easily pass for twice that age—a shrunken, leathery little man with rheumy, cataracted eyes and a flat, drooping face. There was little about him that was heroic, now. He was just a dying old man.

The needles of an intravenous feed-line penetrated his body at various points. He no longer had the strength to swallow or to digest. It was difficult to believe that this man had made the first successful round-trip flight to another planet, back in 1984, and that from his early thirties until his stroke four years ago he had been a figure of world importance, whose words were eagerly rushed into print whenever he cared to make a statement.

He said, "How does it look for next Thursday?"

Harker's jaws tightened. "Pretty good. I hope to be able to swing it."

"How have you set it up?"

Harker drew the papers from his portfolio. "Twenty million is to be established as a trust fund for your grandchildren and for the children of your grandson Frederick. Thirty million is to be granted to the Bryant Foundation for Astronautical Research. Fifty thousand is to be divided among your children, ten thousand to each."

"Is that last bit necessary?" Bryant asked with sudden ferocity.

"I'm afraid it is."

"I wanted to cut those five jackals off without a penny!" he thundered. Then, subsiding, he coughed and said, "Why must you give them so much?"

"There are legal reasons. It makes it harder for them to overthrow the will, you see."

The old man was reluctant to accept the idea of giving his children anything, and in a way Harker could see the justice of that. They were a hateful bunch. Bryant had garnered millions from his space-journey, and had invested the money wisely and well; there had been an undignified scramble for the old hero's wealth when a stroke appeared to have killed him in '28. He had confounded them all by recovering, and by cutting most of them out of his revised will—a document that was being contested in the courts even while the old man still lived.

At three-thirty, the penguinish doctor knocked discreetly at the bedchamber door, poked his head in, and said, "I hope you're almost through, Mr. Harker."

At that moment old Bryant was trying to sign a power-of-attorney Harker had prepared; his palsied hand could barely manage the signature, but in time he completed it. Harker looked at it: a wavy scrawl that looked like a random pattern on a seismograph drum.

"I'm leaving now," Harker told the doctor.

Bryant quavered, "What time is the hearing next Thursday, Harker?"

"Half past eleven."

"Be sure to call me when it's finished."

"Of course. You just relax, Mr. Bryant. Legally they can't trouble you at all."

He reaped a harvest of sour glances as he made his way through the trophy-cluttered halls to the elevator. It was a depressing place, and the sight of the shattered hero always clouded his mind with gloom. He was glad to get away.

Riding a cab downtown to Grand Central, he boarded the 4:13 express to Larchmont, and eleven minutes later was leaving the Larchmont tube depot and heading in a local cab toward his home. At quarter to five, he stepped through the front door.

Lois was in the front room, standing on a chair and doing something to the ceiling mobile. Silently Harker crept in; standing with arms akimbo at the door, he said, "It's high time we junked that antique, darling."

She nearly fell off the chair in surprise. *"Jim!* What are you—"

"Home early," Harker said. "Had an appointment with old Bryant and the medics tossed me out quick, so I came home. Gah! Filthy business, that Bryant deal."

He slipped out of his jacket and loosened his throat-ribbon. He paused for a moment at the mirror, staring at himself: the fine, strong features, the prematurely iron-gray hair, the searching blue eyes. It was the face of a natural leader, an embryo President. But there was something else in it now—a coldness around the eyes, a way of quirking the corners of his mouth—that showed a defeated man, a man who has climbed to the top of his string and toppled back to the ground. With forty years of active life ahead of him.

"Hello, Dad. Want a drink?"

It was the already-deepening voice of twelve-year-old Chris that drew him away from his reverie. In recent months he had let the boy prepare his homecoming cocktail for him. But today he shook his head. "Sorry, son. I don't happen to be thirsty tonight."

Disappointment flashed briefly in the boy's handsome face; then it faded. Minor setbacks like this meant little to a boy who had expected once to live in the White House, and who knew now it wouldn't be happening.

"Where's Paul?" Harker asked.

"Upstairs doing his homework," Chris said. He snorted. "The ninny's learning long division. Having fits with it, too."

Harker stared at his son strangely for a moment; then he said, "Chris, go upstairs and give him some help. I want to talk to Mum."

"Sure, Dad."

When the boy had gone, Harker turned to his wife. Lois at forty, three years his junior—was still slim and attractive; her blonde hair had lost its sheen and soon would be shading into gray, but she seemed to welcome rather than fear the imprint of age.

She said, "Jim, why did you look at Chris that way?"

In answer, Harker crossed to the table near the window and his fingers sought out the tridim of dead Eva, its bright colors losing some of their sharpness now after nine years. "I was trying to picture him as a teenage girl," he said heavily. "Eva would have been fifteen soon."

Her only outward reaction was a momentary twitch of the lower lip. "You haven't thought of her for a long time."

"I know. I try not to think of her. But I thought of her today. I was thinking that she didn't have to be dead, Lois."

"Of course not, dear. But it happened, and there was no help for it."

He shook his head. Replacing Eva's picture, he picked up instead a tiny bit of bric-a-brac, a kaleidoscopic crystal in whose depths were swirling streaks of red and gold and dark black. He shook it; the color-patterns changed. "I mean," he said carefully, "that Eva might have been saved, even after the accident."

"They tried to revive her. The pulmotor—"

"No. Lois, I had a—a person visit me this morning. A certain Dr. Lurie, from a certain research laboratory in New Jersey. He claims they've developed a technique for bringing the dead back to life, and he wants me to handle promotion and legal aspects. For a fat fee, I might add."

She frowned uncertainly. "Reviving the dead? What kind of crazy joke is that?"

"I don't know. But I'm not treating it as a joke; not until I've seen the evidence, anyway. I made an appointment to go out to Jersey and visit their lab on Friday."

"And you'll take the job, if they've really hit on something?"

Harker nodded. "Sure I'll take it. It's risky, of course, and there's sure to be a lot of public clamor in both directions—"

"And haven't we had enough of that? Weren't you satisfied when you tried to reform the state government, and wound up being read out of the party? Jim, do you have to be Quixote all the time?"

Her words had barbs. Harker thought bleakly that being able always to see both sides of a question, as he could, was a devil-granted gift. Wearily he said, "All right. I tried to do something I thought was

right, and I got my head chopped off as a result. Well, here's my second chance—maybe. For all I know they're a bunch of lunatics over there. I owe it to myself and to the world to find out—and to help them, if I can."

He pointed at the tridim of Eva. "Suppose that happened *now*—Eva, I mean. Wouldn't you want to save her? Or," he said, making his words deliberately harsh, "suppose Paul dies. Wouldn't you want to be able to call him back from—from wherever he had gone?"

For a moment there was silence.

"Well? Wouldn't you?"

Lois shrugged, turning her hands palm outward. "Jim, I don't know. I don't know."

CHAPTER THREE

AT THREE minutes past two on Friday afternoon Harker's secretary buzzed him to let him know Dr. Lurie had arrived. Harker felt momentary apprehension. Cautious, even a little conservative by nature, he felt uneasy about paying a visit to a laboratory of—for all he knew—mad scientists.

He turned on an amiable grin when Lurie arrived. The scientist looked less gawky than before, more sure of himself; he wore what seemed to be the same rumpled clothing.

"The car's downstairs," Lurie said.

Harker left word at the front desk that he was leaving for the day, telling the girl to refer all calls to one of the other partners in the firm. He followed Lurie into the gravshaft.

The car idled in the temporary-parking area outside—a long, low, thrumming '33 turbo-job, sleekly black and coming with a $9000 price tag at the least. There were three men inside. Lurie touched a knob; the back door peeled back, and he and Harker got in. Harker looked around.

They were looking at him, too. Minutely.

The man at the wheel was a fleshy, hearty-looking fellow in his late fifties, who swiveled in a full circle to peer unabashedly at Harker. Next to him was a thin, pale, intense young man with affectedly thick glasses (no reason why he couldn't wear contacts instead, Harker thought) and sitting at the far side in back was the third, a coolly self-possessed individual in black clothes.

The fleshy man at the wheel said, "How do you do, Governor Harker. I'm Cal Mitchison—no scientist I, heh-heh! I'm public-liaison man for Beller Labs."

Harker smiled relatively courteously.

Mitchison said, "Man next to me is Dr. David Klaus, one of Beller's bright young men. Specialty is enzyme research."

"H-h-hello," Klaus said with difficulty. Harker smiled in reply.

"And to your left is Dr. Martin Raymond. Mart's the Director of Beller Labs," Mitchison said.

"Pleased to meet you," said Raymond. His voice was deep, well modulated, even. Harker sensed that this was a man of tremendous inner strength and purpose. Raymond was a type Harker had seen before, and respected: the quietly intense sort that remained in the background, accumulating intensity like a tightening mainspring, capable of displaying any amount of energy or drive when it was needed.

"And you already know Ben Lurie, of course," Mitchison said. "So we might as well get on our way."

The trip took a little over an hour, with Mitchison making a cross-town hop via the 125th Street Overpass, then ducking downtown to 110th Street and taking the Cathedral Avenue rivertube across the Hudson into New Jersey. The Village of Litchfield turned out to be one of those Jersey towns of a thousand souls or so that look just like every other small Jersey town: a railroad siding, a block or two of shopping center, bank, post office, then a string of old split-levels rambling away from the highway in every direction.

Mitchison, handling his big car with an almost sensuous delight, drove on through the main part of town, into the open country again, and about a mile and a half past the heart of the village suddenly turned up a small road prominently labeled PRIVATE: KEEP OUT. TRESPASSERS WILL BE PROSECUTED.

The road wound inward through a thick stand of close-packed spruce for more than a thousand feet, at which point a roadblock became evident. Two apparently armed men stood guard at either side of the road.

Mitchison opened the doors and the five occupants of the car got out. Harker took a deep breath. The air out here was sweet and pure, and not with the mechanical purity of Manhattan's strained and filtered atmosphere. He liked the feel of fresh air against his nostrils and throat.

Lurie said to the guards, "This is Mr. James Harker. We've brought him here to visit the labs."

"Right."

The guard who had grunted assent took a red button from his pocket and jammed it against Harker's lapel. It adhered. "That's your security tag. Keep it visible at all times or we can't answer for the consequences."

"What if it falls off?"

"It won't."

Harker and his companions followed round the roadblock while Mitchison took the car somewhere to be parked. Harker saw three large buildings, all of them very old, and several smaller cabins behind them, at the very edge of the encroaching forest.

"Those are the dormitories for the researchers," Lurie said, pointing to the cabins. "The big building over here is the administrative wing, and the other two are lab buildings."

Harker nodded. It was an impressive setup. The group turned into the administrative building.

It was every bit as old-fashioned on the inside as outside. The lighting was, of all things, by incandescent bulbs; the air-conditioners were noisily evident, and the windows did not have opaquing controls. Harker followed the other three into a small, untidy, book-lined room—and, suddenly, he realized that Dr. Raymond was taking charge.

"This is my office," Raymond said. "Won't you be seated?" Harker sat. He reached for his cigarettes and Raymond interjected immediately, "Sorry, but no smoking is permitted anywhere on the laboratory grounds."

"Of course."

Raymond sat back. Klaus and Lurie flanked him. In a quiet, terribly calm voice, Raymond said, "I think Dr. Lurie has explained the essentials of our situation."

"All I know is that you claim to have perfected a process for restoring the dead to life, and that you want me to act as legal adviser and public spokesman. Is that right?"

"Indeed. The fee will be $600 per week for as long as your services will be required."

"For which you'll insist on my full-time participation, I expect."

"We have confidence in your ability, Mr. Harker. You may apportion your time as you see fit."

Harker nodded slowly. "On the surface, I don't see any objections. But naturally I'll expect a thorough demonstration of what you've achieved so far, if I'm to take on any kind of work for you."

Levelly Raymond said, "We would hardly think of employing you unless we could take you into our fullest confidence. Come with me."

He opened an inner door and stepped through; Harker walked around the desk to follow him, with Klaus and Lurie bringing up the rear.

They now were in a large room with the faint iodoform odor Harker associated with hospitals; it was brightly, almost starkly lit, and Harker saw two lab tables, one empty, one occupied by a dog, both surrounded by looming complex mechanical devices. A bearded, grave-looking young man in the white garb of a surgeon stood by the dog-laden table.

"Are we ready, Dr. Raymond?"

Raymond nodded. To Harker he said, "This is Dr. Vogel. One of our surgeons. He will anesthetize the dog you see and kill it."

Harker moistened his lips nervously. He knew better than to protest, but the idea of casually killing animals in science's name touched off a host of involuntary repugnance-reactions in him.

He watched stonily as Vogel fitted a mask over the dog's face—it was a big, shaggy animal of indeterminate breed—and attached instruments to its body.

"We're recording heartbeat and respiration," Raymond murmured. "The anesthetic will gradually overcome the dog. In case you're concerned, the animal feels no pain in any part of this experiment."

Some moments passed; finally Vogel peered at his dials, nodded, and pronounced the dog in full narcosis. Harker fought against the inner tension that gripped him.

"Dr. Vogel will now bring death to the dog," Raymond said.

With practiced, efficient motions the surgeon slit the animal's blood vessels, inserted tubes, adjusted clamps. An assistant glided forward from the corner of the room to help. Harker found a strange fascination in watching the lifeblood drain from the dog into dangling containers. The needle registering the heartbeat sank inexorably toward zero; respiration dropped away. At last Vogel looked up and nodded.

"The dog is dead," he declared. "The blood's been drained off. This pump will ensure oxygenation of the blood during the period of the animal's death. We will now proceed to the next table—"

Where, Harker saw, another dog had been placed while his attention had been riveted on the death scene. This dog lay in a slumped furry heap that grotesquely reminded Harker of Eva as she had looked when they pulled her from the sea. His throat felt terribly dry.

"This animal," Vogel said stiffly, "underwent the killing treatment nine hours and thirteen minutes ago. Its blood has been stored during that time. Now—"

Spellbound, Harker watched the surgeon's busy hands as he and the assistant fastened tubes to the dead animal's body and lowered a complicated instrument into place. "We are now restoring blood to the dead animal. When the indicator gauge reads satisfactorily, injection of adrenaline and other hormones will restore 'life' to the animal. The blood is being pumped back at the same rate and rhythm that the animal's own heart uses."

"In some cases," Raymond remarked, "we've restored dogs dead nearly thirty-six hours."

Harker nodded. He was forcing himself to a realization of the gulf that lay between these calmly efficient men and himself. Yet they needed him and he needed them; neither type of mind was complete in itself.

The resuscitation of the second dog took fifteen minutes.

At length Vogel nodded, withdrew the reviving apparatus. The heartbeat indicator was fluttering; respiration was beginning. The dog's eyes opened wearily. It wagged its tail feebly and almost comically.

Lurie remarked, "For the next several hours the dog will show signs of having undergone a serious operation—which it has. In a day or two it'll be as good as new—once the stitches have healed, of course. In Lab Building Two we can show you dozens of dogs that have been through the killing process and were returned to life, happy, hearty—"

"This dog," Raymond said calmly, "is the *son* of a dog we temporarily 'killed' two years ago. The period of death doesn't seem to interfere with later mating or with any other life process."

While they spoke, Vogel was repeating the process of revivification on the dog that had been killed twenty minutes before. This time Harker watched with less revulsion as life returned to the animal.

In a dry voice he said, "Your experiments—are—well, impressive."

Raymond shook his head. "On the contrary. We've merely repeated work that was carried out more than eighty years ago. These techniques are far from new. But our application of them to—"

"Yes," Harker said weakly. "To *human* life. That's—that's the clincher, I'd say."

Harker realized that Raymond was staring at him coldly, appraisingly, as if trying to read his mind before proceeding to the next demonstration. Harker felt his face reddening under the scrutiny.

"We're lucky enough to be able to—ah—*clinch* things," Raymond said.

"With a human being?"

Raymond nodded. "You understand that getting human specimens for research has been our gravest problem. I'll have to ask you not to voice any of the questions that may arise in your mind now."

Harker nodded. He could recognize a security blanket when it was lowered.

Raymond turned and said in a mortuary voice, "Bring in Mr. Doe."

Two attendants entered, carrying a sheet-shrouded form on a stretcher. They deposited the figure on the vacant lab table that had held the second dog. Harker saw that it was a man, in his late sixties, bald, dead.

"Mr. Doe has been dead for eleven hours and thirteen minutes," Raymond said. "He died of syncope during an abdominal operation. Would you care to examine the body?"

"I'll accept the evidence on faith, thanks."

"As you will. Dr. Vogel, you can begin."

While Vogel worked over the cadaver, Raymond went on, "The process is essentially compounded out of techniques used for decades with varying success—that is, a combination of pulmotor respiration, artificial heart massage, hormone-injection, and electrochemical stimulation. The last two are the keys to the process: you can massage a heart for days and keep it pumping blood, but that isn't restoration of life."

"Not unless the heart can continue on its own when you remove the artificial stimulus?"

"Exactly. We've done careful hormone research here, with some of the best men in the nation. A hormone, you know, is a kind of chemical messenger. We've synthesized the hormones that tell the body it's alive. Of course, the electrochemical stimulation is important: the brain's activity is essentially electrical in nature, you know. And so we devised techniques which—"

"Ready, Dr. Raymond."

Harker compelled himself to watch. Needles plunged into the corpse's skin; electrodes fastened to the scalp discharged suddenly. It was weird, terrifying, laden with burdensome implications for the future. All that seemed missing was the eerie blue glow that characterized the evil experiments of stereotyped mad scientists.

He told himself that these men were not mad. He told himself that what they were doing was a natural outgrowth of the scientific techniques of the past century, that it was no more terrifying to restore life than it was to preserve it with antibiotics or serums. But he sensed a conflict within himself: he knew that if he accepted this assignment, he could embrace the idea intellectually but that somewhere in the moist jungle-areas of his subconscious mind he would feel disturbed and repelled.

"Watch the needles," Raymond whispered. "Heartbeat's beginning now. Respiration. The electroencephalograph is recording brain currents again."

"The test, of course, is whether these things continue after your machinery is shut off, isn't it?" Harker asked.

"Of course."

Time edged by. Harker's overstrained attention wandered; he took in the barren peeling walls of the lab, the dingy window through which late-afternoon light streamed. He had heard somewhere that the old-fashioned incandescent bulbs emitted a 60-cycle hum, and he tried unsuccessfully to hear it. Sweat-blotches stippled his shirt.

"Now!" Vogel said. He threw a master lever. The equipment whined faintly and cut off.

The heartbeat recorder and the respiration indicator showed a momentary lapse, then returned to their previous level. The EEG tape continued recording.

Harker's eyes widened slightly. A slow smile appeared on Raymond's face; behind him, Harker could hear Lurie cracking his knuckles nervously, and bespectacled Dr. Klaus tensely grinding his molars together.

"I guess we did it," Vogel said.

The dead man's arms moved slowly. His eyelids fluttered, but the anesthetic insured continued unconsciousness. His lips parted—and the soft groan that came forth was, for Harker, the clincher he had been half-hoping would not be forthcoming.

The man groaned again. Harker felt suddenly weary, and turned his head away.

CHAPTER FOUR

HARKER'S SHOCK reaction was violent, instinctive, and brief. He quivered uncontrollably, put his hands to his face, and started to lose his balance. Raymond was right there; he caught him, held him upright for a moment, and released him. Harker wobbled and grinned shamefacedly.

"That's strong stuff," he said.

"I've got stronger stuff in my office. Come on."

He and the lab director returned to the adjoining room. Raymond closed the door and clicked it; Lurie and Klaus remained in the lab. Raymond reached into his bookcase, pushed a thick black-bound volume to one side, and withdrew a half-empty bottle of Scotch. He poured a double shot for Harker, a single for himself, and replaced the bottle. Harker swallowed the liquor in two frantic gulps. He gasped, grinned again, and shakily set down the glass. "God. I'm roasting in my own sweat."

"It isn't a pleasant sight the first time, I guess. I wish I could share some of your emotional reaction, but I'm blocked out. My dad was a biochemist, specialty life-research. He had me cutting up frogs when I was three. I'm numb to any such reactions by now."

"Don't let that trouble you," Harker said. He shivered. "I could live very happily without seeing another demonstration of your technique, you know."

Raymond chuckled. "Does that mean you're convinced we aren't quacks?"

Harker shrugged. "What you've got is incredible. I wonder if I've got the voltage needed to handle the job you want me to do."

"You wouldn't be here if we didn't think so."

"I was fourth on the list," Harker said. "Lurie told me."

"You were my personal choice. I was outvoted. But I knew you'd accept and the other three would turn us down without even coming out here to investigate."

"I haven't said I've accepted," Harker pointed out.

"Well? Do you?"

Harker was silent for a moment, his mind returning to the impact of the scene he had just witnessed. There was still plenty he had to know, of course: the corporate setup of this lab, including knowledge of the powers that had "outvoted" the director; the financial resources behind him; the possible bugs in the technique.

A dozen implications unfolded. His mind was already at work planning the campaign. He was thinking of people to see, wires to pull, angles to check.

"I accept," he said quietly.

Raymond smiled and reached into his desk. He handed Harker a check drawn on a Manhattan bank for $2400, payable to James Harker, and signed *Simeon Barchet, Treasurer.*

"What's this?"

"That's four weeks salary, in advance. Barchet's the trustee who administers the Beller Fund. I had him write the check yesterday. I was pretty confident you'd join us, you see."

Harker spent a quietly tense weekend at home with his family. He told Lois about the assignment, of course; he never kept things from her, even the most unpleasant. She was dubious, but willing to rely on his judgment.

He worked off some of his physical tension by playing ball in the back yard with his sons. Chris, entering adolescence, was developing an athlete's grace; seven-year-old Paul did not yet have the coordination needed for catching and throwing a baseball, but he gave it a good try.

On Sunday the four of them drove upstate to a picnic-ground, ate out, even went for a brief swim though it was really too early in the season for that. Harker splashed and laughed with his sons, but there was an essential somberness about him that Lois quietly pointed out.

"I know," he admitted. "I'm thinking."

"About the Beller Labs business?"

He nodded. "I keep finding new angles in it. I try to guess what the reaction of the organized churches will be, and what political capital will be made. More likely than not the parties will take opposite stands. Somebody will dig up the fact that I used to be a National Liberal bigwig, and that'll enter into the situation. After a while it'll become so confused by side-issues that—" He stopped. "I don't sound very enthusiastic about this job, do I?"

"No," Lois said. "You don't."

"I guess I really haven't made up my mind where I stand," he said. "There are too many tangential things I don't know about yet."

"Like what?"

Harker shook his head. "I'm trying not to think about them. This is my day off, remember?"

On Monday he polished off his routine work early, by half-past-ten, and stepped out of his office. He walked down the beige corridor to the door inscribed WILLIAM F. KELLY and knocked.

"Bill? Me, Jim."

"Come on in, boy."

Kelly was sitting back of an impeccably clear mahogany desk, looking well barbered, well manicured, well fed. He was the senior partner of the law firm that now called itself Kelly, Harker, Portobello, and Klein. In his late fifties, ruddy-faced, quick-witted, Kelly was by religion a loyal Catholic and by politics a determined maverick.

He said, "How's the ex-Governor this morning?"

Harker grinned. Kelly was the one man who could not offend him with those words. "A washed-up has-been, as usual. Bill, I've got a big offer to do some work for a Jersey outfit. I think it's going to tie me up for the next few months. I thought I'd let you know."

Kelly blinked, then grinned, showing even white teeth. "Full-time?"

"Pretty near."

"How about your pending cases?"

Harker said, "I'm keeping the Bryant case. Fuller and Heidell will have to be handed over to someone else, I'm afraid."

"I guess you know what you're doing, Jim. Who's the big client?"

"Hush-hush. Nice pay, though."

"Can't even tell old Bill, eh? Well, I know better than to pry. But how come you're telling me all this, anyway? I don't give a damn what work you take on, Jim. You're a free agent here."

Calmly Harker said, "I thought I'd let you know because the account's a controversial one. I want you to realize that I'm doing it on my own hook and not as a member of K.H.P. & K. When and if the boomerang comes around and hits me in the face, I don't want you and Mike and Phil to get black eyes too."

Dead seriousness replaced the amiable grin on Kelly's pink face. "Have I ever backed off a hot item, Jim?"

"You might back off this one."

Kelly leaned forward and turned on all his considerable personal charm. "Look here, son, I'm a decade older than you are and a damned sight cagier. Maybe you better talk this thing out with me. If you're free for lunch—"

"I'm not," Harker said doggedly. "Bill, let's drop the whole thing. I know what I'm getting into and I didn't come here for advice. Okay?"

Kelly began to chuckle. "You said the same damn thing the night you were elected Governor. Remember, when you started telling me about how you were going to turn the whole State machine upside-down? I warned you, and I warn you again, but you don't learn. The only thing that got turned upside-down was you."

"So I'm a fool. But at least I'm a *dedicated* fool."

"That's the worst kind," Kelly drawled amiably. As Harker started to leave the older man's office Kelly added, "Good luck, anyway, on whatever you're getting your fool feet tangled up in."

"Thanks, Bill. Sorry I have to be so tight-mouthed."

On his way back to his office he passed the reception desk; Joan looked up at him and said, "Oh, Mr. Harker—call just came in for you. Mr. Jonathan Bryant's on the phone. He's waiting."

"Switch it into my office," Harker told her. His brows contracted. *Jonathan? What does that particular vulture want?*

Harker cut round the desks in the outer office and let himself into his sanctum. He activated the phone. There was the usual three-second circuit-lag, and then the gray haze of electronic "noise" gave way to the fishbelly face of Jonathan Bryant.

"Hello, Harker," he said abruptly. "Just thought I'd call you up to let you know that I've obtained a stay of the hearing on my father's will. It's being pushed up from the 16th to the 23rd."

Harker scowled. "I don't have any official notice of that fact yet."

"It's on its way via court messenger. Just thought I'd let you know about it."

"Go ahead," Harker said. "Gloat all you want, if it gives you pleasure. Your father's will is unbreakable, and you know it damn well. All this stalling—"

"Legal delay," Jonathan corrected.

"All this stalling is just a waste of everybody's time. Sure, I know you're hoping the old man will die before the hearing, but I assure you that can't influence the outcome. If you're that anxious to collect, stop obtaining postponements and just pull the old man's feeding-plugs out. It'll save a lot of heartache for all of us, him included."

"Harker, you lousy politico, you should have been debarred twenty years ago."

"The word you want to use is *disbarred,*" Harker said coldly. "Suppose you get off my line and stop bothering me now? I'd call you a filthy jackal except that I'm too busy for slander suits just now, even suits that I'd win."

Angrily he snapped off contact and the screen blanked. *Nuisance,* he thought, referring both to Jonathan and to the postponement of the hearing. He didn't seriously believe that the Bryant heirs were going to upset the old man's will, and the quicker he got the case off his personal docket the faster he would be free for full-time work on the Beller Labs account.

He took a doodle-pad from his desk and scrawled three names on it:

Winstead.
Thurman.
Msgnr. Carteret.

Leo Winstead was the man who had succeeded him in the Governor's mansion in Albany—a steady, reliable National Liberal party-line man, flexible and open in his views but loyal to the good old machine. He would be one of the first men Harker would have to see; Winstead would give him the probable Nat-Lib party-line on the resurrection gimmick, and he could be trusted to keep things to himself until given the official release.

Clyde Thurman was New York's senior Senator, a formidable old ogre of a man with incalculable influence in Washington. Harker had been a Thurman protégé, fifteen years ago; publicly old Clyde had soured on Harker since his futile attempt at political independence, but Harker had no idea where the old man stood privately. If he could win Thurman over to his side, Senate approval of revivification legislation was a good bet. The Nat-Libs controlled 53 seats in the 123rd Congress; the American-Conservatives held only 45, with the other two seats held down by self-proclaimed Independents. In the House, it was even better: 297 to 223, with twenty Independents of variable predictability.

Harker's third key man was Monsignor Carteret. The Father was a highly-respected member of New York's Catholic hierarchy, shrewd and liberal in his beliefs, and already (at the age of 38) considered a likely candidate for an Archepiscopacy and beyond that the red hat.

Harker had met Father Carteret through Kelly. While he was no Catholic himself, nor currently a member of any other organized group, Harker had struck up a close friendship with the priest. He could rely on Carteret to give him an accurate and confidential appraisal of the possible Church reaction to announcement of a successful technique for resuscitating the dead.

Harker ripped the sheet off the doodle-pad and pocketed it. He hung poised over his desk, deep in thought, his active mind already picturing the interviews he might be having with these people.

After a moment he reached for his phone and punched out the coordinates of Father Carteret's private number. Might as well begin with him, Harker thought.

A pleasantly monkish face appeared on the screen after several rings. "Yes? May I help you?"

"I'd like to speak to Father Carteret, please. My name is James Harker."

"Pardon, Mr. Harker. Father Carteret is in conference with Bishop O'Loughlin. Would you care to have him call you when he's free?"

"When will that be?"

"A half hour, I'd say. Is your matter urgent?"

"Reasonably. Tell the Monsignor I'd like to make an appointment to see him some time today or tomorrow, and ask him to call me at my office."

"Does he have your number?"

"I think so. But you'd better take it anyway, just to make sure. MON-4-38162."

He blanked the screen, waited a moment, and dialed the number Raymond had given him to use when calling the Laboratory. The pale, goggle-eyed face of David Klaus appeared on the screen.

"I'd like to talk to Raymond."

"Dr. Raymond's busy in the hormone lab," Klaus said sharply. "Try again in an hour or so."

Harker frowned impatiently; he had taken an immediate dislike to this jittery little enzyme researcher. He said, "You tell Raymond——"

"Just a minute," a new voice said. There was confusion on the screen for an instant; then Klaus' face disappeared and the precise, tranquil features of Martin Raymond took their place.

"I thought you were busy in the hormone lab," Harker said. "Klaus told me so."

Raymond laughed without much humor behind it. "Klaus is frequently inaccurate, Mr. Harker. What's on your mind?"

"Thought I'd let you know that I'm getting down to immediate operation. I'm lining up interviews with key people for today and tomorrow as a preliminary investigation of your legal situation."

"Good. By the way—Mitchison's prepared some publicity handouts on the process. He wants you to okay them before we send them to the papers."

Harker repressed a strangled cough. "Okay them? Listen, Mart, that's exactly why I called. My first official instruction is that the present wrap of ultra-security is to continue unabated until I'm ready to lift it. Tell that to Mitchison and tell him in spades."

Raymond smiled evenly. "Of course—Jim. All secrecy wraps on until you give the word. I'll let Mitchison know."

"Good. I'll be out at the lab sometime between here and Wednesday to find out some further information. I'll keep in touch whenever I can."

"Right."

Harker broke contact and stared puzzledly at the tips of his fingers for a moment. His uneasiness widened. His original suspicion that behind the smooth facade of the Beller Research Laboratories lay possible dissension was heightened by Klaus' peculiar behavior on the phone—and the idea of Mitchison doing anything as premature as sending out press handouts now, before the ground had been surveyed and the ice broken, gave him the cold running shudders.

It was going to be enough of a job putting this thing across as it was—without tripping over the outstretched toes of his employers.

CHAPTER FIVE

MONSIGNOR CARTERET'S private office reminded Harker somehow of Mart Raymond's. Like Raymond's, it was small, and like Raymond's it was ringed round with jammed bookshelves. The furniture was unostentatious, old and well-worn. As a concession to the 21st Century, Carteret had installed a video pickup and a telescreen attachment to go with his phone. A small crucifix hung on the one wall not encumbered with books.

Carteret leaned forward and peered curiously at Harker. The priest, Harker knew, suffered from presbyopia. He was a lean man with the sharp facial contours of an ascetic: up-thrust cheekbones, lowering brows, grizzled close-cropped hair turning gray. His lips were fleshless, pale.

Harker said, "I have to apologize for insisting on such a prompt audience, Father."

Carteret frowned reprovingly. "You told me yesterday it was an urgent matter. To me urgency means—well, *urgency*. My column for the *Intelligencer* can wait a few hours, I guess."

His voice was dramatically resonant. He flashed his famous smile.

Harker said, "Fair enough. I'm here seeking an ecclesiastical opinion."

"I'll do my best. You understand that any *real* opinion on a serious matter would have to come from the Bishop, not from me—and ultimately from Rome."

"I know that. I wouldn't want this to get to Rome just yet. I want a private, off-the-record statement from you."

"I'll try. Go ahead."

Harker took a deep breath. "Father, what's the official Church position on resurrection of the dead? Actual physical resurrection here and now, I mean."

Carteret's eyes twinkled. "Officially? Well, I've never heard Jesus being condemned for raising Lazarus. And on the third day after the crucifixion Jesus Himself was raised, if that's what you mean. I don't see—"

"Let me make myself clear," Harker said. "The Resurrection of Jesus and of Lazarus both fall into the miracle category. Suppose— suppose a mortal being, a doctor, could take a man who had been dead eight or nine hours, or even a day, and bring him back to life."

Carteret looked momentarily troubled. "You speak hypothetically, of course." When Harker did not answer he went on, "Our doctrine holds that death occurs at the moment of 'complete and definitive separation of body and soul.' Presumably the process you discuss makes no provision for restoring the soul."

Harker shrugged. "I'm not capable to judge that. Neither, I'd say, are the men who have developed this—ah—hypothetical process."

"In that case," Carteret said, "The official Church position would be that any human beings revived by this method would be without souls, and therefore no longer human. The whole procedure would be considered profoundly irreligious."

"Blasphemous and sacrilegious as well?"

"No doubt."

Harker was silent for a moment. He said at length, "How about artificial respiration, heart massage, adrenaline injections? For decades seemingly dead people have been brought back to life with these techniques. Are *they* all without souls too?"

Carteret seemed to squirm. His strong fingers toyed with a cruciform paperweight on his desk. "I recall a statement of Pius XII, eighty or ninety years ago, about that. The Pope admitted that it was impossible to tell precisely when the soul had left the body—and that so long as the vital functions maintained themselves, it could be held that the person in question was not dead."

"In other words, if resuscitation techniques could be applied successfully, the patient is considered never to have been dead?"

Carteret nodded slowly.

"But if the patient had been pronounced dead by science and left in that state for half a day or more, and *then* reanimated by a hypothetical new technique—?"

"In that case there has been a definite discontinuity of the life-process," Carteret said. "I may be wrong, but I can't see how the Vatican could give such a technique its approval."

"Ever?"

Carteret smiled. "Jim, it's a verity that the Church is founded on a Rock, but that doesn't mean our heads are made of stone. No organization lasts two thousand years without being susceptible to change. If in the course of time we're shown that a reanimation technique restores both body and soul, no doubt we'll give it approval.

At present, though, I can foresee only one outcome."

Harker knotted his fingers together tensely. The priest's response had not been a surprise to him, but he had hoped for some wild loophole. If any loophole existed, Carteret would have found it.

Quietly he said, "All right, Father. I'll put my cards on the table now. Such a process *has* been invented. I've seen it work. I've been retained as legal adviser for the group that developed it, and I'm shopping around for religious and secular opinions before I let them spring the news on the public."

"You want my secular opinion, Jim, now that you've had the religious one?"

"Of course."

"Drop it. Get out of this thing as fast as you can. You're asking for trouble."

"I know that. But I can only see this process as a force for good— for minimizing tragedy in everyday life."

"Naturally. And I could offer you six arguments showing how it'll *increase* suffering. Is it a complex technique requiring skilled operators?"

"Yes, but—"

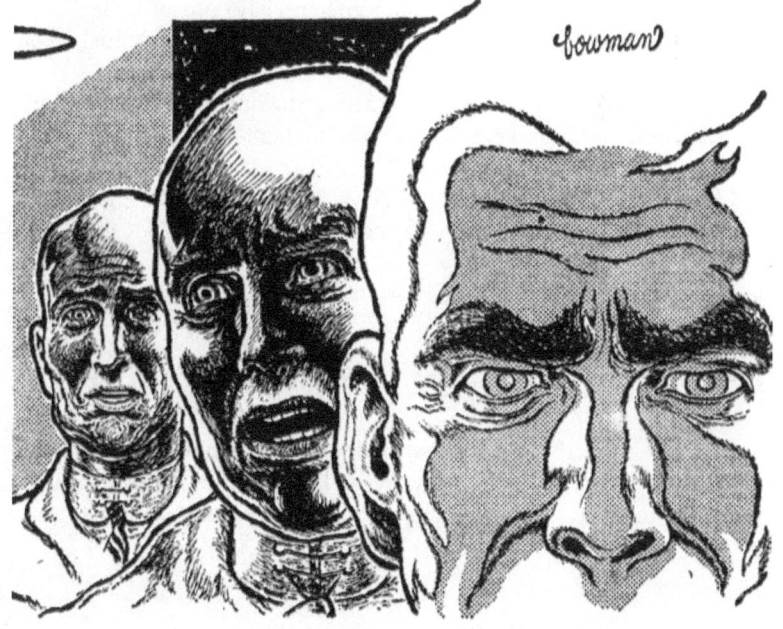

"In that case it won't be available to everybody right away. Are *you* going to decide who lives and who stays dead? Suppose you're faced with the choice between a good and virtuous nobody or an evil but talented creative artist."

"I know. I don't have any slick answers to that, Father. But I still don't think it's any reason to suppress this thing."

"Maybe not. On a purely secular level, though, I tell you it's sheer dynamite. Not to mention the opposition you're bound to get from religious groups. Jim, listen to me: you had a wonderful career once. You wrecked it. But now you're continuing your headstrong ways right to the point of self-destruction."

"Which is frowned upon by your Church," Harker snapped, irritated. "But—"

"I'm not talking about my Church!" Carteret thundered. "I'm talking about you, your family, the rest of your life. You're getting into very deep waters."

"I'll shoulder the responsibility myself."

"I wish you could," the priest murmured. "I wish any of us could. But we can't ever do that, of course."

He shrugged. "Go in peace, Jim. Any time you want to talk to me, just pick up the phone and call. I guarantee no proselytizing."

"Of course everything we've just said is confidential, you understand."

Carteret nodded. He lifted his arms, shaking the sleeves of his cassock back. "Observe. No concealed tape-recorders under my garments. No telespies in the wall."

Chuckling, Harker opened the door and stood at the threshold a moment. "Thanks for talking to me, Father. Even if I can't agree with you."

"I'm used to disagreement," Carteret said. "If everyone who came in here agreed with everything I said, I think I'd lose my faith. So long, Jim."

"Goodbye, Father."

Harker emerged on the steps of the old cathedral where Carteret had his office, paused for a few deep breaths, and looked around. Fifth Avenue was humming with activity, here at noontime on a Tuesday in mid-month.

He thought: *Tuesday, May 14, 2033. A pleasant late-spring day. And any time I decide to give the word, the entire nature of human philosophy will change.*

Harker walked downtown to 43rd Street, stopped in for a quick coffee, and headed toward the Monorail Terminal. Puffing businessmen clutching attaché cases sped past him, each on some business of no doubt vital importance, each blithely shortening his lifespan with each new ulcer and each new deposit of cholesterol in the arteries. Well, before long it would be possible to bring these fat executives back to life each time they keeled over, Harker thought. What a frantic speedup would result *then!*

He bought a round-trip ticket to Litchfield and boarded the slim graceful yellow-hulled bullet that was the New Jersey monobus. He sat back, cushioning himself against the first jolt of acceleration, and waited for departure.

The eleventh commandment: *thou need not die.* Harker shivered a little at the magnitude of the Beller project; each day he realized a little more deeply the true awesome nature of the whole breakthrough.

Mitchison was waiting for him at the Litchfield monobus depot in the big black limousine. Harker climbed in, sitting next to the public-relations man on the front seat.

"Well?" Mitchison jammed his cigar into one corner of his mouth. "What did the padre have to say?"

"Precisely what we all expected."

"Nix?"

"His unofficial feeling is that the Church will condemn this thing the second it's announced."

"Umm. Take some heavy thinking to cancel *that* out. How about the politicos?"

The car pulled into the Beller Labs private road. Harker said, "I'm going to Albany later in the week to see Governor Winstead. After him I'll go after Senator Thurman. Depending on what they say—"

"The hell with that," Mitchison growled. "When do you figure we can release this thing to the public?"

Harker turned round in his seat. In a level voice he said, "When you're planning to touch off a fusion bomb, you look around first and make sure you won't get scragged yourself. Same here. This project's been kept under wraps for eight years, and I'm damned if I'll release anything now until I see exactly where we all stand."

"And you'll pussyfoot around for months?"

"What do you care?" Harker demanded. "Are you getting paid by the week or by the amount of publicity you send out?"

Mitchison grunted something but made no intelligible answer. They pulled up at the roadblock and Harker got out at the right; the guards nodded curtly to him this time but made no attempt to interfere as he headed toward the administration building. Mitchison took his car to the parking area.

Knocking at Raymond's door, Harker said, "You there, Mart?"

The door opened. A diminutive hatchet-faced man peered up at him. "Hello, Harker."

Taken off balance, Harker blinked a moment, then said, "Hello. I don't think we've met."

"You've seen my name. At the bottom of your check. I'm Barchet. Administrator of the Beller Fund."

Harker smiled at the little man and looked past him to Raymond. He shook his head. "It's no go, Mart. The Father says the Church will oppose us."

Raymond shrugged. "We could have figured on that, I guess. You see Winstead on Friday?"

Harker nodded. "I hope for better luck there."

"Doubtful," Barchet snorted. His voice was an annoying saw-edged whine. Harker wondered whether the little man was going to be around the Litchfield labs very often; he had a deep dislike for moneymen.

Ignoring Barchet's comment, Harker said to Raymond, "Mart, how solid is the tenure of the people in this organization?"

"What do you mean?"

"Do all the affiliated men have verbal contracts like me, or are some inked in black-and-white?"

"Most of the research men have verbal agreements."

"How about Mitchison?"

Barchet turned to peer at Harker. Raymond frowned and said, "Why Mitchison?"

"I'll be blunt," Harker said. "I'd like to bounce him. He doesn't seem very capable and he's awfully trigger-happy about releasing data on the project. If it's okay with you, I'd like to bring in a couple of the boys who handled my gubernatorial campaign. They—"

Interrupting icily, Barchet said, "Seems to me we have more than enough people of radical political affiliation working for us now. Any who handled a Nat-Lib campaign would be no asset to our work."

Harker goggled. *"I* was a Nat-Lib Governor! You hired me, and you think that two press-agents—"

"I might as well tell you," Barchet said. "You were hired over my definite objections, Mr. Harker. Your party happens to be the one in power, but it definitely does not represent the main ideological current of American enterprise. And if we succeed in our aims, I like to think it will be *despite* your presence on our team, not because of it."

"Huh? Who the hell—"

"Wait a minute, Jim," Raymond cut in. "And you too, Simeon. I don't want any fighting in here!"

"I'm simply stating views that I expound regularly at our meetings," Barchet said. "For your information, Mr. Harker, Cal Mitchison is the best publicity-agent money can buy. I will not consent to his dismissal."

"You may have to consent to my resignation, then," Harker said angrily. "Dammit, Mart, if I knew this outfit was run by—"

"Watch yourself, Mr. Harker," Barchet warned.

"Calm down, Jim." Raymond disengaged himself from his desk and, glowering down at Barchet, said, "Simeon, you know damned well Harker was approved by a majority of the shareholders. You have no business raising a squabble like this now. He was hired and given free rein—and if he wants to fire Mitchison, it's within his province."

"I insist on bringing the matter before the Board—and if Mitchison is dismissed without full vote, I'll cause trouble. Good day, Dr. Raymond."

The little man sailed past Harker without a word and slammed the door. Harker grinned and said, "What was *he* so upset about?"

Raymond slumped wearily behind his desk. "Barchet's the official voice of old Beller in this outfit—and Beller was as conservative as they come. He thinks you're an arch-radical because you held office for the Nat-Libs. And the little bugger carries a lot of weight on the Board, so we have to humor him."

Harker nodded. He understood now what Raymond had meant when he said he had been "outvoted" in the matter of hiring Harker as first choice. It did not increase his opinion of Beller Research Laboratories.

"I wouldn't blame you if you quit today," Raymond said suddenly. "With Mitchison on pins and needles to give the word to the public, and that idiot Klaus battling for my job because he's tired of enzyme work—"

"Klaus? But he's just a kid!"

"He's twenty-nine, and for an ex-prodigy that's ancient. Degree from Harvard at fifteen, that sort of thing. I have to keep close watch on him or he'll put a scalpel in my back."

"Why not fire him?" Harker suggested.

"Two reasons. He's got a contract, for one—and for another I'd rather have him with us than agin' us, if you know what I mean. Lesser of two evils."

Raymond sighed. "Great little place we have here, Jim.

Sometimes I feel like closing the windows and turning up the gas." He shook his head reflectively. "But it wouldn't work. Someone would drag me next door and bring me back to life again, I guess."

He reached into the bookshelf and produced the liquor bottle. "One quick shot apiece," he said. "Then I want to take you round back to show you the rest of the lab."

CHAPTER SIX

THE GRAND tour of the laboratory grounds was as disturbing as it was stimulating. Seemingly tireless, Raymond marched him through room after room where elaborate experiments were going on.

"Serotonin-diffraction goes on in here. This room's plasma research; remind me to bring you back some time when the big centrifuge is running. Fascinating. This is Klaus' enzyme lab, and down here—"

Harker puffed along behind the lab director, listening to the flow of unfamiliar terms, dazzled by the array of formidable scientific devices. He saw kennels where lively dogs bounded joyfully up and down and struggled to lick his hands through the cage; it was a little jarring to learn that every dog in the room had been "dead" at least once, for periods ranging from a few minutes to twenty-eight hours. He met a grave little rhesus monkey that held the record; it had been dead thirty-nine hours, two months before.

"We had a pair of them," Raymond said. "We brought this fellow back at the 39-hour mark, and held the other off for nine more hours in hopes of hitting a full two days. We didn't make it. The surviving monkey moped for days about it."

Harker nodded. He was swept on; into a large room lined with ledgers, which Raymond said contained all the records of the Beller Laboratories since its opening in 2024. Whitesmocked researchers turned to look up as Harker and his guide passed through into a long, well-lit lab room, then out into the afternoon warmth and across to the other building, for more of the same.

"Well," Harker said finally, after they had returned to Raymond's office. "It's a busy place."

Raymond nodded. "We keep it moving. And it gets results. Despite everything, it gets results."

Despite everything. Harker didn't like the implications of that. He was beginning to form a picture of Raymond as an able man surrounded by stumbling-blocks and obstacles, and bulling his way through none-the-less. He wondered how it would be once he got the campaign into full swing, not too many weeks from now.

Harker leaned back, trying to relax. Raymond said, "Is it too early for you to give me an outline of the program you're planning?"

Harker hunched his shoulders forward uneasily. "It's still in the formative stage. I'm seeing Governor Winstead on Friday, as you know, and early next week I'll go down to Washington and talk to Senator Thurman. If we get them on our side, the rest is relatively easy."

"And if we don't?"

Harker did not smile. "Then we have a fight."

"Why do you say that? Can't we just set up an instruction center and start resuscitating?"

"Pardon me, Mart, if I say that your approach is a naive one. We *can't* do any such thing. Not even if you limit use of the apparatus to fully qualified M.D.s. You see, anything as radical as this will have to be routed through the Federal Health Department, and they'll simply boot it on up to the President, and he'll refer it to Congress. What we need is a law making use of your technique legal."

"Is there any law saying it's *illegal* to reanimate the dead?" Raymond asked.

"Not yet. But you can bet there'll be an attempt to ram one through, before long. Which is why we have to put through a law of our own."

Raymond fell silent; his blue-cheeked face looked grave.

An idea occurred to Harker and he said, "Do you have any idea how big our public-relations budget is?"

Raymond shrugged. "Pretty big. I guess you can have three or four hundred thousand, if you need it."

"Three or four hundred *million* is more in line with what we'll need," Harker said. He saw the stunned expression on Raymond's face and added, "Certainly at least a million, to begin with."

"But why? Why should it be necessary to *sell* the idea of restoring life? You'd think the people of America would rise up and acclaim us as saviors."

"You'd think so, wouldn't you?" Harker shook his head bleakly. "It doesn't work that way, Mart. For one thing, they'll be afraid to try it. There'll be plenty of 'zombie' jokes, and behind those jokes will be unvoiced fear. Uh-uh, Mart. If we're going to put this thing across, we'll need a big public-relations budget. And we can't let a bubblehead like Mitchison handle the job."

"It'll take a little time to fire him."

"Why?"

"You heard Barchet. Mitchison's Barchet's man. We'll have to go through shareholder channels to get rid of Mitchison."

"How long will that take?"

"Two weeks, maybe three," Raymond said. "Will that hold things up too badly?"

"We'll manage," Harker said tiredly.

Harker spent the next morning, Wednesday, at his office, tidying up unfinished business. The delayer on the Bryant hearing had come through, and he read the document carefully, scowled, and jammed it into his desk drawer. He phoned the Bryant home and learned that the old man was very low; the doctor refused to let Harker speak with him. Harker suspected the fine hand of Jonathan Bryant lurking behind that ukase, but there wasn't much he could do about it. The old man wasn't going to last forever, anyway—but Harker genuinely wanted him to hold out until after the hearing, at least.

Nasty business. Jonathan had deliberately obtained the stay of hearing with the hope that his father would die before the case came up.

He left the office at noon, spent some time downtown in the public library trying to find some books that would give him a little scientific background, and headed for home about four that afternoon.

His home life had been suffering, a bit, in the week since he had plunged himself fully into the Beller Labs project. He had been coming home at odd hours, which upset Lois' routine, and his attitude was one of withdrawn introversion, which made things tough on the children. Still, they all were very cooperative about it, Harker thought. He hoped he could make it up to them when the pressure let up.

If the pressure ever let up.

Thursday passed slowly. Harker remained at home, in his study, and tried to read the books he had brought from the library. He was surprised to learn that formal resuscitation research dated from the middle years of the past century. He traced down a few of the terms Raymond had thrown at him, and learned a bit about the mechanics of the Beller reanimation technique.

But, he realized when he put the books down, he knew very little in detail. He had simply skimmed the surface, acquiring a veneer of terms, which he could use to impress the even-less-educated.

A politician's trick, he thought. But what else could he do?

He woke early on Friday, before six, and made breakfast for himself. By the time he had turned off the autocook and set the kitchen-servo to mop-up, Lois and the children were moving about upstairs. They had come down for breakfast before he was ready to leave.

"Morning, Dad," Chris said. "Up early, eh?"

"I have to make a 9:30 jet," he explained. "It's the last one before noon."

Paul appeared, thumbing his eyes, yawning. "Where you going, Daddy?"

"Albany," Harker said.

The seven-year-old looked awake immediately. "Albany? Are you Governor again, Daddy?"

"Hush, stupid!" Chris said savagely.

But Harker merely smiled and shook his head. "No, I won't be Governor any more, Paul. I'm going to visit Mr. Winstead. *He's* the Governor now."

"Oh," the boy said gravely.

Harker reached the West Side jet terminal at ten after nine. The big 150-seater was out on the field, surrounded by attendants. It would make the trip to Albany in just under thirteen minutes.

It was a silly business. It took him twice that long to get to the terminal from his home. But modern transportation was full of such paradoxes.

At nine-thirty-five the great ship erupted from the landing strip; not much later it was roaring over Westchester, and not very much after that it was taxiing to a smooth and uneventful landing just outside Albany.

Thirteen minutes. And it took twenty-five minutes more for the jetport bus to bring them across the Hudson into Albany proper after the flight.

His appointment with Governor Winstead was for eleven that morning. Declining the public transport service, Harker walked through town to the governor's mansion—a walk that he had come to know well, in his four years in Albany.

The town hadn't changed much. Still third-rate, dirty, bedraggled; one of his proposed reforms had been to move the Capital downstate to New York City, where it really belonged, but naturally the force of sentiment was solidly against him, not to mention the American-Conservative Party, whose New York stronghold Albany was.

He smiled at the memory. He had fought so many losing battles, in his four years as Governor.

The guards at Winstead's mansion recognized him, of course, and tipped their hats. Harker grinned amiably at them and passed through, but he felt inward discomfort. *Their* jobs were pegged down by civil-service regulations; his was not, and he had lost his. In an odd way it made him feel inferior.

He travelled the familiar journey upstairs to the Governor's office. Winstead was there to greet him with outstretched hand and a faintly abashed smile.

"Jim. So glad you could come up here."

"It's not a courtesy call, Leo. I'm here to ask some advice."

"Any way I can help, Jim, you know I will."

Harker experienced a moment of disorientation as he took a seat facing Winstead across the big desk that had been his until a few months ago. It was strange to sit on this side of the desk.

He looked for ways to begin saying what he had come here to say. He sensed the other man's deep embarrassment, and shared it in a way, because the awkwardness of this first meeting between Governor and ex-Governor was complex and many-leveled.

Winstead was ten years his senior: a good party man, a reliable workhorse who had come up through the ranks of the Manhattan District Attorney's office, and who had turned down a judgeship because he thought he had a shot at the race for Governor. But the party had chosen the bright, meteorically-rising young Mayor, James Harker, to be the standard-bearer instead, and an avalanche of Nat-Lib votes from downstate had swept Harker in.

Then it had been necessary to discard Harker four years later, and good dependable old Leo Winstead was trotted out of private law practice to take his place. The Nat-Lib tide held true; Winstead was elected, and now it was the ex-prodigy who entered private law practice instead of using the Governorship as a springboard into the White House.

Harker said, "Leo, you carry weight with the party. I don't any more."

"Jim, I—"

"Don't try to apologize, Leo, because it's my own fault and none of yours that I'm where I am now. I'm simply asking you to exert some influence on behalf of a project I'm involved in."

It was a naked attempt at lobbying. Harker hoped Winstead's unconscious guilt-feelings would lead him to support the Beller people.

"What sort of project, Jim?"

"It's—it's a sort of revolutionary breakthrough in science, Leo. A process to reanimate people who have been dead less than twenty-four hours."

Winstead sat up. "Are you serious?"

"Dead serious. I'm going down to Washington next week to see Thurman. This thing really *works*—and I want to get it legally approved."

"And where do I come in?"

"You're a powerful official, Leo. If you came out in praise of this new development—"

"Dangerous business, Jim. The Church—"

"I know all about the Church. And you can bet our friends the American-Conservatives will make some kind of political capital about the news. The Nat-Libs will *have* to take a favorable stand on this."

"Suppose we don't?" Winstead asked. His voice was tense and off-center; he ran his knotty hands nervously through his bushy shock of white hair. "You know as well as I do that this is no time to hop off supporting anything too farfetched."

Harker began to feel a definite sense of exasperation. "Farfetched? Leo, I saw a dead man come back to life right in front of me. If you think—"

"I don't think anything. Thinking's not my job. If you'll pardon my saying so, Jim, you did too much thinking for your own good when you were in Albany. This thing has to be handled with kid gloves. It wouldn't surprise me if the government clamps down and bottles it all up until it's been fully explored."

"Federal Research Act of '92," Harker said thinly. "It guarantees freedom of research without government interference, as you know well enough."

Winstead seemed to be perspiring heavily. "Laws can be repealed or amended, Jim. Listen here: why don't you go see Thurman? Find out how *he* stands on the matter. Then come back here and maybe we can talk about it again."

It was obviously a dismissal. Winstead had no intentions of getting involved with something that had so many ramifications as this.

Tiredly Harker rose. "Okay. I'll see Thurman."

"Good."

"One more thing, Leo—this project hasn't been announced to the public yet. Since you're aware of the fuss it's going to kick up, I hope you'll be thoughtful enough to keep your mouth shut until we're ready to spring it ourselves."

"Of course, Jim. Of course."

CHAPTER SEVEN

IT WAS a very long weekend.

Harker reached his home at five-thirty that evening, having left Winstead around noon. He had had a miserable chlorella-streak lunch on the wrong side of State Street and spent the early afternoon strolling around Albany, easing the inner tension that gripped him. He made the 4:15 jet back to New York.

Chris was watching the video when he came in; it was a weekend, and the boy had no homework. He hopped up immediately and said, "Drink, Dad?"

"Martini. *Very* dry."

The boy busied himself with the pushbutton controls of the autobar while Harker hung up his hat and jacket. Lois appeared from the general vicinity of the kitchen.

"Did you see Winstead?"

He nodded. "Yeah, I saw him. He isn't interested, I guess."

"Oh, Dr. Raymond called, from the labs. He wanted to know if you were back yet. I told him you'd call as soon as you came home."

Harker picked up the phone, yanked down on the long-distance switch, and punched out Raymond's number. He waited, hoping Raymond himself would pick up and not Klaus or Barchet or someone like that.

Raymond did. He looked inquisitively out of the screen and Harker told him exactly what Winstead had said. When he had finished the flat, weary recital, he added, "I'm going to Washington on Monday. But if Thurman gives me the brush-off, we may be in trouble."

Raymond grinned with unconvincing heartiness. "We'll get through somehow, Jim. Have faith."

"I wish I could," Harker said.

He sipped the drink Chris put in his hand, and after a little of the cold gin had filtered into his bloodstream he felt better. It was a false comfort, he knew, but it was comfort all the same. He went upstairs to the sitting room, picked out a music tape almost at random, put it on. The selection was a mistake: Handel's *Messiah*, Part III. He listened to the big alto aria that opened the section:

> *...I know that my redeemer liveth, and that he shall stand at the latter day upon the earth:*
> *And though worms destroy this body, yet in my flesh shall I see God.*
> *For now is Christ risen from the dead...*

After the final notes of the aria had died away came the Chorus, slow, grave:

> *...Since by man came death, by man came also the resurrection of the dead.*
> *For as in Adam all die, even so in Christ shall all be made alive...*

The jubilant tones of *"Even so in Christ"* sent startling shivers of illumination through him; it was as if he had never listened to these words before *("Since by man came death, by man came also the resurrection of the dead...").* The words pursued him everywhere.

Twenty minutes later, after the last melisma of *"Amen,"* he abruptly turned the set off; dinner was about ready, or at least it should be. It was. He ate quietly, deep in thought.

On Saturday he was a little more lively; he worked around the house, took Chris and Paul for an hour-long hike in the early afternoon, spent some time before dinner watching the telecast of the Yankee-Dodger interleague game from Los Angeles. He and Lois visited neighbors in the evening; it was a pleasant, relaxed three or four hours. He was beginning to think he could forget about the problem that was starting to grow.

But Sunday his short-lived forgetfulness ended. It was breakfast-time, Paul was struggling under the bulk of the Sunday *Times*, which had, been left in the box outside, and Lois was bringing the pancakes to the table. As he took the paper from his youngest son, Harker turned to Chris and said, "Switch on the audio. Let's see what the morning news is like."

There was a click. A resonant, almost cavernous voice said:

"...he saith unto them, Our friend Lazarus sleepeth; but I go, that I may awake him out of sleep. Then said his disciples, Lord, if he sleep, he shall do well. Howbeit Jesus spake of his death: but they thought that he had spoken of taking rest in sleep. Then said Jesus unto them plainly, Lazarus is dead. And I—"

Impatiently Chris reached out and changed the station.

Harker shook his head, annoyed. "No, Chris. Get that back. I want to hear it."

"The *Bible*, Dad?"

Harker nodded impatiently. As Chris searched for the original station Lois said, "That's St. Matthew, isn't it?"

Chuckling; Harker said, "St. John, unless I've forgotten all my Sunday Schooling. Your father ought to hear you say a thing like that."

Lois' father had been a stern Bible-reading Presbyterian; he had never approved of Harker. The radio preacher said:

"...Then they took away the stone from the place where the dead was laid. And Jesus lifted up his eyes, and said, Father, I thank thee that thou hast heard me. And I knew that thou bearest me always: but because of the people which stand by I said it, that they may believe that thou hast sent me. And when he thus had spoken, he cried with a loud voice, Lazarus, come forth! And he that was

dead came forth, bound hand and foot with grave clothes; and his face was bound about with a napkin. Jesus said unto them—"

"All right," Harker broke in suddenly. "You can change the station now."

Chris said, "How come you wanted to hear that, Dad?"

"It's a very famous passage." Harker smiled. "And I have a feeling we're all going to get to know it pretty well before summer comes."

After supper Sunday he packed for his trip to Washington; he took an extra change of clothes, because Thurman's secretary had warned him that the Senator was very busy and might not be able to see him until Tuesday. Harker reflected privately that that was fine treatment to accord a man who had once been virtually the titular head of the party, but complaining would have done him less than no good.

He came downstairs again after packing, and spent the next several hours watching video with the family: a silly, mindless series of programs, ideally designed to give the mind a rest.

At quarter past nine, in the middle of an alleged ballet sequence, the screen went blank. Harker frowned, annoyed; then an announcer's face appeared.

"We interrupt this program to bring you a special announcement from our newsroom.

"Richard Bryant, hero of Earth's first successful voyage to another planet, died quietly in his sleep an hour ago, in his Manhattan apartment. He would have been seventy-four next month.

"He was assured of immortality on the first of August, 1984, when he radioed from Mars the triumphant message, 'Have landed Mars One safely. Am on way back. Mars is pretty dreary.' From that day on, Rick Bryant was a hero to billions.

"We return you now to the regularly-scheduled program."

Cavorting dancers returned to the screen. In a soft, barely audible voice, Harker cursed eloquently.

"Gee, Dad! Rick Bryant died!" Chris exclaimed.

Not long after he had taken the case, Harker had induced the old man to autograph a copy of his book *I Flew to Mars* for Chris; since then, the boy had taken deep interest in Bryant's career.

Harker nodded. To Lois he said, "They didn't even give him a chance. The hearing would have been last Thursday, but his son got it postponed."

"Do you think this will affect the outcome, Jim?"

"I doubt it. That document was pretty solid. Damn, I wanted old Bryant to have the satisfaction of knowing he died on top." Broodingly he stared at his slippers. "If any of them had any guts, they would have lied to him, told him his will was upheld. But of course they didn't. They're just so many vultures. Hell, I guess I'd better phone. As the old man's lawyer, I'd better get in touch."

He went upstairs to his den and switched on the phone. Punching out the Bryant number, he waited a moment; an intercepting service took the call and said, "We represent the Bryant family. Only friends of the family and immediate relatives can be put through just now, sir."

"I'm the late Mr. Bryant's lawyer," Harker said, staring at the monogrammed pattern on the screen. "James Harker. Will you put me through?"

There was a momentary pause; then—"I beg your pardon, sir. Your name does not seem to be on the list. You understand that in a time of grief such as this the Bryant family accepts your condolences in the sincere spirit in which they are offered, and regrets that it cannot devote personal time to you as yet. We suggest that you call back tomorrow, when the shock of Mr. Bryant's departure has lessened."

The intercepting-service monogram disappeared from the screen. Harker scowled.

The cold-blooded lice. Hiring a service to dish out all that unctuous crap, meanwhile making sure I don't have a chance to talk to anybody there.

He took a deep breath and punched out another number: the home phone of District Judge Auerbach, who was scheduled to conduct the Bryant hearing next Thursday.

Auerbach appeared on the screen, plump, sleepy-looking. Harker said, "Sorry to disturb you on a Sunday night, Tom. You've heard about the Bryant business?"

Auerbach nodded. "Too bad, I guess. He was very sick."

"No doubt of that. Look, Tom, his sons are being sticky about their phone. I'm on the blacklist and can't get through to them. Has Jonathan phoned you tonight?"

"No. Is he supposed to?"

"I don't know. I just want to notify you that I'll be out of town on business tomorrow and maybe Tuesday, in case you or he or anybody is trying to reach me. But I'll be back in plenty of time for the hearing on Thursday. There isn't another motion for a postponement, is there?"

"Not that I know of," Auerbach said. "Be seeing you in court on Thursday, then?"

"Right."

He returned to the television room. The ballet was still going on.

"Well?" Lois asked.

"I couldn't reach the Bryants. They hired an intercepting service," Harker said darkly. "I spoke to Tom Auerbach, though. The hearing's still scheduled for Thursday. Jonathan just didn't want the old man to be alive when it was held."

I wouldn't put it past them to murder old Bryant, he thought. *Cold-blooded bunch.*

He stared at the screen, but the colorful images only irritated him.

Idlewild was a busy place the following morning. Harker got there at half-past-nine, and the sprawling buildings were jam-packed.

"Flight 906 leaving for London via TWA in fifteen minutes— Flight 906 leaving for London via TWA in fifteen minutes—"

He heard a deep-bellied boom; someone next to him said, "That's a cross-country job, I'll bet."

Sure enough, the loudspeaker said, *"Now departing, Flight 136 for San Francisco—"*

Above him a neon board flashed. The bright letters said: *Flight 136. Lv Idlwld 0932, Ar SF 1126.*

Less than two hours across the continent. Harker thought: the plane that had just taken off two minutes ago was probably somewhere over Pennsylvania or Ohio by now.

"Attention, please. Flight 199, United AirLines, for Washington D.C., departure 0953, now boarding—"

That was his plane. Leaving in about twenty minutes, and arriving in Washington only about twenty minutes after that. Harker looked up and saw a great golden stratocruiser coming in for a landing on a distant runway. All around him he felt the nervous urgency of people traveling.

Inwardly he began to grow tense. He had checked off two of the three names on his scrawled list; neither had been of much encouragement. Only Senator Clyde Thurman remained, and Thurman represented the old-guard conservative wing of the Nat-Lib party; there was no telling how he would react to the news that a technique had been developed for—

"Attention, please. Telephone call for Mr. James Harker. Mr. James Harker, please report to any ticket desk. Telephone call for James Harker—"

Puzzled, Harker shoved his way through the crowd to the desk in the foreground and said to the uniformed clerk, "I'm James Harker. I was just paged for a phone call."

"You can pick it up in there."

Harker stepped through into a waiting room and picked up an extension phone-audio only, no visual. He said to the operator, "I'm James Harker. There's a phone call for me."

"One moment, please."

There was the sound of phone-jacks being yanked in and out of sockets. Then Mart Raymond's voice said, "Hello? Jim?"

"Harker here. That you, Mart?"

"Oh, thank God I caught you in time! I phoned your home, and your wife said you'd gone to the airport to make a 9:53 jet! Another few minutes and you'd have been aboard the plane, and—"

Harker had never heard Raymond this excited before. "Whoa, boy! Calm down!"

"I can't. Cancel your trip and get out here right away!"

"How come? I'm on my way down to see Thurman."

"The hell with Thurman. Haven't you heard the news?"

"What news? About Bryant, you mean? How—"

"No, not about Bryant," Raymond snapped. "I mean about the *project*. Hell, I guess you haven't heard yet. It only broke about five minutes ago."

Harker stared strangely at the receiver in his hand. In as level a voice as he could manage he said, "Mart, what are you trying to tell me?"

"Mitchison!" Raymond gasped. "Mitchison and Klaus—they issued a public statement about five minutes ago, telling the world all about the project! The lab is swarming with reporters! Jim, you've got to get out here at once!"

He hung up. Harker let the receiver drop into its cradle.

He moistened his lips.

The mask of secrecy was off. From now on, they were accountable to the world for their every move.

HARKER HAD thought Idlewild was in a state of confusion, but he realized he still had a lot to learn about ultimate chaos when he reached Litchfield, an hour later. Cars clogged the highway for a quarter of a mile on each side of the private road leading to the laboratories. He saw television cameras, sound trucks, men who looked like reporters.

He ducked through the milling mob and tried to slip unobtrusively along the spruce-bordered dirt road to the administration building. But it was a foolhardy attempt; he hadn't taken more than ten steps before someone yelled: Hey! There's Governor Harker!"

A dozen of them surrounded him in a minute. Harker recognized a few of the faces from his mayoralty days—a *Times* man, one from the *Star-Post,* one from the Hearst combine. Harker strode doggedly along, trying to ignore them, but they blocked his path.

"What are *you* doing here, Governor?"

"What's your opinion on the reanimation bit? You think they're serious?"

"How will the Nat-Libs react?"

"Do you figure there'll be a congressional investigation?"

They crowded around him, waving their mini-recorders and notebooks. In a loud voice Harker said, "Hold on, all of you! Quiet down!"

They quieted.

"In answer to half a dozen of your questions, I'm here because I'm legal adviser to Beller Laboratories. The statement that was released to the press earlier today was an unofficial and possibly inaccurate one. I'll have an official statement for you as soon as things are under control here."

"Does that mean the reanimation process doesn't actually exist?"

"I repeat: I'll have an official statement later." It was the only way to handle them. He spun, pushed his way forcefully but with care between the *Times* and Scripps-Howard-Cauldwell, and made his way up the hill.

The roadblock still functioned—only this time there were five guards there instead of two, and three of them held multishot rifles, the other two machine-pistols. Harker approached and said, "How come the firearms?"

"It's the only way we can keep them back, Mr. Harker. You better go in. Dr. Raymond wants to see you."

Harker nodded grimly and stepped through the cordon. He half-trotted the rest of the way.

Raymond's office was crowded. Barchet was there, and Lurie, and two or three of the other researchers. Raymond, his face gray and stony, sat quietly back of his desk.

"Here," he said. "Read this. It's the text of the handout Mitchison released."

Harker scanned it.

"Litchfield, N.J., 20 May (for immediate release)—security wraps today came off an eight year old project that will be the greatest boon to mankind since the development of modern medicine. A process for bringing the dead back to life has left the experimental stage and is now ready for public demonstration, according to famous biochemist David Klaus, 29, a Harvard graduate who has spearheaded the project in recent months.

"Klaus stated, 'The technique developed at this laboratory will make possible restoration of life in all cases where death has taken place no more than twenty-four hours before the reanimation attempt, provided no serious organic damage was the cause of death. A combination of hormone therapy and electrochemical stimulation makes this astonishing and miraculous process possible.'

"The Beller Research Laboratories of Litchfield, established in 2024 by a grant from the late Darwin F. Beller, was the birthplace for this scientific breakthrough. Further details to come. Cal Mitchison, publicity."

Harker dropped the sheet contemptuously to Raymond's desk. "Bad grammar, bad writing, bad thinking—not even a good mimeograph job. Mart, how the dickens could a thing like this have happened?"

"Klaus and Mitchison must have cooked it up last night or early this morning. They handed copies of it to the local press-service stringers in town, and phoned it in to all the New York area newspapers."

"We didn't even have time to fire him," Harker muttered. "Well? Where is he now?"

Raymond shrugged. "He and Klaus are gone. I sent men looking for them as soon as I found out about the newsbreak, but no sign of them."

"Operation Barn Door," Harker snapped. "Most likely they're in Manhattan getting themselves interviewed on video. I see Mitchison didn't bother to mention anyone's name but Klaus' in this alleged handout."

"What would you expect?"

Harker whirled on Barchet, who looked very small and meek suddenly, with none of his earlier blustery self-assurance. *"You! You're the one who brought Mitchison into this outfit!"*

In a tiny voice Barchet said, "Recriminations are useless now, Mr. Harker."

"The hell with that. Did you tell Mitchison I was going to have him sacked?"

"Mr. Harker, I—"

"Did you?"

Helplessly Barchet nodded. Harker glared at him, then turned to Raymond and said, "There you have it, Mart. Mitchison heard he was getting canned, so he whipped this thing out now, while he could get fat on us. Well, we're stuck with this statement. There are 500 hundred reporters on the front lawn waiting for official word from us."

Raymond had not shaved that morning. He ran his fingers through a blue-stubbled growth of beard and then locked his hands over his forehead. In a sepulchral voice he said, "What do you suggest? Deny the Mitchison release?"

"Impossible," Harker said. "The word has gone out. If we deny it, the public will never believe a further word we say. Uh-uh."

"What then?"

"Don't worry about it. First thing is to prepare a release saying that the early announcement was premature, that Mitchison and Klaus are no longer connected with this organization—"

"Klaus has a contract."

"The contract has a clause in it about insubordination or else it isn't worth a damn. Have somebody send a special-delivery letter to Klaus informing him that his contract is voided. Keep a couple of carbons. Send a letter of dismissal to Mitchison, too."

Harker paused to wipe sweat from his face. Even in the small room, the air-conditioners had little effect.

He went on, "Next thing: I'll draft a release confirming the fact that you've developed this technique, and I'll sign my name to it.

When I'm done, have it mimeographed and distributed to everybody out there. That cancels out Mitchison's poop, anyway. After that—" he frowned—"do you have any human cadavers around the place? Revivable ones, I mean?"

Raymond shook his head.

"Too bad. Find one. We'll give a demonstration of the technique to any of the pressmen who have strong enough stomachs to want to watch. And then—"

"Don't you think that's a little risky?" Lurie asked mildly.

"What? The demonstration?"

Lurie nodded, grinning foolishly. "Well, I mean, something might go wrong—"

"Like what?"

"There are flaws in the process," Raymond cut in. "We haven't fully perfected it. I was meaning to talk about them to you, but of course this thing coming up makes it impossible to iron the bugs out in time, and—"

"Hold it," Harker said. He felt a chill start to rise up his back. In a flat voice he said, "You gave me the impression that this process worked all the time. That if the body was in good enough shape to live, and hadn't started to decay, you could revive it. Suppose you tell me about these so-called 'bugs,' right here and now."

There was a brief, ominous silence in the room. Harker saw Raymond glare sourly at Lurie, who cowered; the other staff researchers looked uneasy, and Barchet nibbled at his nails.

At last Raymond said, "Jim, I'm sorry. We didn't play it square with you."

"Go on. Bare your soul to me now, Raymond. I want to know everything."

"Well—ah—the process *doesn't* always work. About one out of twenty times, we can't bring the patient back to life."

"Understandable. If that's the whole trouble—"

"It isn't. Jim, you have to understand that death is a tremendous shock to the nervous system—the biggest shock there is. That goes without saying. Sometimes the shock is so great that it short-circuits the brain, so to speak. And so even though we can achieve physiological reanimation, the mind—ah—the mind is not always reanimated with the body."

Harker was stunned as if by a physical blow. He took one step backward, groped for a chair, and lowered himself into it. Forcing himself to keep calm he said, "Just how often does this happen?"

"About one out of every six tries, so far."

"I see." He drew in his breath sharply, cleared his throat, and fought to hang on to his self-control. The whole thing had taken on an unreal dreamlike atmosphere in the past two hours. And this was the crusher.

So one out of six revivifications produced a live idiot? *Great,* Harker thought. *So a public demonstration will be like a game of Russian Roulette. One chance out of six that the whole show will blow up in our faces.*

"How long will it take you to iron this thing out?" he asked.

"All I can say is that we're working toward it."

"Okay. Forget the demonstration. We don't dare try it until things calm down. Remind me to cut your throat for this, Mart. Later."

There was a knock on the door. Harker nodded to Barchet, who opened it. One of the laboratory guards stood outside.

"The reporters are getting out of hand," he said. "They want to know when they're getting their statement."

Harker stood up and said, "It's five minutes to eleven now. Tell them that I'll have a statement for them before noon."

"Yes, sir."

"Get me a typewriter," Harker said to Raymond.

A typewriter was produced. Harker fed a sheet of paper in, switched on the current, and began to type. He composed a hasty 250-word statement disowning Mitchison, crediting Raymond as head of the project, and declaring that full details of the technique would be released as soon as they were ready.

He signed it *James Harker,* and added parenthetically, *(Former Governor of New York—now legal adviser to Beller Research Laboratories.)*

"Here," he said, handing the release to Raymond. "Read this thing through and approve it, Mart. Then get it mimeographed and distributed to that wolfpack out there. Is there a vidset around anywhere?"

"In A Lounge," Lurie offered.

A Lounge was in the small dormitory in back Harker said, "I'm going there to pick up the news reports. Lurie, I'm requisitioning you to set up office space for me someplace in Dormitory A. I want a phone, a vidset, a radio, and a typewriter. And I don't care who has to get pushed out of the way."

"Yes, sir."

"Good."

He jogged across the clearing toward Dormitory A, pausing only to look back briefly at the horde of newsmen straining at the barrier down the hill. A Lounge was packed with lab researchers, clustered around the video. They moved to one side as Harker entered.

He recognized Vogel and said to the bearded surgeon, "Has there been much about us on yet?"

Vogel laughed. *"Much?* Hardly anything but!"

Harker stared at the screen. A newscaster's solemn face stared back. *"...a discovery of staggering importance, if we can credit this morning's release. Further details will be brought to you as bulletins the moment information is received at the network newsroom."*

Harker wrenched the channel-selector dial one turn to the left. A new voice, equally crisp and solemn, was saying: *"...called for an immediate Senate investigation. The cry was echoed by Nat-Lib Senator Clyde Thurman, who declared that such a scientific finding would have to be placed under careful Federal regulation."*

A third channel offered: *"...the President had no comment on the news, pending further details. Vice-President Chalmers, attending a meeting in Detroit, commented: 'This is not as incredible a development as superficial appearances would indicate. Science has long had the power to save human lives; this is merely the next step. We should not lose our sense of proportion in considering this matter.'"*

Harker felt a sudden need for fresh air. He muscled his way through the crowded lounge and out onto the dormitory porch.

Confusion reigned everywhere. His tentative plans for making a careful survey of the situation had gone up in one puff of press-agentry; from now on, he would have to improvise, setting his course with desperate agility.

He tried to tell himself that things would quiet down before long, once the initial impact had expended itself. But he was too well schooled in the study of mass human behavior to be able to make himself believe any such naive hope.

The man in the street could only be thinking one thing now: that the power of death over humanity had ended. In future days, death would have no dominion.

But how would they react? Jubilantly, or with terror? What would they say when they learned five times out of six, life could be restored—but the sixth time a mindless idiot was the product?

Fear and trembling lay ahead, and days of uncertainty. Harker let the warm mid-May sun beat down on him; he stared up at the sky as if looking into tomorrow.

The sky held no answers. Confusion would be tomorrow's watchword. And there was no turning back, not for any of them.

CHAPTER NINE

HARKER held his first news conference at three-thirty that afternoon, in the hastily rigged room that was now his Litchfield office.

By that time, it had occurred to him that he had become, not only the legal adviser of the laboratories, but the public spokesman, publicity director, and chairman of the board as well. Everyone, Raymond included, seemed perfectly willing to delegate responsibility to him.

He made a list of eight selected media representatives—three newspapers, both press services, two video networks and one radio network, and invited them to send men to his conference. No others were allowed in.

He told them very concisely what the Beller technique was, how it had been developed, and what it could do. He used a few technical terms that he had picked up from his weekend reading. He didn't mention that the technique was not without flaws.

When he had finished his explanation, he called for questions. Surprisingly few were forthcoming. The news seemed to have stilled the tongues of even these veteran reporters.

At the close of the conference he said, "Headquarters for further Beller news will be right here. I'll try to make myself available for comment about the same time every afternoon."

He watched them go. He wondered how much of what he had said would reach the public undistorted, and how much would emerge in garbled and sensationalized form.

Toward evening, he started finding out.

Harker reached his home in Larchmont about seven p.m., utterly exhausted. Lois was at the door, anxious-faced, tense.

"Jim! I've been listening to the news all day. So have the boys. Your name's been mentioned every time."

"That's nice," Harker said wearily. He unsnapped his shoes and nodded hello to his sons, who stared at him strangely as if he had undergone some strange transformation during the day.

"I'll be spending most of my time at Litchfield until things get calmer," he said. "I may even have to sleep out there for a while."

The phone rang suddenly. Harker started to go for it, then changed his mind and said, "Find out who it is, first. If it's anybody official tell them I'm not home yet. Except Raymond."

Lois nodded and glided off toward the phone alcove. When she returned, she looked even more pale, more tense.

"Who was it?"

"Some—some crank. There've been a lot of those calls today, Jim."

He tightened his lips. "I'll have the number changed tomorrow. Nuisances."

The late editions of two of the New York papers lay on the hassock near his chair. He picked up the Seventh Edition of the *Star-Post*. A red-inked banner said, CAN LIFE BE RESTORED? READ NOBEL WINNER'S OPINION!

Harker glanced at the article. It was by Carlos Rodriguez, the Peruvian poet, winner of the Nobel Prize for Literature in 2018. Evidently it was a philosophical discussion of man's right to bring back the dead. Harker read about three paragraphs, then abruptly lost interest when another headline at the lower right-hand corner caught his eye. It said,

RICK BRYANT REMAINS DEAD,
SAY SPACE PIONEER'S HEIRS

New York, May 20—The body of 73-year-old Richard Bryant, early hero of the space age, will be cremated on schedule tomorrow morning, according to a family spokesman. Commenting on the growing public sentiment that the famed Bryant be granted a reprieve from death for his epochal flight to Mars, Jonathan Bryant, his oldest son, declared:

"The feeling of my family is that my father should go to eternal rest. He was an old and sick man and frequently expressed the desire to sleep forever. We em-

phatically will not subject his remains to the dubious claims of the so-called re-animators currently in the headlines.'"

Harker looked up. "Listen to this hogwash, Lois!" He read her the article, bearing down with sardonic malice on Jonathan's more cynical remarks.

She nodded. "I heard about it before. Seems some people got up a quick petition to bring old Bryant back to life. Jonathan's statement was broadcast about five this afternoon."

Scowling, Harker said, "You can bet they'll rush him off to the crematorium in a hurry. They waited four years for him to die, and they'd be damned before they let him be brought back to life!"

The phone rang again. Lois slipped away to answer it, while Harker busied himself with the papers. She returned in a moment, looking puzzled, and said, "It's a Father Carteret. He begged me to let him talk to you. What should I tell him?"

"Never mind. I'll talk to him."

He picked it up in the foyer, where the phone was audio only. "Father Carteret? Jim Harker speaking."

"Hello there, Jim." Carteret sounded troubled. "I—I guess you meant what you said, that day you saw me. It's all over the papers."

"I know. Some knucklehead sprang the thing prematurely, and we're stuck with it now."

"I thought I'd let you know that ecclesiastic circles are in a dither," Carteret said. "The Archbishop's been on the phone to Rome half the day."

Harker's throat tightened. "Any news?"

"Afraid so. The Vatican has issued a hands-off order: no Catholic is to go near your process in any way whatever until the Church has had ample time to explore the implications. Which means a few months or a few centuries; there's no telling."

"So it's a condemnation, then?"

"Pretty much so," Carteret agreed softly. "Until it's determined whether or not reanimation is sinful, no Catholic can let a member of his family be reanimated—or even work in your laboratories. I hope everything works out for you, Jim. There's nothing you can do now but stick to your guns, is there?"

"No," Harker said. "I guess not."

He thanked the priest for the advance information and hung up. Storm clouds were beginning to gather already. His earlier mood of gloom and desperation had washed away, he found, much to his surprise.

He knew why. The battle had been joined. No more behind-the-scenes skulking; he was out in the open as the standard-bearer of Beller Labs. It promised to be a rough fight, but that didn't scare him.

"This is my second chance," he said to Lois. She smiled palely. "I don't understand, Jim."

"I was elected Governor of New York on a reform platform that nobody in the party organization took seriously except me. I waded in and started to make reforms, and I got my teeth rammed down my throat for it. Okay. I lost Round One. But now I'm in the thick of the fight again, fighting against ignorance and fear and hysteria. Maybe I'll lose again—but at least I'll have tried."

She touched his arm, almost timidly. Harker realized that he had never really seen into his wife before; seen the contradictions in her, the caution, the timidity, and the core of toughness that was there too.

"This time you'll win, Jim," she said simply.

It didn't look that way in the morning...

THURMAN SPEARHEADS REANIMATION INQUIRY

...the *Times* announced, and the story revealed that Senator Clyde Thurman (N-L, N.Y.) had urged immediate Congressional investigation of the claims of Beller Research Laboratories, and from the tone of Thurman's statements it was obvious that he was hostile to the whole idea of reanimation. "Sinful...possibly a menace to the fabric of society..." were two of the terms quoted in the newspaper.

The *Times* also printed a full page of extracts from editorials of other newspapers throughout the country, plus a few comments from overseas papers that had arrived in time for the early editions.

The prevailing newspaper sentiment was one of caution. The East Coast papers generally suggested that careful scrutiny be applied to the alleged statements of Beller Labs before such a process be used on any wide scale. The Far West papers called for immediate scientific study of the Beller achievement, and most of them implied that it would be a tremendous boon to humanity if the claims were found to be true.

The Midwest papers, though, took a different approach, in general. The Chicago *Tribune* declared: "We fear that this new advance of science may instead be a step backward, that it may sound the trumpet-call for the decline of civilization as we know it. A society without the fear of death is one without the fear of God"—and so on for nearly a full column.

The overseas notices were mixed: the Manchester *Guardian* offered cautious approval, the London *Daily Mirror* ringing condemnation. From France came puzzled admiration for American scientific prowess; the Germans applauded the discovery, while no word was forthcoming from Russia at the moment. The Vatican statement was about what Carteret had predicted it would be.

He reached the Litchfield headquarters about quarter past ten that morning. There was the usual gaggle of newsmen cluttering up the highway, even though the skies held a definite threat of rain. However someone had had enough sense to rope off the approach to the laboratory grounds, and so he had no trouble getting past the gauntlet of reporters and into the area.

Raymond and Lurie were in the office when Harker got there. They had a huge pile of newspapers spread out all over the floor.

"Makes interesting reading," Harker said amiably.

Raymond looked up. "We never expected this, Jim. We never expected anything like this."

Harker shrugged. "Death is the most important word in the language, right after birth. What comes in between is immaterial; everybody goes through his days remembering that all his life is just a preparation for the moment of his death. You've changed all that. Did you expect the world to take it calmly?"

Lurie said, "Show him the letters, Mart."

Raymond sprang to his feet and shoved a thick file-folder at Harker. "Take a look at these, will you? It's enough to break your heart."

"They come in truckloads," Lurie said. "The Litchfield postmaster is running hourly deliveries down to us because he doesn't have room for the stuff up there."

Harker reached into the folder and pulled out a letter at random. It was written painstakingly by hand on blue-lined yellow paper. He read it.

"Dear Sirs,

You will probably throw this letter in the wastebasket but I beg you to consider it sincerely. My wife age 29 and the mother of our four children is sick in the Hospital with cancer and the Dr. says she will not live more than 1 more week.

We have all been praying for her but so far she shows no sign of getting well and does not recognize us. I read of your miracle discovery in this morning's paper and hope now you can bring my Lucy back to life when she is gone. I enclose a self-addressed envelope so you can let me know if such would be possible, I will immediately upon her death bring her to you so you can give her back to me. I speak for our children Charles age 6 Peggy age 4 Clara age almost 3 and Betsy age fourteen months. May God bless all of you and keep you from suffering what I have been suffering, and I will live in hope of hearing from you.

Yours gratefully,
Charles Mikkelsen
R.F.D. #1, Deleware, Minne.

Harker put the letter down, feeling a strange sense of bitter compassion. He said nothing.

Raymond said, "We have hundreds like that. Some of the damndest things, too. People with relatives dead ten years want to dig them up and bring them to us."

Harker shook his head. "There's no chance you can help any of these people? How about this woman?"

"The cancer one? Not a chance. If it's as bad as he says it is, the malignancy has probably metastasized right up and down her body by now. Maybe we could bring her back to life, but we couldn't keep her alive afterward."

"I see. How about other diseases?"

Raymond shrugged. "If the organic damage is beyond repair, we can't do a thing. But if it's reparable, you can figure a good chance of success. Take a patient with cardiac tissue scarred by repeated attacks. One more attack will finish him—and so would any operation to correct the condition. But now we can 'kill' him ourselves, install an artificial heart, and reanimate. He could live another thirty years that way."

"In other words—"

The phone rang. Raymond swiveled around and scooped it lightly off its cradle without activating the video. He frowned, then said,

"Yes. Yes. I get you. No, we won't make any such concessions. Go ahead, then. Sue, if you like. We'll countersue."

He hung up.

"What the blazes was *that?"* Harker demanded.

"Do you know a lawyer named Phil Gerhardt?"

Harker thought for a moment, then said, "Sure. He's a flashy lawsuit man, about as honest as snow in the Sahara. What about him?"

"He just called," Raymond said, scratching the lobe of one ear thoughtfully. "Seems he's representing Mitchison and Klaus. They got their dismissal notices and they're suing for a million bucks plus control of the Labs. Isn't that lovely?"

CHAPTER TEN

HARKER LOOKED up the phone number of Gerhardt's New York office, called, and spoke briefly with the lawyer. It was not a very pleasant conversation. Gerhardt seemed almost offensively bubbling with confidence, gloating as he informed Harker that it was only a matter of days before the court tossed Raymond and Harker out of control of Beller Labs and reinstated Klaus and Mitchison. No, Harker was told, he would *not* be given the present whereabouts of the two dismissed employees. And yes, the suit had already been filed—control of the labs and $1,000,000 in punitive damages.

"Okay," Harker said. "I'll prepare a counter-suit against your clients on grounds of malfeasance, insubordination, and half a dozen other things. I don't mind fighting, Gerhardt."

He hung up. After a moment's thought he pulled a sheet of notepaper from a desk drawer and started to jot down notes for the counteroffensive. This was an additional nuisance; things grew more complicated by the moment.

And Gerhardt was a prominent member of the American Conservative Party's national committee. Harker could see the battle-lines beginning to form—with Klaus and Mitchison, Gerhardt, the American-Conservatives, the organized churches, Jonathan Bryant, and Senator Thurman on one side, and, at the moment, nobody but Harker, Raymond, and the staff of Beller Labs on the other.

During the day tension rose at the Litchfield headquarters. The phone rang constantly; from time to time the mail-truck arrived with more letters, and Harker found it necessary to clear out one of the less important lab rooms to store them.

"Have a couple of men start going through them," he told Lurie. The gangling biologist had slipped easily into the role of messenger-boy and general go-between. "Have all the letters pleading for revivification of long-dead relatives burned immediately. Likewise the ones asking for miracles we can't perform, like that cancer business."

"How about the abusive ones?"

"Save those," Harker said. "It helps to know who our enemies are."

The afternoon papers again devoted most of their front-page space to the news, and the *Times* in addition ran a wellhandled four-page symposium in which many noted scientists discussed the entire concept of reanimation with varying degrees of insight. Harker skimmed through it rapidly and paled when he came across a comment by Dr. Louis F. Santangelo of Johns Hopkins. He read it aloud to Raymond:

"There is the distinct possibility that death causes irremediable damage to the brain. So far the Beller researchers have been extremely silent on the subject of the mental aftereffects of reanimation. We must consider the chance that the process may produce living but mindless bodies—in short, walking corpses, or the zombies of legend."

Raymond looked up, troubled. "Santangelo's a brain surgeon, and a good one. Too damn good, Jim. He's smack on the nose."

Harker shook his head. "I don't like this for two reasons. One is that it happens to be accurate; two is that it puts the 'zombie' stigma again, this time thanks to a reputable scientist." He reached for a fresh sheet of notepaper. "Mart, give me the figures on human reanimations so far, will you?"

"To date seventy-one attempts. Successful resuscitation in sixty-seven cases."

"Uh-huh. And how many of your sixty-seven suffered no mental aftereffects?"

"Sixty-one," Raymond said.

"Which leaves six zombies." Harker felt a sudden chill. The frenzy of the first few days of publicity had left him no time to discover some of the vital information about the laboratory. "What did you do with the six?"

"What could we do? We chloroformed them and returned them to the source. It was the merciful thing to do—and it's no crime to kill a man who's already been pronounced dead."

"Where'd you get these seventy-one?"

Raymond looked evasive. "Locally. We got a few from a hospital in Jersey City. That's where we got the man you saw revived. Some came from auto accidents in the neighborhood. Medical supply houses, too. Three of the bodies were of staff-men at the labs who died naturally."

"And where are the sixty-one successful revivees?" Harker asked.

"It's all in the records. Twelve of them are in hospitals, re-cuperating. Death really jolts the nervous system, you know. It takes two or three months to make a full recovery. Twenty have returned to normal life. Six of these don't even know they were dead, incidentally. We keep careful watch over them."

"How about the rest?"

"The recent ones are still on the premises, in Lab B. I guess I didn't get a chance to show you the ward."

"I guess not," Harker said wryly. "Well, we're going to have to issue a general statement on your experiments so far. Get Vogel and Smathers to write it up, and I'll revise it into releasable form. Tell them not to say anything about the six idiots, but it's okay to mention the fact that four of the cadavers couldn't be revived."

Vogel delivered the first draft of the statistical summary about one-thirty that afternoon. Harker read it through once, made a couple of changes, and typed it out. He stressed the fact that many of the reanimatees had returned to normal life. He did not mention that six of the revivals had been unsuccessful, and that the patient had had to be destroyed.

The release was mimeographed and was ready in time for his daily three-o'clock press conference. He handed out the sheets and waited.

Times said, "Could we have the names of the successful revivifications?"

"Flatly impossible. This is to protect them, naturally. They still aren't in perfect health."

"When was the first successful reanimation?" asked Associated Press.

Harker glanced at Raymond, who said, "Exactly ten months ago. To be exact, it was at 3:30 in the afternoon on Tuesday July 17 of last year. Dr. Vogel operated."

"What was the name of the patient?" United Press shot out quickly.

Harker laughed. "Good try, but no score. Patients' names will not be revealed."

"How many unsuccessful attempts were there before the July 17 success?" *Times* wanted to know.

"I don't have the exact figure," Harker said, because Raymond had neglected to give it to him. "Mart, what would you say? About—"

He hesitated. Raymond caught the hint and said, "I'd estimate approximately thirty attempts over a period of two years."

"And there have been seventy-one tries since then?" Transcontinental TV said.

"Right. With sixty-seven reanimations."

"All completely successful?" the sharp *Times* man said. Harker looked vague.

"Varying degrees of success," he replied ambiguously.

"Would you care to elaborate on that, Mr. Harker?"

"Not just now."

Video cameras recorded his statement. He was used to the televised press conference, from long experience in public office, and he maintained a perfectly guileless expression while uttering the evasion.

The Scripps-Howard-Cauldwell man said, "As you know, Senator Thurman is pressing for a detailed Senate investigation of your laboratory. Would you welcome such an investigation?"

"If it's conducted fairly and without prejudice," Harker said, "of course we'd welcome it. We're not trying to fool anyone. We've discovered something wonderful and we want the people of the world to share in it."

"How do you feel about the American-Conservative party stand on reanimation?" *Times* asked.

"I wasn't aware there was one."

"They issued a statement at noon today. It implies that the National-Liberal Party is going to exploit the discovery for its own personal advantage. They point to your presence as legal adviser as proof of that."

Harker smiled, but beneath the smile was sudden bitterness. So it would be political capital too? He said, "This comes as a big surprise to me. I don't have any formal affiliation with the National-Liberals, though of course I generally support their program. I'm not even a member of the national committee. And we've received no encouragement or anything else from them."

"But you were a former Nat-Lib governor, Mr. Harker. Doesn't that make you a major figure in the party hierarchy?" Scripps-Howard-Cauldwell asked.

It was a loaded question. Harker mopped the sweat from his forehead, glared straight into the eye of the video camera, and said, "I still vote Nat-Lib, if that's what you mean. But ex-governors are just ex-governors, period."

"How about the claim of Cal Mitchison and David Klaus that there have been unethical practices in this lab?" Transcontinental TV asked slyly.

Harker said, "I hardly think that's worth talking about. Mitchison and Klaus are former employees who didn't perform competently and who were discharged. It's as simple as that."

"You were the lawyer for the late Richard Bryant," said the *Times* man. "Did you make any attempts to have Mr. Bryant resuscitated?"

"I did not. The family issued a statement expressing no desire to have Mr. Bryant revivified, and at no time did anyone here suggest that he should be. The movement to revive Richard Bryant was strictly unofficial."

Harker was starting to weary under the barrage of questions. He looked at his watch; the half-hour he allotted to these conferences had elapsed. He felt as if he were wrung dry.

"I'll have to ask you to cut it short now," he said. "Unless there are any other very urgent questions, we'll stop here."

Times said, "One question, Mr. Harker. Have any reanimations taken place since the announcement of the process yesterday morning?"

Harker shook his head. "The answer is no. Until the legal status of reanimation is settled, we're not proceeding with further experiments on human beings"—he regretted the unfortunate word *experiments* as soon as it passed his lips, but by then it was too late—"although we're continuing with other phases of our research. We've been bombarded with requests for reanimations, but we don't intend to attempt any. Obviously a legal decision on the validity of our process is needed first. The death-certificate laws, for instance; they'll have to be considered. And a host of other things. Well, gentlemen, I think our time is just about up."

The fearsome blaze of the video cameras died away, and the newsmen packed up their pocket recorders and left. Harker sank down wearily behind the desk and looked at Mart Raymond.

The scientist smiled admiringly. "Jim, I don't know how you do it. Stand up to those eagles, I mean. The pressure doesn't let up for a second."

"I'm used to it," Harker said with forced casualness. His stomach felt knotted, tight; his throat was dry and seemed to be covered with hundreds of small blisters. His legs, under the desk, quivered of their own volition.

Gradually, as the minutes passed, he recovered his poise.

The press conference had been a sort of purgative; he had put forth all the thoughts that had been boiling within him during the day.

The battle, he saw now, would be fought on a number of fronts— but the essential standpoint was a politico-legal one. They *had* to secure congressional approval for the process. And they had to win friends and influence people in a hurry, before the various splintered opponents of reanimation, the Beller Labs, and James Harker could join forces and provide a united front.

What would happen if reanimation lost? No doubt the technique would survive, no matter what the legal verdict was. But it would become an undercover, furtive activity, as abortion had been before the permissive laws of the late twentieth century. And undercover meant dangerous, illegal equated with deadly. The tools of medicine are *always* deadly in unskilled hands.

No doubt about it, the fight was on. It was, thought Harker, the old, old struggle—the battle to give humanity something it craved, despite the obstacles provided by fear, greed, and ignorance. The essential fact—that of the conquest of death—could easily be clouded over by half-truths, distortions, and the well-meant fanaticism of self-righteous pressure groups.

I fought this fight once before, Harker thought. *And I let myself be beaten. But this time I'm not giving up. There's too much at stake.*

CHAPTER ELEVEN

THE NEXT morning—Wednesday—Harker found a neatly typed note sitting on his desk when he reached his office in Dormitory A. It was from Raymond. It said simply, *"We got a call from Washington at 0800. Investigating committee headed by Thurman is on its way north to snoop around the lab. They're arriving noon today."*

Methodically Harker destroyed the note and turned his attention to the morning papers. He felt tense, but not unduly so; the Senatorial investigation could be the beginning of success in their campaign, and in any event it would put an end to these days of doubt. He would know at least how the reanimation project stood in the eyes of the Senate.

On this, the third morning of the Era of Reanimation, almost the entire front page of every paper was given over to a discussion of the subject. His press conference had been given a great deal of space, and as usual the *Times* had printed the full text. He read the other articles with a queasy sense of expanding confusion.

MANHATTAN—*The late Richard Bryant was cremated here today despite a demonstration urging his reanimation. At least fifty banner-waving demonstrators attempted to interfere with the ceremony, but police maintained order.*

" We are sure Father would never have approved of such an awakening," declared Jonathan Bryant, 42, oldest son of the space hero—

MONTREAL (UP)—A mob destroyed the home and office of Dr. Joseph Pronovost this afternoon after he refused to resuscitate a 9-year-old girl who had died the night before. Dr. Pronovost, 58, a general practitioner, claimed to have no knowledge of the Beller reanimation technique announced Monday. Despite his statement, relatives of Nancy St. Leger, a victim of leukemia, broke into the doctor's home and attacked him.

Dr. Pronovost was reported to be in good condition at Sacred Heart Hospital—

CORPUS CHRISTI, Tex. (AP)—Four men and two women suffered injuries here this evening as a result of a rumor that a Beller reanimation was taking place at a local funeral home.

More than thirty persons entered the Burr Funeral Parlors in an attempt to prevent the reanimation. A funeral service was in progress, and the injuries resulted when guests turned back the intruders. The funeral continued as scheduled after the disturbance.

There were other similar stories elsewhere in the newspapers: violence on both sides of the controversy, angry and ill-informed people trying to prevent or to bring about reanimations. Harker gloomily put the papers aside.

Dark forces were being unleashed. He suspected there was violence yet to come. The fabric of society had been unbound; anything might happen now.

At twenty minutes to twelve, Benedict Lurie stuck his head in Harker's door and said, "A helicopter full of senators just landed outside. Raymond's talking to them right now."

"How many?"

Lurie shrugged. "There were ten in the copter. I couldn't tell you how many are senators."

"I'll be right out," Harker said.

He filed away the newspapers, cleaned his desk, and self consciously straightened his clothing before he went outside. A little group stood in the clearing formed by the area between the three main buildings. Harker saw Mart Raymond, Vogel, Barchet, and Dr. Smathers, and they were talking to—among others—Senator Clyde Thurman.

Harker joined them. Thurman was the first to notice him; he stared at Harker glintingly and rumbled, "Ah—Harker. Hello, there."

"How are you, Senator?"

"Never better. Harker, you know these men? Senator Brewster of Iowa, Vorys of South Carolina, Dixon of Wyoming, Westmore of California. Gentlemen, you know Mr. Harker—former Governor of New York, of course."

Harker shook hands all around. He knew most of the senators at least casually; Dixon and Westmore represented the Far West branch of the Nat-Libs, while Brewster and Vorys were arch-Conservatives.

Thurman was the chairman of the committee, and would have the deciding vote in case of a tie. Harker felt apprehensive of that. The venerable senator was ostensibly a Nat-Lib; at least he was elected every six years under that label. But in the past decade he had been trending increasingly toward conservative ways of thinking, and away from the party he had helped to found forty years earlier, in the great political upheaval and reshuffling of the 1990's.

Each of the senators was accompanied by a staff assistant. That made ten in all.

Thurman said, "The hearings will begin next week, Mr. Harker. We're here for a preliminary look-see, you understand."

"Of course." Harker glanced at Raymond and said, "Mart, have you been introduced?"

Raymond nodded.

Harker went on, "Mr. Raymond is the director of the labs. He'll conduct you wherever you would like to go, on the premises."

Raymond looked worried; Harker had seen the faint harried expression growing on the dapper lab director's face in the past few days. It troubled Harker. Raymond was a good organizer, a levelheaded scientist-but he was showing alarming signs of crumbling under the sudden pressure brought about by Mitchison's treasonous press release.

Harker edged close to him and murmured, "What's on the schedule for the senators?"

Through tight lips Raymond replied, "The main event's a cadaver."

"You're going to risk it?"

Raymond shrugged. Worry-lines tightened his cheeks. "We'll have to do it sooner or later. Why not now?"

Harker made no reply. Attempting a human reanimation in front of the senators was a long-shot gamble, even with odds of five to one in favor of success.

If the experiment succeeded, they had gained very little; if it failed, they had lost everything right at the start. The odds of five to one were highly deceptive. But Harker decided to go along with Raymond, just this one time.

He said, "Shall we begin our tour, gentlemen?"

Raymond had evidently been working frantically all morning to set things up. The labs were spotlessly clean, everything well ordered and well dusted. The researchers had received their instructions, too; every one of them looked Constructively Busy, doing something scientific-looking no matter how trivial. In reality, most of them spent a good half their time staring into space, making doodles on scrap paper, or thumbing through textbooks—but senators could never be expected to believe that such idle acts were part of genuine scientific research.

The tour began with a rapid and exhausting general survey of the labs; Raymond served as guide, giving forth bristling scientific terminology at every possible opportunity. The senators looked impressed.

The senators also looked increasingly weary—all except Thurman, who strode along next to Raymond and Harker and put forth a never-ending string of questions, some of them pointless and others embarrassingly perceptive.

As he struggled to keep pace with Thurman, Harker felt a surge of new admiration for the Nat-Lib patriarch. Thurman was a ruggedly built man, well over six feet tall and still erect of bearing; his face was a craggy affair dominated by massive snowy-white eyebrows and a thatch of silver hair, and his voice was a commanding rumble.

It was Thurman who had completed the destruction of the old Democratic and Republican parties by serving as organizer for the National-Liberal Party that carried the 1990 congressional elections; he had then persuaded the incumbent President Morrison to run for re-election on the Nat-Lib, rather than Democratic ticket, in '92—and, by '94, the obsolete political parties had vanished, replaced by a more logical alignment of liberal against conservative.

Now, Harker thought, the party lines were blurring again; perhaps it was an inevitable force at work. There were liberals in the American-Conservatives, and some early Nat-Libs, especially Thurman, were with increasing regularity voting for Conservative-sponsored measures. Perhaps in another fifty years' time a further reorganization would be needed; it seemed to be necessary about once a century, judging by past performance.

As they explored the enzyme lab and watched the big centrifuge at work in the serotonin room, Harker wondered how he stood with Thurman now. Fifteen years ago, he had virtually been a son to the senator, serving for a while as his private secretary before being tapped for prominence in the New York Nat-Lib organization. Thurman had guided him up through the Mayoralty, saw him into the governor's mansion in Albany—and then, when the party decided to ostracize him, Thurman had not said a word in his defense. It was more than a year since he had spoken to the veteran legislator.

"These dogs," Senator Vorys said as Raymond and Vogel demonstrated reanimation on a pair of spaniels—"they feel no pain?" Vorys was a waspish, bald little man, with seemingly a lifetime tenure as American-Conservative Senator from South Carolina.

"Absolutely none," Raymond assured him.

"Animal experiments are legal," remarked Senator Westmore, the Californian Nat-Lib. "No grounds for objecting there."

"I wasn't objecting," snapped Vorys. "Merely inquiring."

Harker smiled to himself.

The dogs were cleared away in due time; Harker saw the tension-lines reassert themselves on Raymond's face, and he knew the main event was about to begin.

When Raymond spoke, his voice was thin and strained.

"Gentlemen, I know you've come here for one main purpose—to see if human life can be restored. The time has come for us to demonstrate our technique."

Raymond licked his lips. Tension mounted in the lab room. The senators stirred in anticipation; the five staff men scribbled notes furiously. Harker felt dry fingers clutching at his windpipe. It was a feeling he remembered having felt on two election nights, at that moment just after the polls had closed—when, with the die irretrievably cast, there was nothing to do but wait until the electronic counters had done their job and announced the winner.

He waited now. Two white-smocked assistants rolled in an operating-table on which a covered cadaver lay.

In a harsh, edgy voice Raymond said, "We secure most of our experimental cadavers from local hospitals. We have permits for this. The body here is approximately the one hundredth we have used in our work, and the seventy-second since the first successful reanimation."

The covers were peeled back. Harker flinched slightly; the body was that of a boy of about twelve or thirteen, and it was not a pretty sight.

"This boy drowned late yesterday afternoon in a nearby lake," Raymond said hoarsely. "All conventional methods of resuscitation were tried without success."

"You mean artificial respiration, heart massage, and things like that?" Senator Dixon said.

"Yes. The boy was worked over for nearly eight hours, and pronounced dead early this morning. When I phoned the hospital to arrange for a demonstration specimen for you gentlemen, I was allowed to speak to the boy's father, who gave permission for this experiment."

Five mini-recorders on five secretarial wrists drank in Raymond's words. Harker felt growing anxiety; still, he had to admit that using a boy for the experiment was a good touch—if the experiment worked.

He was not afraid of total failure; that could always be explained away and accepted tolerantly. It was the one-out-of-six chance that frightened him, the worse-than-failure of restoring the boy's body and not his mind.

Raymond nodded to Vogel, who again was presiding over the reanimation. The bearded surgeon clamped the electrodes to the boy's temples and wrists, and lowered the great hooded bulk of the re-animator.

"The initial attack will come simultaneously through the electrodes and through hormone injections," Raymond said droningly. "Heart massage will follow, as well as artificial operation of the lungs. Keep your eyes on these instruments; they measure heartbeat, respiration, and the electrical activity of the brain."

The room was terribly silent. Vogel moved swiftly and smoothly, confidently, without tension. He threw three switches. The archaic light-bulbs overhead dimmed slightly at the instant of power-drain.

Driblets of sweat rolled down Harker's face. The five senators watched eagerly; he wondered what they were thinking now, how they were reacting as electrical currents rippled through a dead brain and hormones raced through a stilled bloodstream.

The boy was dwarfed by the hovering instrument that simultaneously clung to his exposed heart, pumped his lungs, jolted his brain, fed awakening substances to his blood. The needles on the indicator gauges began to flicker gently.

Harker felt little of the earlier revulsion this sight had caused in him. Now he stared at the slim thin-limbed body of the boy, his skin mottled with the blue imprint of asphyxiation, and waited for the miracle to take place.

Minutes passed. Once Thurman coughed and it was like a physical blow. Needles rose on dials, wavered, fell back as Vogel decreased power, stepped forward again as the delicate fingers nudged the rheostat a few fractions of an inch upward.

"Watch the EEG indicator," Vogel murmured.

The needle was tracing out an increasingly more agitated line. The calmness of sleep was ending.

"Respiration approaching normal. I'm shutting off the lung manipulators."

The heart-pump followed. Frowning, Vogel moistened his lips and yanked down on toggle-switches, finally drawing the main rheostat back to point zero.

"Artificial controls are withdrawn," Vogel said. "The life-process continues."

The boy lived. Raymond said quietly to Harker, "The EEG patterns are normal ones. The boy's mind is okay. We did it."

We did it. Harker felt a sharp sense of triumph, as if he personally had accomplished something. The senators would *have* to react favorably to something like this, he thought.

He glanced at Thurman. The old man was gray-faced, disturbed. Harker said, quietly, "Well, Senator? You've just seen a miracle."

He wasn't prepared for the reply, when it came. Thurman shook his great head slowly from side to side like a dying bison and said, "Jim, this is nightmarish. In the name of all that's good, boy, why did you get mixed up in it?"

CHAPTER TWELVE

TWO HOURS later, the Senate committee had gone, but the gloom of their presence still hovered darkly over Harker.

A delayed reaction having nothing to do with the visit of the senators had struck him. The old wounds of that day at the beach were open once again; once again he huddled Eva's cold little form against his.

Somewhere else on the laboratory grounds, surgeons were working over a twelve-year-old boy, stitching together the surgical apertures that had been made to permit resuscitation. By tomorrow, the boy would be out of anesthesia. In a few weeks, he would be walking around, healthy, recalled to life after twenty hours of death.

Eva had drowned. She had not been saved.

"I don't understand it," Mart Raymond exclaimed vehemently. "It just doesn't make sense."

Drawn for a moment from his painful memories, Harker said, "What doesn't make sense?"

"Thurman. How can he stand there and watch a dead boy come to life, and end up twice as solid against us as he was before?"

Harker shrugged. "I wish I knew. I thought we won them over with that show—until Thurman spoke up. The old fossil is fogged up with age, I guess. He's got some preconceived idea that it's immoral to bring back the dead, and having it done right in front of him just solidified his thinking."

The strain was showing on Raymond, Harker saw. His gray eyes were red-rimmed and bleary; his face had grown thin. He had given up a career in medical research to handle the job of running Beller Labs—and perhaps he was regretting that, now.

He said, "Thurman is supposed to be a Nat-Lib. I could understand those two Conservatives turning up their noses, but I thought—"

"Yeah. So did I. But Thurman's an old man."

"The Conservatives came out against reanimation today, didn't they? Doesn't he realize he's helping the opposition if he fights us?"

"Maybe he doesn't think of them as opposition any more," Harker said. "He's eighty-eight years old. He may *look* alert and bright-eyed, but that's no guarantee against senility."

"If he votes against us," Raymond said, "we're cooked. How can we win him over?"

"The hearings begin next Monday. We've got four days to figure out a line of attack. Maybe the old buzzard will die before Monday." Harker reddened slightly as he spoke the words; the thought of a universe without Clyde Thurman in it was a mind-shaking concept for him.

He looked at his watch. Five minutes to three. Right on the button, Lurie stuck his head in and said, "Time for the press conference, Jim."

Leadenly Harker nodded. "Okay. Send them in, Lurie."

He ran through what he had to say in less than half an hour. He told them that the senatorial committee had been there and had watched the successful reanimation of a twelve-year-old boy. He expressed a hope that the demonstration had impressed the senators favorably, and did not mention that Thurman's remarks implied a negative reaction.

There was a brief session of sporadic questions; then Harker pleaded exhaustion and hustled the newsmen out. He felt tremendously weary, but at the same time there was the excitement of knowing he was in a fight, and a tough fight.

He phoned Lois and said he would be home in time for dinner. She was being cooperative beyond the call of wifely duty, he thought. He was hardly ever home these days, and when he did show up at Larchmont he was a pale, exhausted ghost of himself, with little energy left over for family life.

The evening papers came in about half past four. Harker had been preparing a plan of attack for the Senate hearings the next week; he looked up when Lurie silently dropped the stack on his desk.

There was a statement from Mitchison and Klaus in most of the papers, to the effect that the Beller Laboratories were in the hands of—approximately—power-hungry madmen, and that they should be stripped of control immediately.

"I wonder what they hope to gain by that?" Raymond asked. "Even if they *do* succeed in getting control of the labs, they'll have thoroughly loused up the whole idea of reanimation."

Harker nodded. "We'll shut them up soon enough. I spoke to Gerhardt this morning and he said the hearing's coming up soon."

"How about this other thing you're involved with? The Bryant case. When's the hearing on that?"

"Tomorrow," Harker said. "I'll be tied up with that all day, I guess. But then I'll be free to devote full time here."

He skimmed through some of the other papers. More news of mob disturbance; this business of mobbing physicians because they either allegedly had been practicing reanimation or had refused to reanimate some newly-dead person was becoming disturbingly more frequent. There were three instances of it in the late editions—in Idaho, Missouri, and Louisiana. The mobs acted with fine impartiality, rioting on both sides of the question. Harker brooded for a while over that.

The editorial pages universally hailed the decision of the Senate to hold an immediate investigation; the papers seemed divided here too, the Conservative ones urging suppression of reanimation and the Nat-Lib papers pleading for sane consideration and government control.

By now everyone was getting into the act: philosophers, painters, athletes, ministers of foreign countries, were all quoted copiously pro and con reanimation. The Russians at last were heard from: Georgi Aksakov, President-General of the Federated Socialist States, sent a note of congratulations to President McComber on the American conquest of death, and extended hope that America would follow the time-honored custom of sharing its scientific developments with the other nations of the world.

By now word had reached the settlements on the Moon and under the Mars Dome too; by wire came messages of enthusiasm from the two international colonies. It was only to be expected, Harker thought, that the space colonists would welcome the breakthrough with joy. There was no breeding-ground for hysterical anti-scientific reaction on an airless world where only scientific miracles daily insured survival.

It was fast becoming a contest between darkness and light, between education and ignorance—a contest complicated by the presence of educated, intelligent, utterly sincere fanatics in the camp of the opposition.

"We must have regard for the soul," declared the spokesman for the Archbishop of Canterbury. "A limitation has been placed on the term of man's life. We must proceed with care when we destroy a limitation of God."

It was, Harker had to admit, a reasonable attitude—granted a framework of beliefs which he and much of the rest of the world did not share.

"The United States has always been the world pioneer," declared Senator Marshall of Alabama, the elder statesman of the American-Conservatives. "We never show fear as we approach the boundary between the known and the unknown. But we must exert caution in this new step, and take care lest we move recklessly forward and unleash forces which can destroy the bonds of society."

The medical societies had statements, too—sound ones. "The problem," declared an A.M.A. spokesman, "is essentially a soul-searing one. If the Beller process is valid, every physician will have the power to return life to the dead. Shall he make use of this power whenever he can? Or will there be the danger of giving life indiscriminately, to those perhaps who do not merit a reprieve? What will happen if a dead man's family refuses the right of reanimation? Can the physician proceed? And is he guilty of murder if he does not? Who will make the decisions? An entirely new code of medical ethics must be developed before any wide scale practice of reanimation can be permitted."

These were sound viewpoints, and Harker had no issue with them. But there were other, more hysterical voices clamoring in the newspapers, and hundreds of vituperous letters had already descended on the Litchfield post office as well.

People who feared death feared reanimation more. There were those who assumed that reanimation might become the property of an aristocracy that would perpetuate itself over and over, while leaving the common people to death. There were those who dreaded the return to life of a loved one, who were unwilling to face again someone who had been "beyond" and returned.

Fear and ignorance, ignorance and fear. Harker read the letters in the newspapers, and his head swam. The ones received direct were even worse.

...you are violating the command of God brought on us by Adam's fall, Harker. But you will rot in Hell for it...

...you Harker and Raymond and the others there should have been strangled in your cribs. Bringing the dead back from the grave is disgusting. You will fill the world with a race of undead zombies...

...I know what it is to have a loved one die, do you? (Yes, Harker thought.) *But I would not want to touch the lips of one who was dead...*

Harker paused a moment in thought as he read that last letter, wondering how he would feel had Eva been brought back to him there on the beach. He had assumed that he would welcome the idea, but now he remembered Lois' doubtful answer to the question, and it seemed to him that he himself was doubtful too now. Would he be able to embrace a daughter who had died and had been reanimated. Could he—

He shook his head in bitter self-contempt. *I'm overtired, he thought. All this superstitious muck is contagious. The life process stops, it starts again— and is anything lost? Wake up, Harker. Of course you'd have hugged Eva if she had been brought back to life.*

It had been a long day. He riffled through a few more letters, but the emotional impact was too great for him to bear after all the other conflicting events of the day. It was not easy to read letters from people who had pleaded for the reanimation of a loved one on Monday, and who now wrote bitterly to say that the period of grace had passed, and by their silence the re-animators had become murderers.

...my fiancée Joan who was seventeen and electrocuted in a kitchen accident Sunday night could have been saved if you had been willing. But three days have gone by and now she is forever gone...

Even more hellish than watching the slow ebb of life from a dying person, Harker thought, must be the wait while the hours pass after death, and the time for reanimation passes with them. New torments had been loosed upon the world, he saw. He felt like a man riding a tiger that grew larger with each day.

He picked up another one:

...you may remember I mentioned my wife mother of our four children who was close to death from cancer. Well she died the night I wrote to you, and not having heard from you yet I suppose you can not help me in this matter. I understand revival must be done on day of death, since she has now been gone two days I am arranging for her burial. Though I am unhappy and disappointed I do not hold bitterness in my heart against you, may God forgive you for having let Lucy die...

Harker remembered that one: Mikkelsen, from Minnesota. The implied accusation of murder, cloaked as it was by the prayer for God's forgiveness, chilled him. He put the letters away, phoned across the lab to Raymond, and said he was going home for the day.

"Good luck with that hearing tomorrow," Raymond said. "Thanks."

The air was clean and warm as he stepped outside; at five in the afternoon of an almost-summer day, the sun was still bright, the sky blue and curiously transparent. Harker tried to blot away the network of human suffering whose vortex he had apparently become; he drew in a deep breath, expanded his chest, swung his arms loosely at his sides.

A yellow dart crossed the sky and was gone; after it came the abrupt *blurp* of sound. It was a southbound rocket to Florida. No doubt it would be landing in Miami before he had reached his own home.

He remembered the legal fight when rocket service had been instituted on a commercial basis, almost thirty years ago. The jetlines had fought tooth and nail against introduction of rocket service; yet, today, both jets and rockets served the cause of transportation amicably enough.

There had been the Moon wrangle too, back in the trouble-wracked twentieth century. He had cut his legal teeth on the suits and countersuits; they were standard fare in every law-school. The Moon had been reached almost simultaneously by America and Russia in the early 1960's, during a period of international conflict and danger. The Socialist revolution in Russia in 1971 had ended the threat of atomic war, but even so it had not been until 1997 that the United States agreed to join forces with the Federated Socialist States in making the Moon base truly international in character.

There, too, forces of reaction had fought the merger on grounds that seemed to them just and necessary. They had been defeated, ultimately—and now, the Moon base and its newer companion on Mars were hailed as triumphs of the harmony of mankind.

Now reanimation. The old struggle was joined again. Harker told himself that the force of history was on his side, that ultimate victory would be his. But what sacrifices would be made, what campaigns fiercely fought, before then?

He reached his home at six-fifteen. Lois had the video set on, and even as he stood in the doorway the words of a newscaster drifted toward him:

"Senator Thurman of New York and four colleagues today visited the Beller Laboratories and witnessed an actual human reanimation which was successful. Senator Thurman later commented, and I quote, There is no doubt that a restoration of life took place. What is in doubt is whether this power is one that mankind should permit to be used, end quote. Senator Thurman will head a committee to study the implications of reanimation. Hearings begin Monday in Washington—"

Thurman was chairman, and Thurman had already indicated opposition. It was not a good omen. Harker kissed his wife wearily and said to Chris, "Get me something strong to drink, lad. I've had a tough day."

CHAPTER THIRTEEN

THE HEADLINE the next morning, black against the faint green of the paper, was, THURMAN TO OPPOSE LEGALIZED REANIMATION. Harker read the story at breakfast; it seemed the veteran senator had had a chance to think things over, and his conclusion was that reanimation was unmitigatedly evil and should be suppressed.

Harker tried to pretend he had not seen it. It was a staggering setback; it negated any possible gains they might make at the hearing next week. With the vote of the tie breaking chairman already committed to their opposition, Harker thought, what chance did they stand?

He glanced quickly over the rest of the front page. Riot in Des Moines; accusation of reanimation leads to attack on doctor in Missouri. And—Harker nearly choked on his breakfast coffee—what was this?

RETURN TO LIFE A FAILURE
PATIENT SUICIDES

New York—Police are searching the Hudson River this morning for the body of 58-year-old Wayne Janson, who allegedly jumped to his death from the lower level of the George Washington Bridge late last night.

"Wayne was in a state of despondency since submitting to the Beller reanimation technique two months ago," said Jonathan Bryant, of 312 W. 79th St., a close friend of the dead man. "He suffered a stroke in February and placed himself in the hands of the Beller people. I was notified of his death and reanimation early in March, but when he returned to Manhattan he seemed to be entirely changed. His whole personality had changed. He—

"Excuse me," Harker muttered to his wife. Clutching the paper, he ran to the phone and tapped out Mart Raymond's number.

"Mart? Jim. Have you seen this Wayne Janson thing in the paper?"

"What's that?"

Harker rapidly read the article. Raymond was silent for a moment, then said, "Huh? Who does he think he's kidding?"

"What do you mean?"

"We've never had anyone of that name here. Bryant's obviously fabricating something."

"I figured that when I saw his name in the article. You better check the records, though. We've got grounds for a suit if you're right."

"Jim, I tell you we've never carried out any reanimations on anyone named Wayne Janson. Bryant is obviously trying to smear us."

"Smear me," Harker corrected. "But I guess it amounts to the same thing."

"What are you going to do?"

"Nothing yet," Harker said. "I'll wait until the police find the body and then demand proof from Bryant."

"But there *is* no body, Jim! It's just a hoax!"

Grimly Harker said, "It may be a hoax, but I'm willing to bet there's a body. Jonathan isn't *that* foolish!"

The long delayed Richard Bryant will hearing took place at last at half past ten that morning, in the gray-walled, luminalit chambers of District Judge T. H. Auerbach. The affair was almost a farce; it lasted no more than twenty minutes.

Jonathan Bryant was not there. His sister Helen was the official representative of the Bryant children, and she explained curtly that Jonathan was "overcome with grief at the death of a very dear friend last night" and would not attend.

Six other Bryants were in court, all of them hungry for the old man's millions. They had retained a lawyer named Martinson who briefly and concisely explained that the old man had not been in sound mind at the time of making the will, and that it was therefore invalid.

It was a flimsy stand, and Harker said so. He spoke for no more than ten minutes. Judge Auerbach smiled politely, said he had studied the briefs from both sides with care, and ruled in favor of upholding the will.

Just as simple as that. Helen Bryant tossed Harker a glance of molten hatred and flounced out, followed by her younger brothers and sisters. Auerbach leaned forward from his bench and said to Harker, "I'm glad *that's* over with. One more delaying injunction—"

"There wouldn't have been one, Tom. They just were waiting for old Bryant to kick off. Jonathan didn't want to give him the satisfaction of winning while he was alive."

Auerbach shrugged. "They really didn't have a claim to the money. Were they just trying to make trouble?"

Harker nodded. "Trouble's their specialty, Tom."

"Well, you're through with having trouble with the Bryants now, I guess."

Harker shook his head slowly. "No," he said. "Not by a long shot."

He rode uptown from the courthouse and stopped off at his law-office for the first time in a week. The girls in the outer office stared at him strangely, as if he had undergone some frightening apotheosis

and was no longer just the firm's newest partner.

He crossed left and rapped on Bill Kelly's door. The plump lawyer smiled at him as he entered, but without much warmth.

"Morning, Jim. Long time no see."

"I've been busy."

"I know. I know all about it."

Harker ignored Kelly's tone and said, "I've come from the Bryant hearing. Thought I'd let you know it's over. Poof: fifteen minutes!"

"The will was upheld?"

"What else? It was just a case of willful petty obstruction on the part of the Bryant family. They're mean, twisted people, Bill. They've lived all their lives in the shadow of one great man—Rick Bryant— and I guess they chose this time to show him and everyone else just what Great Big Important Persons they really were." He scowled.

There was a pained expression on Kelly's face that seemed to have nothing to do with the Bryant affair. Slowly Kelly said, "Jim, this completes all the current work you're doing here, isn't that right?"

Harker nodded. "I turned over the Fuller and Heidell cases to Portobello. That was to leave me clear for—"

"Yes. I know." Kelly's face reddened even more than normally, and he squirmed wretchedly in his inflated pneumatic desk-chair. "I've been following the papers, Jim. I've been following the whole thing."

"I warned you it was hot."

"I know. I didn't know how hot it was, though. Jim, this hurts me," Kelly said. "I'm going to ask a favor of you. It's a lousy thing to ask, because it shows I don't have guts or the courage of your convictions or something along those lines. But—"

Harker said, "I'll spare you the trouble of putting it into words. The answer is yes. If you think my presence on your firm letterhead will hurt the firm, Bill, I'll resign."

A look of gratitude appeared on Kelly's fleshy sweat-shiny face. "Jim, I want you to understand—that is—look here, I asked you to come in with me when your party booted you out, and don't think I didn't get my wrist slapped for it. But this reanimation thing is too big. I don't want to get associated with it in any way. And so—well it seemed to Portobello and Klein and me—"

Sure, Bill." Harker had a sudden dizzying vision of himself standing at the rim of a bottomless abyss, but he heard his voice saying, calmly, rock-steady, "I'll draft a note informing you that I'm resigning because of the pressure of outside activities."

Hoarsely Kelly said, "Thanks, Jim. And if this thing blows over—if it all works out—we'll have a spot for you here. Don't forget that."

"I won't." *Not even because you don't mean it,* Harker thought. It wasn't possible for Kelly to mean it. It was just a formal ritualistic statement, this implication that he could come back at a future time.

He was through here. Probably he was through with private law practice forever. Kelly was a brave and intelligent man, but Kelly had been afraid to keep the hot potato named James Harker on his letterhead any longer. No one else would welcome him either. Beller Labs was the straw to which he had to cling now.

He stood up.

"Okay, Bill. Glad we got everything cleared up. Just thought I'd tell you about the wrap-up on the Bryant case. I'll clear out my office next week."

"No hurry about it. Oh—nearly forgot." Kelly consulted a memo slip. "Leo Winstead's office phoned here for you earlier today. The Governor wants you to call him back between one-thirty and three this afternoon."

Harker frowned momentarily. *Winstead? What does he want with me?* He said to Kelly, "Thanks, Bill. And so long."

He bought a noontime edition of the *Star-Post* and ate a gloomy little meal by himself in a nineteenth-floor automated restaurant overlooking the East River. He pushed the meal-selector buttons almost at random; the result was largely an assortment of cheap synthetics, but he hardly cared. He ate abstractedly, not looking at his food but at the increasingly more troubling news in the paper.

There was a new statement from Senator Thurman, more doggedly anti-reanimation than the last. Apparently Thurman's views on the subject mounted in vitriol-content in hourly increments; now he said that "reanimation is of dubious value in mitigating human sorrow—a crude and unsatisfactory process that robs life of dignity." Evidently he had read about the Janson suicide. And speaking of that—

Yes. The body had been found and identified, according to a story at the bottom of Page One. Wayne Janson, 58, an unmarried industrialist. Listed as suicide; Jonathan Bryant identified body. Investigation now proceeding as a result of Bryant's statement that Janson had recently undergone reanimation.

And a statement from David Klaus, too, evidently released by Mitchison: "The Janson case proves that the Beller technique can be a dangerous and destructive instrument in the wrong hands." He recognized Mitchison's blunt word-sense, the equating of *technique and instrument*.

At half past one he made his way to a public phone booth, sealed himself in, snapped on the privacy-shield, and called the operator.

"I'd like to make a charge-account call to Albany."

She took his name and home phone, assured him that the call would be billed to his account, and put him through to the Governor's mansion. A relay of secretaries passed him along to Winstead.

The booth's screen was small, a seven-incher, and definition was poor. Even with that handicap, though, Harker could see the rings around Winstead's eyes. New York's Governor obviously had had little sleep the night before.

"I got your message, Leo. What goes?"

Winstead said, "You know about Thurman and his stand on reanimation, don't you?"

"Of course. Thurman visited the lab yesterday."

"And then proceeded to issue a series of statements blasting your project," Winstead said. The Governor looked like a man about to explode from conflicting tensions. In a tight strung voice he said,

"Jim, we held a caucus on the Thurman situation last night. First let me tell you that the Nat-Libs have decided to issue a public statement praising your outfit and asking for careful consideration of reanimation."

Harker smiled. "It's about time someone said he was on our side."

"Don't break your arm patting your back," Winstead warned. "The Amer-Cons forced our hand. It took all night for us to agree to support you. A lot of us aren't in favor of reanimation at all."

"And a lot of you aren't in favor of anything I'm in favor of," Harker said crisply. "But what's this about Thurman, now?"

"He's killing us! How can we come out pro-reanimation when the elder patriarch of our party is issuing statements condemning it?"

Harker shrugged. "I'll admit you have a problem."

"Any such inconsistency would make us look silly," Winstead said. "Jim, would you do us a favor?"

The idea of doing favors to the party leaders who had summarily expelled him less than a year ago did not appeal to him. But he said, in a cautious voice, "Maybe. What do you want?"

"We haven't approached Thurman directly yet. We'd like you to do it."

"Me?"

Winstead nodded. "Go down to Washington and appeal to the old gorilla's sense of sentiment. Plead with him to come back to the fold. Thurman was once very high on you, Jim. Maybe he still is."

Harker said, "I saw Thurman yesterday and he wasn't running over with sentiment. He came, he saw, and he condemned. What more can I say to him?"

Winstead's face grew agitated, Harker wondered what pressures had been exerted on the Governor to make this phone call. "Jim, this is for your sake as well as ours. If you can win Thurman over, Congressional approval of reanimation's a cinch! You're just cutting your own throat by refusing to go down."

"You know I'm not anxious to do favors for—"

"We understand that! But can't you see you'll be helping yourself as well? We'll try to make things easier for you if you convince Thurman."

Harker grinned pleasantly. It was fun to see Winstead squirm. "Okay," he said finally. "I'll go down to see Thurman first thing tomorrow morning."

CHAPTER FOURTEEN

FRIDAY MORNING. Ten-fifteen A.M., on the morning of May 24, 2033.

James Harker stared out the round vitrin porthole at the fleecy whiteness of the clouds over Washington. The two hundred-fifty-mile flight from Idlewild had taken about twenty minutes, by short-range jet.

Now the big passenger-ship plunged down toward the Capital's jetport. Harker felt the faint drag of gravity against his body and thought that a spaceship landing must be something like this, only tremendously more taxing. The ship quivered as its speed dwindled, dropping from 700 mph to less than half that, and halving again, while the 150-passenger ship swooped down from its flight altitude of 40,000 feet.

Harker was seeing Thurman at half past eleven, at the Senator's office. He rolled the phrases round in his mind once again:

"Mr. Thurman, you stuck by me long ago—"

"You owe this to your party, sir—"

"A forward step toward the bright utopia of tomorrow, Senator—"

None of the arguments sounded even remotely convincing. Thurman was a stubborn old man with a bee in his bonnet about reanimation; no amount of cajoling was going to get him to alter his stand. Still, Harker thought, he owed it to himself to try. The hearings began on Monday, under Thurman's aegis. It would not hurt to have the patriarch sympathetically inclined. Nor would it be undesirable to have Leo Winstead and the whole Nat-Lib leadership beholden to him, Harker reasoned.

The yellow light flashed and a soft voice emanating from a speaker next to Harker's ear murmured, "Please fasten your safety belts. We'll be landing in a few minutes."

Mechanically Harker guided the magnetic snaps together until he heard the proper click The ship broke through the thick layer of clouds that blanketed the sky at 20,000 feet, and the white, neat, oddly sterile-looking city of Washington appeared below.

Harker hoped there would be no further difficulty over the Janson case while he was gone. Police investigators had arrived at the labs in mid-afternoon the day before, wanting to know if a reanimation had been carried out on the late industrialist. Raymond had flatly denied it, but at Harker's advice had refused to turn over the laboratory records to the police until subpoenaed to do so.

The inspectors had left, making it clear that the matter was far from at an end. Harker smiled to himself about it; any comprehensive investigation was bound to prove that the whole affair had been staged by Bryant, taking advantage of his bachelor friend's suicide declaration to smear the reanimators.

But the suicide was in the newspapers, and no amount of unmasking ever really cancels out unfavorable publicity. The public would—with some justice—now link reanimation with possible mental deficiency afterward. Harker longed to have Jonathan Bryant's neck between his hands, just for a minute.

Troublemaker!

He leaned back and waited for the landing.

It took nearly half an hour for Harker to make the taxijaunt from the jetport to Capitol Hill, longer than the transit-time between New York and Washington. It was nearly eleven when he reached Senator Thurman's suite of offices—imposing ones, as befitted a senator who not only represented the second most populous state in the Union but who had held office for nearly seven terms.

A pink-faced, well-starched secretary about two years out of law-school greeted Harker as he entered the oak-paneled antechamber.

"Sir?"

"I'm James Harker. I have an appointment with the Senator for half past eleven."

The secretary looked troubled. "I'm sorry, Mr. Harker. The Senator appears to be ill."

"Ill?"

"That's right, sir. He hasn't reported to his office yet today. He's always here by nine sharp, and it's almost eleven now, so we figure he must be sick."

So far as Harker knew, Clyde Thurman had not known a day's illness yet in the twenty-first century. It was strange that he should fall ill this day of days, when Harker had an appointment to see him.

But it was not like Thurman to run away from a knotty problem, either. Harker said, "Have you checked with his home?"

"No, sir." The secretary appeared to resent Harker's question. "The Senator's private life is his own."

"For all you know Thurman died this morning!"

A shrug. "We have not received word of any sort whatever."

Harker paced up and down in the antechamber for fifteen minutes, sitting intermittently, fidgeting, glancing up nervously every time the big outer door opened to admit someone. He thought back thirty-odd years, to the time when eight-year-old Jimmy Harker was reported to his school principal for some obscure, forgotten offense. He had sat in just this manner in the anteroom of the principal's office, waiting for the principal to come back from lunch to administer his punishment—his head popping around every time a clerk opened the big door, his stomach quivering in fear that this might be the principal this time.

In time, he recalled, the principal *had* come—and had not expelled him nor phoned for his father, merely reprimanded him and sent him back to his classroom. Perhaps the same thing might happen today, he thought, perhaps some miraculous change of heart on the part of old Thurman—

But no miracles took place. Eleven-fifteen went by, and eleven-thirty, and there was no sign of Thurman. Clerks serenely went about their routine duties, ignoring the tense, sweating man in the outer office.

At ten to twelve Harker rose and confronted the secretary again. "Any word from Thurman?"

"Not yet, sir," was the bland reply.

Harker crooked his fingers impatiently. "Look here, why don't you phone his home? Maybe he's seriously ill."

"We never disturb the Senator at home, sir."

Harker glared at the man, exhaled exasperatedly, and growled, "I guess you won't give me his home phone number, then."

"Afraid not, sir."

"Is there anything you *will* do? Suppose you phone the office of Senator Fletcher for me, then."

Fletcher was the Senate Majority Leader, another veteran Nat-Lib who was likely to know where to reach Thurman if anyone was. A little to Harker's surprise, the secretary said, "You can use the phone back here. Just pick up and tell the switchboard who you want."

The phone was audio-only. A metallic voice said, *"Your party, please?"* and Harker, resisting the temptation to ask for Thurman's home number (it was probably restricted) said, "Would you connect me with Senator Fletcher's office?"

Four secretaries later, Harker heard the deep, confident voice of Pennsylvania's Fletcher say, "What can I do for you, Harker? Heard you were in town."

"I'm here to see Senator Thurman," Harker said. "Do you know where—"

"Thurman? Where are you now, Harker?"

"At the Senator's office. He isn't here, and I thought you might know—"

"Me? Harker, if I knew where Thurman was I'd be talking to him and not to you. I'm looking for him myself."

Harker's hopes sank. "Have you phoned his home?"

"Yes. Nobody there has seen him since early last evening. If you get any word, Harker, call me back."

The line went dead. Harker stared at the phone thoughtfully a moment, then replaced the receiver. He walked over to the smug secretary and said casually, "You better start looking for a new job. Senator Thurman hasn't been seen since some time last night."

"What? But—"

Interrupting the agitated reply, Harker said, "You better make some quick phone calls. I'll be back later if the Senator turns up."

The next two hours were hectic ones at the Capital. Harker picked up an early afternoon newspaper when he saw the huge scare-head reading WHERE IS SENATOR THURMAN? The article simply said that the 88-year-old Senator had last been seen at his huge bachelor home in nearby Alexandria shortly after dark the previous night, and that nothing had been heard of him since.

Secret Service men were combing Washington and the outlying districts. The three-thirty headlines screamed, THURMAN STILL MISSING!

No word has been received yet of the whereabouts of Senator Clyde Thurman (N-L, N.Y.), who vanished from his home early last evening. The veteran lawmaker is slated to preside over the controversial reanimation hearings beginning Monday, if—

At four o'clock there was still no sign of the missing senator. Harker phoned the jetport, made reservations for a four-thirty flight back to New York. At five, he was at Idlewild; he phoned Lois from there, told her what had happened, and said he was going straight out to Litchfield and would be home later, after supper.

The New York evening papers were full of the Thurman disappearance. Harker thought of phoning Winstead, then changed his mind; the Governor was well aware by now that Harker could not have kept his appointment with Thurman. Instead he rented a cab and travelled quickly out to the Beller Laboratories.

He got there shortly after six. The place was oddly empty; evidently the reporters had grown tired of clustering around the entrance to the dirt road. Three guards, fully armed, stood by the blockade in the yellow-brown light of very late afternoon.

"Hello, Mr. Harker. You can go in."

"Where's Raymond?"

"Main operating lab," the guard said.

Frowning, Harker moved past and headed across the clearing to the lab building. A late-spring breeze whistled down through the spruces, chilling him momentarily; the sun was a dying swollen reddish ball hovering near the horizon. Harker felt a strange foreboding sense of fear.

Three white-garbed medics guarded the lab entrance. Harker started to go past; one of them shook his head and said, "Very delicate work going on in there, Mr. Harker. If you're going in, be sure to keep quiet."

Harker tiptoed past.

Inside, he saw a tense group clustered around the operating table: Raymond, Vogel, Lurie, little Barchet, and a surgeon Harker did not know. There was a figure on the table. Harker could not see it.

Raymond detached himself from the group and came toward him. The lab director's face was pale, almost clammy; his lips hung slack with tension, and his eyes bulged. He looked frightened half into catatonia.

"What's going on?" Harker whispered.

"Experiment," Raymond said, shivering. "God, I wish we hadn't started this."

Raymond seemed close to collapse. Puzzled, Harker edged closer to the table, shunting Barchet to one side to get a better view. Five guilt-shadowed faces turned uneasily to stare at him.

For a long moment Harker studied the exposed face of the cadaver on the table, while billowing shock waves clouded his mind, numbed his body. The enormity of what had been done left him almost incapable of speech for a few seconds.

Finally he looked at Raymond and said, "What have you people done?"

"We—we thought—"

Raymond stopped. Barchet said, "We all agreed on it after you left yesterday. We would bring him here and try—try to convince him that we were right. But he had a heart attack and d-died. So—"

In the yellow light of the unshielded incandescents the lie stood out in bold relief on Barchet's face. It was Lurie who said finally, "We might as well tell the truth. We had Thurman kidnapped and we chloroformed him. Now we're going to revive him and tell him he died of natural causes but was reanimated. We figure he'll support us if—"

Wobbly-legged, Harker groped for a lab stool and sat down heavily, cradling his suddenly pounding head in his hands. The monstrosity of what had been done behind his back stunned him. To kidnap Thurman, kill him, hope that in reviving him he would be converted to their cause—

"All right," Harker said tonelessly. "It's too late for saying no, I guess. You realize you've condemned all of us to death."

"Jim," Raymond began, "do you really think—"

"Kidnapping, murder, illegal scientific experimentation—oh, I could strangle you!" Harker felt like bursting into tears. "Don't you see that when you revive him he's bound to throw the book at us? Why did you have to do this when I was gone?"

"We planned it a long time ago," Barchet said. "We didn't think you'd be back in time to see us doing it."

Vogel said, "Perhaps if we don't carry out the resuscitation, and merely dispose of the body—"

"No!" Harker said, half-sobbing. "We'll reanimate him. And that'll be the end of this grand crusade. Finish." He looked down at Thurman's massive head, imposing even in death. His voice was a harsh hissing thing as he said, "Go on! Get started!"

He watched, numb-brained, as if dream-fogged, while Vogel and the other surgeon prepared the complex reanimating instrument. His heart pounded steadily, booming as if it wanted to burst through his ribcage.

He felt very tired. But now, thanks to this one master blunder, all their striving was at an end. Thurman, awakened, would denounce them for what they had done. After that, they ceased to be scientists and would be mere criminals in the eyes of humanity.

Harker listened to the murmured instructions being passed back and forth over the table, watched the needles entering the flesh, the electrodes being clamped in place. Minutes passed. Vogel's thin hand grasped the controlling rheostat. Power surged into the dead man's body.

After a while Harker rose and joined the group round the table. Needles wavered and leaped high, indicating that life had returned. But—

"Look at the EEG graph," Raymond said hollowly.

The graph held no meaning for Harker. But he did not need to look there to see what had happened.

The eyes of the body on the table had opened, and were staring toward the ceiling. They were not the beady, alert, eager eyes of Senator Thurman. They were the dull, glazed, slack-muscled eyes of an idiot.

CHAPTER FIFTEEN

FOR A MOMENT, no one spoke.

Harker stood some five feet from the operating table, looking away from the creature under the machine, thinking, *These people are like small boys with a new shiny toy. I should never have trusted them alone. I should never have gotten involved in this.*

"What do we do know?" Lurie asked. The gangling biologist was nearing a state of hysteria. Sweat-drops beaded his forehead. "The man's mind is gone."

"Permanently?" Harker asked. "There's no way of restoring it?"

Raymond shook his head. "None. The EEG indicates permanent damage to the brain."

Harker took a deep breath. "In that case, there's nothing for us to do but kill him again and dispose of the body."

The suggestion seemed to shock them. Barchet reacted first: "But that's *murder!*"

"Exactly. And what did you think you were committing the first time you killed Thurman?" There was no answer, so he went on.

"According to the present law of the land, you were all guilty of murder the moment you put the chloroform-mask over Thurman's face. The law needs fixing, now, but that's irrelevant. You made yourselves subject to the death penalty when you abducted him, incidentally."

"How about you?" Barchet snapped. "You seem to be counting yourself out."

Harker resisted the impulse to lash out at the little man who had caused so much trouble. "As a matter of fact, technically I'm innocent," he said. "The kidnapping and murder both were carried out without my knowledge or consent. But there isn't a court in the world that would believe me, so I guess I'm in this boat with you. At the moment we all stand guilty of kidnapping and first-degree murder. I'm simply suggesting we get rid of the evidence and proceed as if nothing had happened. Either that or call the police right now."

Raymond said, "I think you're right." The lab director's face was green with fear; like the rest of them, he was awakening slowly to the magnitude of their act. "We did this thing because we thought we were serving our goal. We were wrong. But the only way we can *continue* to serve our goal is to commit another crime. We'll have to dispose of the body."

"That won't be hard," Vogel said. "We dispose of bodies pretty frequently around here. I'll do a routine dissection and then we'll just make sure the parts get pretty widely scattered through the usual channels."

Raymond nodded. He seemed to be growing calmer now. "Better begin at once. Chloroform him again and do the job in the autopsy lab. Make it the most comprehensive damn autopsy you ever carried out."

Silently Vogel and the other surgeon wheeled the body out, with Lurie following along behind. In the empty operating room, Harker glared at Raymond and Barchet. He felt no fear, no apprehension—merely a kind of dull hopeless pain.

"Well done," he said finally. "I wish I could tell you exactly how I feel now."

Raymond pursed his lips nervously. "I think I know. You'd like to strangle us, wouldn't you?"

"Something like that," Harker admitted. "Why did you have to do it? *Why?*"

"We thought it would help us," said Barchet.

"Help? To kidnap and kill a United States Senator? But—oh, what's the use. Just remember now that there are six of us who know about this. The first one who cracks and talks not only sends all six of us to the gas chamber but finishes reanimation permanently."

Suddenly he did not want to be with them. He said, "I'm going to my office to get some papers, and then I'm going home. Can I trust you irresponsible lunatics for an entire weekend?"

Raymond looked boyishly at his shoes; Barchet tried to glare at Harker, but there was something sickly and unconvincing about the expression. Harker turned and headed out.

He made the long journey from the lab to his home by taxi, an extravagance that he did not often permit himself. Tonight it seemed necessary. He had no heart for facing other people in a public jet, for buying tickets at a terminal, for doing anything else but sitting in the back of a cab, with the driver shrouded off by his compartment wall, sitting alone and staring out at the bright night city lights as he rode home.

Friday, May 24, 2033. Harker thought back to the morning when Lurie had first come to him. That had been a Wednesday; May 8, it had been. Two weeks and two days ago, and in that time so much had happened to him, so many unexpected things.

He had lost his affiliation with the law firm. He had reentered public life, this time as publicity agent, legal adviser, and general champion of a weird and controversial cause. He had become a stranger to his family, a man bound up entirely in the many-leveled conflicts arising out of the simple announcement that a successful reanimation technique had been developed.

He had watched two dogs and two human beings, both of them dead, return to the ranks of the living. He had watched a third man, a great man, a former idol of his, suffer death in the name of this strange cause.

He had become a murderer and a kidnapper. Unintentionally, true, and after the fact; but his guilt was as sure as that of the man who had lowered the chloroform.

Forces ranked themselves against him: Mitchison, Klaus, Jonathan Bryant—petty little men, those three, but they could cause trouble. Barchet, who was on their side and still managed to hurt them with everything he did. The Church; the American-Conservative Party; the ignorant, fearful people of the world, swayed by whatever hysteria happened to be in the air at the moment.

Had it been worth it?

He thought back, putting himself in the shoes of that James Harker of May 8, 2033 who had made the decision to go ahead. The bait had been the image of Eva, drowned, beyond his grasp. Eva might have lived.

Yes, he thought, *it's worth it.*

Abruptly the gloom began to lift from him. He realized that none of the things that had happened to him mattered—not the dismissal by Kelly, nor the crimes for which he had assumed the burden, nor the inner turmoil, which was exhausting him. How transient everything was!

The important fact was reanimation—the defeat of death. The end of death's dominion. That was his goal, and he would work toward it—and if he destroyed himself and those about him in the process, well, there had been martyrs in man's history before. That Evas of tomorrow might live, Harker thought, I will go ahead.

"Larchmont, mister," the driver called out. "Which way do I go?"

Harker gave him the directions. They reached his home a few minutes later; the fare was over $10, and Harker added a good tip to it.

The cab pulled away. Harker stood for a moment outside his home. The sitting-room lights were on, and one of the upstairs bedroom lights. It was shortly before ten, and since it was the weekend Chris would still be up, though young Paul had long since been tucked away.

And Lois probably sat before the video, waiting patiently for her husband to come home. Harker smiled gently, put his thumb to the identity-plate of the door, and waited for it to open.

Lois came to the door to meet him. She looked pale, tired; when she kissed him, it was purely mechanical, almost ritualistic.

"I was hoping you were in that cab, Jim. How'd everything go?"

He shrugged. "I don't know, Lois. I feel beat."

"Come on inside. Tell me about your day."

He followed her into the sitting-room. The autoknit stood to one side; she had been making socks, it seemed. The video blared some hideous popular song:

If I could hold you in my arms, Baby!
And cuddle up and—

Harker jerked a thumb toward the screen. "Is this the sort of junk you've been watching?"

Lois smiled faintly. "It's a good tranquilizer. I just let the sound bellow out and numb my mind."

He thumbed the off-switch set in the table before the couch, and the singing died away, the image shrank to a spot of tri-colored light and then to nothing at all. His hand sought hers.

He found himself wishing she would get up on her back legs and yowl, just once. It would be good for both of them. But she was so wonderfully patient! She had said nothing, or little, when he had stubbornly defied the national committee and gone ahead with the reform program that could only have ended his political career, and did. She had barely objected when he told her of his new affiliation with the Beller people, and she had said nothing in these past ten days, when the pressure of conflicting cross-currents had kept him bottled up within himself, unloving, cold.

He tried to say something affectionate, something to repay her for the suffering he had caused, the lonely evenings, the tense breakfasts.

But she spoke first. "They still haven't found Senator Thurman, Jim. I heard the nine-thirty newscast. Isn't it terrible, an old man like that disappearing?"

Sudden coldness swept through him. "Still—haven't found him?" he repeated inanely. "Well—I guess—ah—that old buzzard's indestructible. He'll turn up."

"How do you think this will affect the hearing on Monday?"

Harker shrugged, only half-listening. He was thinking, *You know damn well where Thurman is, and you're afraid to tell her. Why don't you speak up? Don't you trust your own wife?* He wet his dry lips. "I—I suppose they'll choose a new chairman if something's happened to Thurman. But—"

"Jim, are you all right? You look terrible!"

"Lois, I—want to tell you something. Today—"

He stopped, wondering how to go on. She was staring intently at him, curious but not overly curious, waiting to hear what he had to say.

The phone rang.

Grateful for the interruption, Harker sprang from the couch and darted around back to take the call on the visual set. He activated it; Mart Raymond's face appeared on the screen.

"Well?" Harker said immediately, in a low voice. "Is the evidence all taken care of?"

Raymond nodded agitatedly. "Yes. But that's not what I called about. Barchet's dead!"

"What? How?"

"It happened about five minutes ago. He was getting ready to leave, and we were discussing—you know, what happened tonight. He had a heart attack and just dropped. It must have been all the excitement. His heart was weak anyway, he once said."

Harker could not repress the tide of relief that rose in him. Barchet had been the cause of half of his troubles—Mitchison and Klaus, for one, and the Thurman affair for another. Still, a man was dead, and that was no cause for rejoicing, he told himself coldly.

He said, "That's too bad. Did he have a family?"

"Just a wife, but she died years ago. He was alone."

Harker nodded. "You'd better notify the local police right away."

"Jim, what's the matter with you?" Raymond asked incredulously.

"What do you mean?"

"Barchet's in the operating room now. Vogel's getting ready to try a reanimation on him."

"No!" Harker said instantly.

"No? Jim, we can't just let him die like that!"

"Barchet was a troublemaker, Mart. He was the weak link in the organization. Now we're rid of him; let him stay dead. It's one less witness to the thing that happened today."

In a shocked whisper Raymond said, "You can't mean what you're saying, Jim."

"I mean exactly what you're hearing. Barchet was unstable, Mart. He pressured you into doing all sorts of cockeyed things. If he lived, he'd end up revealing the Thurman business before long. Let him stay dead. That's an order, Mart."

Raymond seemed to shrink back from the screen. "It's—almost like committing murder, Jim! The man could be saved If we—

"No," Harker said, with a firmness he did not feel. "There'll be trouble if you cross me, Mart. Good night."

He broke the contact with a shaky hand.

Lois gasped when she saw him. "Jim! It must be bad news. You're utterly white."

He sat down heavily. "One of the Beller executives just had a heart attack. A man named Barchet—a runty little fellow who enjoyed sticking lead pipes between the spokes of smoothly running machines. I just ordered Mart Raymond not to attempt reanimation."

His hands were quivering. Lois took them between hers. Harker said, "It's like murder, isn't it? To refuse to reanimate a man, when it's possible to do so. But it's better for everyone if Barchet stays dead. Nobody will miss him. God, I feel awful."

"Remember the McDermott case, Jim?"

He frowned, then smiled at her. "Yes," he said. McDermott had been a factory hand, an overgrown moron of 22 who had beaten his 70-year-old father to death one night shortly before Harker had become Governor of New York. The verdict had been speedy, the sentence one of execution. With the boy in the death house and the night of the execution at hand: his aged mother had relented, lost her vindictiveness, pleaded with the new Governor Harker to commute the sentence.

The boy had had a long criminal record. The court had found him guilty. He had murdered his father in cold blood, premeditatedly. He deserved the full penalty.

Harker had refused to commute. But then he had spent the rest of the evening staring at his watch, and at the stroke of midnight had burst into an attack of chills.

He nodded slowly now. "I refused to commute Barchet's sentence. That's all there is to it."

CHAPTER SIXTEEN

THE NEWSPAPERS Saturday morning gave full play to the Thurman disappearance. Several of them ran biographies of the missing senator, tracing his political career from the early founding days of the National-Liberal Party to his present anti-reanimation stand.

The police and FBI statements were simply mechanical handouts, repeats of last night's assurances that no stone would be left unturned. Harker read them with some amusement. He had slept well, and a good deal of last night's tension had departed from him.

He had come to a calming conclusion: Raymond and Barchet had done a violent thing, but these were violent times. Somehow he would have to forget about the shocking Thurman affair and continue along the path already entered upon.

The obituary pages contained one item worth note:

SIMEON BARCHET

Simeon Barchet of 210 Princeton Road, Rockville Centre, L.I., treasurer of the Beller Research Laboratories, died of a heart attack at the Beller office in Litchfield, New Jersey yesterday. His age was 61.

Mr. Barchet joined the organization of the late oil operator D. F. Beller in 2014, after serving as a vice-president of the Chase Manhattan Bank. Upon Mr. Beller's death ten years later, he became a trustee of the Beller Fund and participated actively in the operation of the laboratory in Litchfield.

He left no survivors. His wife, the former Elsie Tyler, died in 2029.

Harker felt inward relief. Raymond had not dared to defy him; the reanimation of Barchet had been stopped as he had ordered.

It was only to be expected that some keen-eyed reader would read the Barchet obit and wonder why an official of the Beller Laboratories had been allowed to die on the premises, when reanimation equipment was right there. No doubt the question would be raised in the afternoon papers, since any news of the Beller researchers rated a good play.

He was not mistaken. At noon Mart Raymond called; he stared somewhat reproachfully at Harker out of the screen and said, "Some reporters just phoned up, Jim. They saw Barchet's obit and want to know how come he wasn't reanimated. What am I supposed to tell them—the truth?"

Harker scowled. "Don't tell them anything. Let me think. Ah—yes. Tell them Barchet was despondent over personal affairs, and left a memo imploring us not to reanimate him. Naturally, we abide by his last request."

"Naturally," Raymond said acidly. "Okay. I'll tell them. It sounds halfway plausible, anyway."

The newspapers moved fast. By nightfall the story had been promoted to the front pages, generally headed with something like BELLER MAN CHOOSES DEATH. The editorial pages of the *Star-Post's* evening edition had an interesting comment:

NATURAL DEATH OR SUICIDE?

Yesterday Simeon Barchet, an executive of the now-famous Beller Research Laboratories, died suddenly of a heart attack. According to his colleagues at Beller, Mr. Barchet had been in a despondent frame of mind and left instructions that he was not to be reanimated.

The situation exposed a new facet of the already explosive reanimation situation. Can willful refusal to undergo reanimation be considered suicide? According to time-honored principles of law, suicide or attempted suicide is an illegal act. In this case, the odd paradox arises of a man already dead committing what can only be termed suicide. Should reanimation be given the cachet of legal approval during the forthcoming Congressional hearings, then it is clear that a testament forbidding reanimation will reach beyond the grave to bind the dead man's survivors, counsel, and physicians in a conspiracy to abet suicide.

Obviously this is an impossible state of affairs. It demonstrates once again that the staggering Beller Laboratories success, which renders death in many cases merely temporary, will unavoidably bring about a massive revolution in our codes of legal and medical ethics, and indeed a change in our entire manner of life.

As he looked through the heap of newspapers, Harker began to feel that the tide was turning. The hysteria was dying down. Men were realizing that reanimation was no grisly joke, no hoax, but something real that had been developed and which could not be stamped out.

There were relatively few cries for wholesale suppression of the process. A Fundamentalist minister from Kansas had got his name into the papers by demanding immediate destruction of all equipment and plans for reanimation apparatus, but his was an isolated voice.

The tone of the *Star-Post* editorial seemed to be the tone of the consensus. Men of intelligence were saying, *Reanimation exists, for good or evil. Let's study it for a while and find out what it can do and how it will change society. Let's not scream for its suppression, but let's not unleash it entirely before we know what we're letting loose.*

The most authoritative of the secular anti-reanimation voices had belonged to Clyde Thurman, and that voice now was stilled. The act had been one of colossal audacity and thoughtlessness, and even now Harker found it difficult to endure the memory of the noble old warrior's mindless eyes; but, he had to admit, it had silenced a potent force for suppression.

Perhaps these were times for violence and audacity, Harker thought.

In that case I'm the wrong man for my job. But it's too late to help that now.

Sunday's papers continued the general trend toward reasonable consideration of the reanimation case, and also reported no progress in the search for the missing senator. It was learned that the reanimation hearings would begin as scheduled on Monday—not in Washington, though, but in New York. Late Sunday evening a messenger appeared at Harker's door and handed him a document.

It was a subpoena, requesting him to be present at 10:00 the following morning at the Hotel Manhattan, where the Congressional hearings would begin.

Harker arrived there half an hour early. The hearings were taking place in a meeting-room on the nineteenth floor of the big hotel. Federal law required the presence of the press at Congressional hearings; television cameras were already set up, and at the back of the room Harker saw the four senators who had visited the labs: Brewster, Vorys, Dixon, Westmore. Two American-Conservatives, two National-Liberals. The fifth seat had been left vacant, obviously for Thurman; but Thurman would not be likely to take part in the hearings, though only a few men knew that fact with any certainty.

Mart Raymond was there already, wearing not his stained lab smock but a surprisingly natty tweed suit. Vogel had been subpoenaed too, but not Lurie. Next to Raymond sat a plumpish woman Harker had never seen before; she was middle-aged and dressed in an obsolete fashion.

"Jim, I want you to meet someone," Raymond called to him as soon as Harker entered. He crossed the room to the front row of seats and Raymond said, "This is Mrs. Beller. She's acting as representative for the Beller Fund since Barchet died."

"Dreadful, about poor Mr. Barchet," the woman said, in a highly masculine baritone. "Pleased to meet you, Mr. Harker. I've heard so much about you. My late husband was deeply interested in your career."

I'm damned sure of that, Harker thought. For as many years as he could remember, the name of Darwin F. Beller had headed the list of contributors to the annual American Conservative Party campaign fund. He said aloud, "How do you do, Mrs. Beller."

He looked toward the platform where the senators sat. Brewster looked grim, Vorys peeved; Dixon and Westmore, the Nat-Lib members of the commission, both wore identical uneasy smiles.

Television cameramen seemed to be under foot everywhere, checking camera angles, adjusting mike booms, testing the lighting. A small, harried-looking man with close-cropped hair came scurrying up to him, jabbed a microphone under his nose, and said, "Mr. Harker, would you mind saying a couple of words into this?"

"What do you want me to say?"

"That's fine, sir. Now you, Mr. Raymond, and then after that I'd like to hear the lady speak."

It was a voice-test. Someone yelled out, "Harker's fine! Raymond could stand more resonance!"

"Would you mind getting more *chest* into your voice, Mr. Raymond?"

"I'll do my best," Raymond said.

The man with the microphone scurried away.

Harker watched the time on the big clock above the dais. Ten minutes to ten. The room was slowly filling up, not only with newspapermen. Raymond pointed out a couple of well-known medical men; Harker spotted two lawyers, including one who had issued a ringing denunciation of reanimation a week before.

At ten sharp Senator Westmore rose, smiled apologetically at the video camera, and said, "Good morning, ladies and gentlemen. As acting chairman of the Senate Special Investigating Committee dealing with the problem of the discoveries of the Beller Research Laboratories, I hereby ask for your attention and call this hearing to order."

The room fell silent. In the hush, the throbbing purr of the official stenographer's recording machine was clearly audible. After a pause Westmore went on, "We begin this session in the absence of our chairman, Senator Thurman of New York. I'm sure you'll all join me in the hope that the beloved senator is safe, wherever he is, and that his unusual absence will soon be explained. However, the—shall we say—delicate nature of the Beller discoveries makes it imperative that this Committee elicit facts and present its findings to Congress immediately, and so we are proceeding on schedule despite our chairman's absence.

"Our purpose is to draw forth information on the subject of reanimation. First I think it is well to question the director of the laboratory which developed the technique, Dr. Martin Raymond."

Raymond rose, a trifle awkwardly, and as he did so Senator Vorys requested permission to question him. Permission was granted.

Vorys said, in this thin, penetrating voice, "Dr. Raymond, you recognize me, do you not, as a member of the group of United States Senators who visited your laboratories recently?"

"I recognize you. You were there."

"In our presence you applied your reanimation technique to a twelve-year-old boy. Am I correct?"

"You are."

"The boy was dead?"

"He had drowned the day before."

"And where is this boy now?"

Raymond said, "Recuperating from the aftereffects of his experience. He's in good health, but still pretty weak."

"Ah. Would it be possible for you to bring this boy to a session of this Committee?"

"I don't believe so, Senator. The boy's not ready for any travelling yet. And it would violate our policy to present him to the video audience. We try to keep the identity of our patients secret."

"Why do you do that?"

"To protect them. Reanimation is still in its early stages. The social implications are still unclear."

"Ah. Would you object if the members of this Committee paid the boy a visit, then, to ascertain the current state of his health?"

"That could be arranged," Raymond said.

There was a moment of silence. Vorys stared keenly at Raymond and said, "Would you trace briefly for us the history of your laboratory, the nature of your process, and the results you have obtained so far."

Speaking easily and freely now, Raymond told of the original Beller bequest, the gathering-together of the laboratory staff, the early failures. He outlined a rough sketch of the technique as it was now practiced. "To date we've had about seventy successful reanimations," he finished.

"And how many failures?"

"About ten out of the seventy. Previous to our first successful reanimation we had thirty consecutive failures."

"I see. And what is the nature of these failures?"

Raymond began to fidget. "Ah—well, we don't succeed in restoring life."

"The body remains inanimate?"

"Yes. Most of the time, that is. I mean—"

It was too late. Vorys pounced on the slip gleefully and said, "Most of the time, Dr. Raymond? I don't quite understand. Does that mean that some of your failures result in actual reanimation, or *partial* reanimation? Will you make yourself clear?"

Panicky, Raymond glanced at Harker, who shrugged and nodded resignedly. *It had to come out eventually,* Harker thought.

The squirming Raymond was a pitiful sight under the merciless lights. He said in a hopeless voice, "I guess I ought to be more specific."

"That would help, Dr. Raymond."

"Well," Raymond said, "Counting the boy we reanimated when you were at the labs, Senator, we've had 72 reanimations since the first success. No, 73. In 62 of those cases, we've had complete success. In four others, it was impossible for us to restore life at all. And in the remaining seven"—*now it comes out,* Harker thought—"we achieved reanimation with partial success."

"In what way partial?" Vorys pressed.

Raymond had run out of evasions. He said, "We restored the body to functional activity. We were unable to achieve a similar restoration of the mind, in those seven cases."

CHAPTER SEVENTEEN

THE NEWSPAPERS had a field day with Raymond's unwilling revelation. Even the traditionally sedate *Times* devoted six of its eight columns to a banner headline about it, and a story that began,

Public faith in the Beller reanimation process was seriously shaken today by the surprising revelation that reanimation sometimes produces a mentally deficient individual.

Dr. Martin Raymond, head of the Beller research organization, made the statement in New York at the opening session of Senate reanimation hearings. He

declared that seven out of seventy-three experimental reanimations had produced "mindless beings." In four other instances, neither body nor mind was successfully recalled to life.

In the other papers, it was even worse. The *Star-Post*, which had been growing more sympathetic each day, demanded atop its editorial column, WHY HAVE THEY BEEN HIDING THIS? The Hearst papers, which had never been sympathetic to the cause of reanimation, grew almost apoplectic now; their key slogan was the label, "The Zombie-Makers," which they used in reference to the Beller researchers not only in the editorial (a vitriolic one) but even in several of the news columns.

At the Litchfield headquarters, the flood of abusive mail threatened to overpower the local postmaster. It was impossible to read it all, and after Harker picked up a scrawled letter that threatened assassination for him and his entire family unless reanimation experiments ceased, he decided to read none of it at all. They stored it in one of the supply-buildings in back, and Harker gave orders that any overflow was to be destroyed unread.

On the second day of hearings, new faces were in the auditorium. They were faces Harker did not enjoy seeing. They belonged to Cal Mitchison and David Klaus, and with them was their lawyer, Gerhardt.

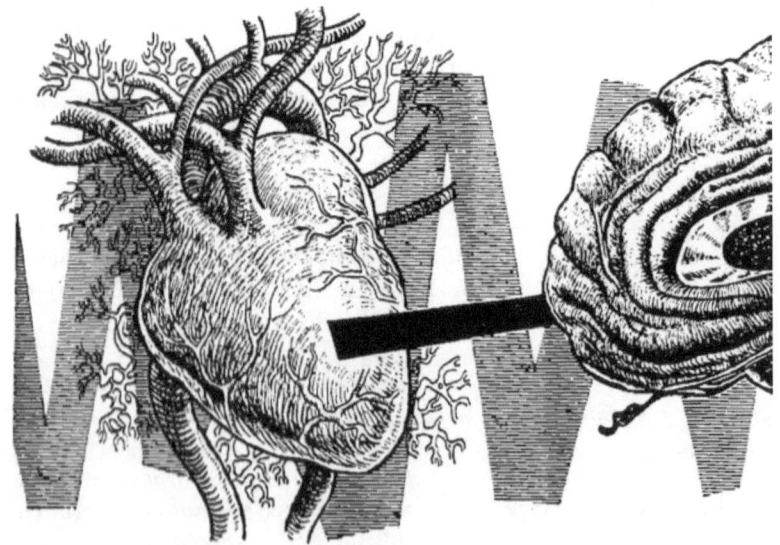

With Senator Thurman still not found, Brewster presided over the second session—a heavy-set, slow-moving man with the ponderously tenacious mind that went with those physical characteristics. With the

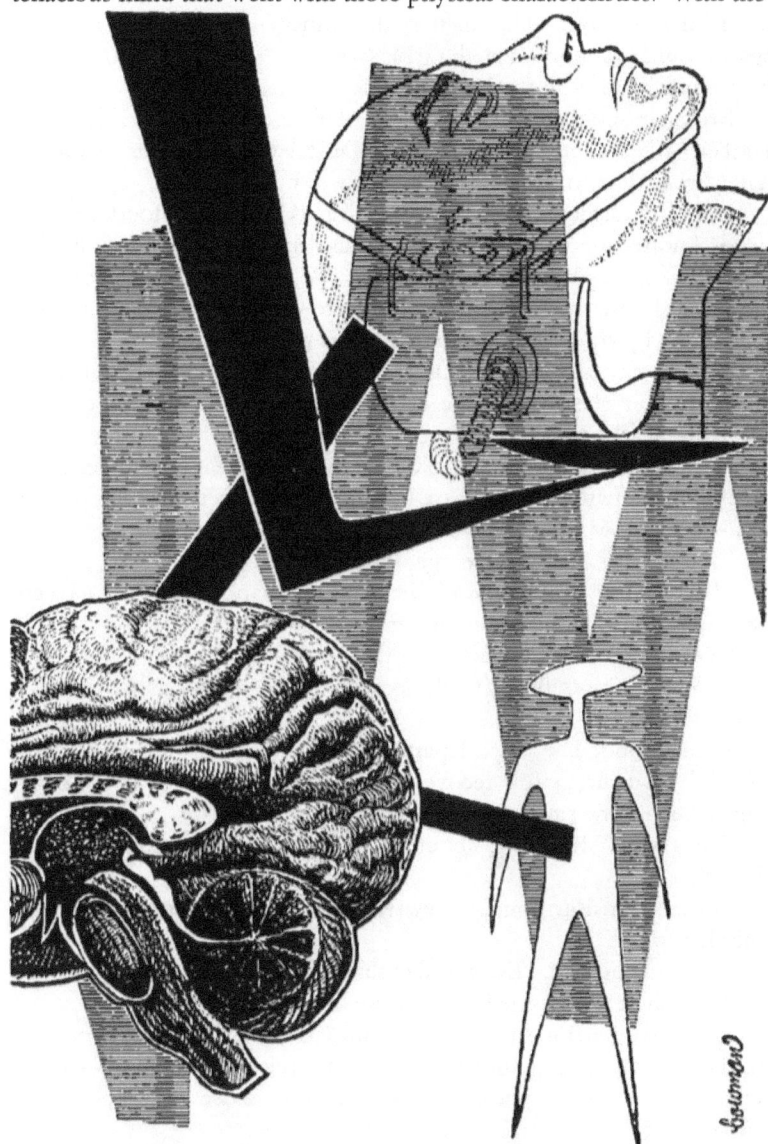

opening formalities out of the way, Brewster said, "We'd like to hear from Dr. David Klaus, formerly of the Beller Research Laboratories."

Harker was on his feet immediately. "Senator Brewster, I'd like to enter an objection. This man is the principal in a lawsuit pending against our laboratory. Anything he says in his favor this morning may be prejudicial to us in the lawsuit."

Brewster shook his head slowly. "This is not a court of law, Mr. Harker. We are interested in hearing Dr. Klaus' statements. You will have ample time to refute them later, if you wish."

Harker subsided. Brewster looked at Klaus, who stood with his hands knotted nervously together, a thin, slab-jawed, scrawny bright-young-scientific-prodigy type. "Dr. Klaus, you were formerly employed by the Beller Laboratories, were you not? Would you mind telling us why your employment there was terminated?"

Stammering as usual, Klaus said, "I was discharged by order of James Harker shortly after he came to work there. It was a purely malicious act."

Harker fumed, but Brewster waved imperiously at him to keep him quiet. The Senator said, "Please keep personal differences out of this, Dr. Klaus. How long were you employed at the laboratories?"

"Three years. I was in charge of enzyme research."

"I see. And you were aware that the reanimation experiments were occasionally producing—ah—idiots?"

"Yes, sir. We all were aware of that."

"Were attempts being made to safeguard against this unfortunate result, Dr. Klaus?"

Klaus nodded. "My department was working on a chemical method of insuring full recovery of mental powers. I don't know what's been done since my dismissal."

"He's lying!" Raymond shouted. "His group never had anything to do with—"

"Please, Dr. Raymond," Brewster said fiercely. "Your outburst is uncalled-for."

To Klaus he said, "Do you feel that this hazard of the reanimation process can be overcome in the course of further research?"

"Definitely. But the present management of the laboratories is heading in the wrong direction. They've rejected my ideas—which were close to being perfected—and instead chose to suppress the whole affair."

Harker felt his pulse mounting. Klaus seemed icily calm up there, speaking now with cold precision—most unusual for him. He sounded as if he had rehearsed this speech all morning.

Brewster said, "It would seem to me that the directors of the Beller Laboratories were guilty of an act of bad faith. Wouldn't you agree, Dr. Klaus?"

"Definitely, sir."

"Thank you. We would like to hear from Mr. James Harker, now."

Moistening his lips, Harker rose and took his place in the spotlight. Brewster gave place to Dixon, for which Harker was thankful; the American-Conservative Senators had a way of conducting hearings as if they were representatives of the Spanish Inquisition.

Dixon said, "Would you tell us how you became affiliated with the Beller outfit, Mr. Harker?"

"I was approached by Dr. Lurie of Beller," Harker said. "I had retired to private law practice after conclusion of my term as Governor of New York State. Dr. Lurie requested me to handle the legal aspects of reanimation."

"Ah. How long have you been connected with Beller, then?"

"Dr. Lurie first approached me on May 8. Roughly three weeks ago, Senator Dixon."

"And you have acted as spokesman for the laboratory since May 8?"

"No, sir. My first public statement for Beller appeared on May 20. It was occasioned by the premature and unauthorized release of information to the public by Dr. Klaus and our then public-relations agent, Mr. Mitchison. This was the act of insubordination for which they were dismissed from the laboratory."

"You infer that the first public announcement of the Beller reanimation experiments was made without your consent or knowledge?"

"That's right, sir."

"Why did you intend to maintain continued secrecy?"

"The process was not quite perfect, sir. A few more weeks of work and we could have eliminated the possibility of mental loss. It was my plan not to bring the matter to the public notice until then—but Dr. Klaus took it upon himself to inform the world without my knowledge."

Harker glanced at Brewster and Vorys. They were frowning; perhaps he had gotten through to them. He wondered if his words would counteract the tide of unfavorable reactions already swelling.

Dixon said, "Could you tell us how close you are to actual elimination of the hazard of insanity?"

"Sorry, I can't. That would be Dr. Raymond's province. But I will say that research at our laboratory has virtually ceased during this period of uncertainty."

There was a whispered conference at the dais, and abruptly Vorys replaced Dixon as interrogator.

"Mr. Harker, does the name Wayne Janson mean anything to you?"

Brewster and Vorys had evidently primed themselves well for the attack. Harker said, "Yes, Senator Vorys. Janson was an industrialist who committed suicide last week."

"It means nothing else to you?"

"No."

"No one of that name underwent reanimation at the Beller Laboratories?"

"No, sir."

Vorys paused momentarily. "The late Mr. Janson was supposed to have undergone reanimation several months before your employment at Beller. Is it possible that he *did* experience treatment there, and that you don't know about it?"

"I've examined the list of patients at Beller since the beginning of experiments there. No one named Janson is on the list."

"Perhaps he entered under another name."

"We have photographs of all patients, Senator. None of them corresponded to the photo of Mr. Janson published in the newspapers."

"In other words, you deny that he was ever a patient of the laboratories?"

"Exactly."

"But a close friend of the late Mr. Janson claims that he *did* secretly enter the Beller laboratories of his own will shortly before his death of natural causes, was reanimated, and suffered such mental disturbance afterward that he took his own life."

Harker said quietly, "It's obvious that one party is lying, isn't it? Our records indicate that no such person ever entered the labs for treatment. The burden of proof, I believe, rests with the other party."

"We have only your word for this," Vorys went on obstinately. "And you are not even under oath. Will you make these records of yours available for public inspection?"

"It would be against our policy."

"We could subpoena the records," Vorys warned.

Harker shrugged. "That's within your rights, of course. But exposure of the names of our patients would probably have adverse effects on them, psychologically and otherwise."

"That sounds very good, Mr. Harker. But it could also be an excuse for hiding something."

Resisting the impulse to lose his temper—for Vorys was obviously deliberately baiting him—Harker said, "I believe it would be possible to grant you and your three colleagues access to our records, to prove the fraudulent nature of the Janson matter. But public exposure of the names would not be necessary, would it?"

"Quite possibly not. Thank you, Mr. Harker. We will recess for one hour now."

As soon as Harker had left the stand, Mart Raymond approached him and said, "Things are getting rough, eh?"

Harker nodded. "Vorys and Brewster are out for our scalps. The American-Conservatives must be preparing to come down hard."

"I'm sorry about letting that statistic slip yesterday, Jim—"

"Forget it. It had to come out sooner or later, and maybe if we had announced it at the start we wouldn't be having so much trouble now. Well, it couldn't be helped. Let's go get some lunch."

As they rode downward in the gravshaft toward the hotel dining room, Harker said, "Exactly how close are you to getting the bugs out of the process?"

Raymond looked vague. "A week, a month, maybe a year. We know what causes the mental breakdown—most of the time. It's a matter of hormone impurity, generally. Of course, in some cases the brain suffers severe damage in the process of dying, and we'll never be able to lick that any more than we can revive a man who's been blown apart by dynamite. But I'm pretty sure we can lick the defects in our own system soon."

"And what probability of success would you predict after that?"

Raymond shrugged and. said, "Who knows? Nine out of ten successes? Ninety out of a hundred? Until we have ten or twenty thousand case histories behind us, our statistics don't mean anything."

Harker nodded thoughtfully. The meal was a quiet one; neither man said much. Harker was going back over the morning's session, trying to pick out the phrases the press would leap on.

He hoped he had discredited the Mitchison-Klaus combine and Bryant by his refutation. Surely the public would see that Mitchison and Klaus were vengeful power-seekers and nothing more, and that the whole Janson affair was nothing but a malicious hoax.

But he overestimated the public's ability to distinguish truth from slung mud, it seemed. The early afternoon papers were already on sale by the time the hearing resumed for the afternoon.

The headline on the *Star-Post* was, KLAUS SAYS HARKER FIRED HIM; CHARGES BELLER 'BAD FAITH'

The story, slanted heavily in Klaus' direction, implied that the enzyme man had been on the verge of a brilliant discovery when Harker maliciously sacked him. As for the Janson case, it referred to Harker's "uncomfortable evasions."

The tide was turning. The public fancy had seized on the one fact, grotesque and horrifying enough, that in a few cases reanimation resulted in dreadful mindlessness. On that slim base, a massive movement aimed at the total suppression of reanimation was beginning to take form and grow in strength.

Harker had seen the phenomenon before, and had been helpless before it. The great insane raging tide of public opinion had sprung up from what had been a smoothly-flowing stream, and once its mighty power had been channeled toward a definite end, there was no standing against it.

He had the uncomfortable feeling that only a miracle could save things, now. And miracles were not easy to come by, in this secular age.

CHAPTER EIGHTEEN

AS THE hearing ground along into its third day, and its fourth, and then its fifth and sixth, things grew even worse. The "zombie" phrase became a favorite, not only of the press and the public, but even of Brewster and Vorys. The fact that seven of the seventy-three reanimation subjects had been revived sans intellect had become the main issue. In his rare moments of relaxation, Harker wondered how the world would react if it were ever learned that one of those seven had been none other than the missing Senator Thurman.

Very much as Harker had expected, the American-Conservative Party intensified its previous belief in "caution" into what amounted to condemnation of the whole process. Maxwell of Vermont, the Senate Minority Leader, delivered an off-the-cuff but probably carefully-rehearsed speech at a Chicago gathering of American-Conservative committeemen, in which he referred to reanimation as "That mess engineered by a one-time lame duck of a National-Liberal, that unholy conspiracy against human dignity."

Later the same day, the chairman of the Nat-Lib national committee was quick to announce that James Harker had voluntarily severed his party connections in January, was now a private citizen, and in no way represented the membership of the National-Liberal Party. It was a neat disavowal that took the Nat-Libs off the hook in case the reaction against reanimation grew stronger, but left them an avenue of entry just in case public opinion should swing back in favor of Harker.

Work at the lab had come practically to a standstill. "If we only had a few more weeks," Raymond mourned, "we might be able to lick the remaining defects and get public approval. But they won't leave us alone to work."

A delegation of FBI men and the four investigating senators visited the laboratory a week after the hearings had begun, and Raymond and Harker reluctantly showed them the data on the revivifications so far-excluding that of Senator Thurman, which had not been recorded in any way whatever.

They checked through the photos, compared them with those of Wayne Janson, and left. That night the FBI issued an official statement, which read in part, *"Examination of the Beller Laboratories' records does not indicate that the late Mr. Janson ever received treatment there. Since there is nothing in Janson's own private papers that leads us to believe he as much as knew of the existence of the Beller organization prior to its public announcement, we must conclude that no reanimation did take place."*

This left Jonathan Bryant in an ambiguous position, since he continued to maintain that Janson *had* undergone reanimation, and had suffered a severe change in personality as a result, leading to his suicide.

"This ought to settle Jonathan for good," Harker crowed when the text of the FBI exoneration reached him. After all, it had to be obvious to everyone that Bryant had perpetrated a hoax designed solely to discredit reanimation and arouse popular fears against it.

But again Harker was wrong. The day after publication of the FBI statement, Jonathan Bryant was subpoenaed to appear before the investigating committee. The questioner was Senator Vorys. The interchange between Bryant and Vorys was widely reported in the late editions that day:

SENATOR VORYS: *You knew the late Wayne Janson well?*

BRYANT: *I was his closest friend.*

VORYS: *When did he first mention reanimation to you?*

BRYANT: *About January. He said his doctor had told him about the experiments going on in Litchfield.*

VORYS: *What is the name of this doctor?*

BRYANT: *I'm sorry, I don't know, Senator Vorys.*

VORYS: *Very well. Go ahead.*

BRYANT: *Well, Wayne suffered a stroke in February and he told me then that he was going to Litchfield, that he felt close to death and was volunteering for reanimation.*

VORYS (Interrupting): *The FBI did check and found that Janson had been away from home during February and March.*

BRYANT: *Yes, sir. Well, Janson came home late in March and told me of his experiences. He seemed moody, depressed, very different from usual. I tried without success to cheer him up. Then one night several weeks ago he phoned me and said he was going to end it all, to jump off the George Washington Bridge. In his conversation he attributed his desire for death to a morbid change that had come over his mind as a result of the Beller treatment.*

VORYS: *You're aware, are you not, of the FBI statement which says that to the best of their knowledge Janson never had any contact with the Beller people?*

BRYANT: *Of course. The key phrase there is "to the best of their knowledge." I have no doubt that the Beller people have suppressed this case as they've suppressed so many other things since James Harker started running them.*

The ten-minute colloquy between Vorys and Bryant, widely quoted and republished everywhere, served not only to discredit the FBI statement utterly, but to convince the public that Harker had indeed suppressed the records of the Janson reanimation.

A magnificent scientific discovery discredited because of a ten percent imperfection. An FBI investigation thrown into the rubbish-heap because of one man's bitter determination to crush an old enemy.

Harker studied the newspapers each day with increasing bitterness. The original importance of the Beller process seemed to be getting lost under the welter of side-issues, the jackal-like snapping of Klaus-Mitchison and Bryant, the political fencing of the two great parties, the hysteria of the people faced with something beyond easy acceptance.

Only one issue had not been raised yet—luckily, for it was the deadliest of all, having a basis of truth. No one had accused the Beller people of murdering Senator Thurman.

It was a logical accusation, against the background of insane charges already raised. After all, Thurman had been the most vigorous and most important of the enemies of reanimation, and he had disappeared on the eve of the hearings themselves! It seemed obvious to Harker that *someone* would think of implying that the Beller group had done away with their tough, intractable enemy.

But no one raised the cry, perhaps because it was too obvious. A thousandth time, Harker was grateful for that momentary impulse of steely purposefulness that had led him to condemn Barchet to continuing death. Of the six people who had known the fate of Senator Thurman, only Barchet was likely to crack and reveal the truth—and Barchet was out of the picture now.

The eighth day of the hearing came and went; Vorys grilled poor Lurie mercilessly on minor scientific details, while Brewster got Vogel to explain some of the surgical fine-points of the reanimation technique.

"You have to admire those two boys," Harker said after that session. "They've really brushed up on the pertinent subjects."

"I haven't had a quizzing like that since I left medical school," Vogel said, nervously tugging at the dark strands of his beard.

"And for what?" Raymond wanted to know. "Just to use up the taxpayers' money. They've found out all they want to know about us."

Harker nodded gloomily. You only had to pick up any newspaper, listen to any reasonably right-wing news commentator, attend any church, even walk in the street and talk to people at random.

The response was the same. Fear.

Fear of reanimation; fear of that one-chance-out-of-six that the result would be a so-called "zombie." Desperately Harker tried to counteract the swelling tide of fear. He scraped up money for a full-page ad in the *Times*, headed, THROW OUT THE BABY WITH THE BATHWATER?

His line of argument was that the reanimation process should not be condemned for its failures, but praised for its successes. It was in the early stages, the experimental years. What if aviation had been suppressed because of the early crashes? Research had to go on.

The response to the advertisement was a lessening of hysteria in responsible places; the *Times* itself echoed his feelings in its own editorial the next day. But he sensed he was not reaching the people. And the people feared reanimation. There was no doubt of that, now.

The hearing rolled along into early June, and then one day Dixon announced that this was the last week; the committee would enter private deliberations preparatory to delivering its findings to the Senate as a whole.

Harker approached Senator Dixon privately and said, "Tell me, Senator—how are our chances?"

The Wyoming liberal frowned quizzically. "Hard to say. The Committee's deadlocked two-and-two, you see. We may fight all summer about it."

"Vorys and Brewster are dead against it?"

"Absolutely. They heed the voice of the people, you see. Every minority party has to. It's the way they became a majority again."

Harker said doubtfully, "How's the feeling in high Nat-Lib circles?"

Dixon shrugged. "Right now, the feeling runs toward taking the Beller labs over and continuing reanimation research under federal supervision—with you and Raymond still in charge, of course."

"Fine!"

"Not so fast," Dixon warned. "We've got a Congressional majority, but that doesn't mean a thing. The way the people are murmuring, it looks pretty bad for getting that measure through."

"You mean you may have to switch your stand?"

Dixon nodded. "Jim, you know all about political expediency. You tried to knock down the stone wall when you were Governor, and got nowhere. If the people say, junk reanimation, then we'll have to junk it."

Hotly Harker said, "Junk it? The way I was junked as Governor?"

Dixon smiled. "I'm afraid so. It's this business of the seven idiots, Jim. That scares people more than you can imagine."

"But we can lick that problem—eventually!"

"Maybe you can. But the voters don't believe that. All they see is the short-range possibility. And they're more afraid of having a loved one turn into a zombie than they are of death. After all, you can't very well kill your wife or son or father if you've had him reanimated and he turns out to be an idiot. You have to go on supporting him. It's pretty frightening."

Doggedly Harker said, "I think we can get over that particular hump."

"Then reanimation's in. Jim, I'm not so foolish as to think that we can ever go back to where we were two months ago. The Beller process exists; it can't be destroyed. But it can be batted around in committee and side-channeled and circumvented until the time is ripe for popular acceptance. And the Party may have to do that to you, though I hope it doesn't happen."

"Do you think it will, though?"

Again the sad smile. "Read the newspapers, man. Read your mail!"

Harker read his mail.

He ploughed through hundreds of vicious, sweat-provoking letters. He sorted them out: favorable on one side, unfavorable on the other. The *unfavorable* pile grew so high it toppled over, and he started a new one; the pile of encouraging letters was no more than three inches thick.

They were letters of raw hate, most of them. The kind of thing that went, *My beloved* mother-father-sister-brother-son-daughter-aunt-uncle-grandmother-grandfather-died last week, and I want to tell you she/he had a decent Christian burial and went to his/her eternal repose. Naturally I feel *sorrow at my loss, but I'd rather be dead myself than let a loved one of mine get into your hands. Sure, maybe you'll bring him/her back to life—but who wants to see the hollow mindless shell of someone you once loved? Not me, brother. Not me.*

It was an enlarging experience to read those letters. Even when he had held public office, Harker had never received so many, nor such loaded ones.

It was astonishing. They gloated in the triumph of death, they thanked God they had not allowed their beloved ones to be reanimated, they extended curses for Harker and his whole family. *He* was the target of their hate, the symbol for reanimation.

At first he was irritated, then angered; anger passed, and turned into compassion. Perhaps some of these same people had written to him a month ago, pleading to have a loved one restored to them by the new miracle of science. Now, confused by the haze of conflicting tales, of lies and partial truths, their earlier willingness turned to repulsion.

Harker wearily baled the letters up again, and left Litchfield to spend some time with his puzzled, unhappy family. They were accustomed to seeing their father's name in the headlines; it was old stuff to them. But this public hatred was new to them, and difficult for them to understand.

It was not too late, Harker thought. The forces of confusion could be put to rout; the dominion of death could at last have boundaries staked out.

But the public faith had to be regained. Some spectacular demonstration, some act of faith that would capture their imagination and end the sway of ignorance.

But what? How?

Harker had no answer. And the answer, when it came, arrived from an unexpected quarter.

CHAPTER NINETEEN

AT LITCHFIELD again, the next day, Harker was reading through a lab report, comprehending not very much of it, when a diffident knock sounded outside his door.

Probably Lurie with the papers, he thought. "Come in!"

A slim figure in ecclesiastical robes entered. Harker blinked and said, "I didn't expect to see *you* here, Father Carteret."

"Nor I. But I thought I would make the trip."

"Sit down," Harker urged. "What's on your mind?"

"Jim, I asked you to come to me if you ever had any troubles. You have them now. I thought I'd stop over and find out if I could be of any help."

Harker felt faintly irritated. He liked the priest, but he felt no desire for unasked advice. "Father, if you've come to tell me I ought to quit this outfit while I still have my soul, forget it."

"The time for telling you that is past."

Harker stared at the priest coolly. "Then why are you here?"

"To help you. I have a suggestion for you—a rather strange one. But first: let me tell you that the Church is reconsidering its stand."

"What?"

Carteret smiled gently. "The Church moves slowly; don't anticipate anything for the next several years. But I have it on good understanding that as soon as your technique is perfect—that is, as soon as you can restore body and mind every time—the Church will no longer withhold its approval from reanimation."

Harker chuckled. "I'd say that bet was pretty well coppered. The *if* there is a pretty big one."

"I know. But a necessary one. I'm praying for your success, Jim."

"You? But you warned me away from this thing!"

Carteret nodded. "You took the step, anyway. And perhaps I made an original error in judgment."

"Well, that's neither here nor there. Reanimation is going to be squashed by Congress anyway."

"What do you mean?"

"Simply that the defect in the process has aroused such public horror that Congress is afraid to legislate in our favor."

"And you don't expect to overcome that defect?"

"Not immediately. Another six months, maybe—but by that time it'll be too late."

Carteret steepled his long thin fingers reflectively. "You tell me, then, that your real problem is a failure of public relations. If you could sell your product to the people, Congress would follow along."

"In a word, that's it."

"I thought so."

"You said you had a suggestion to make," Harker reminded the priest.

"I did. It's an idea for capturing the stream of public opinion. I'm anxious to see your project succeed, Jim. It may sound strange, coming from my lips, but that's the truth. I suffered to reach this opinion."

"And what's your idea?"

An odd smile appeared on Carteret's thin face. "It's one that bears the test of time, Jim. Our Savior went meekly to the Cross, and on the third day he rose. It was an act that has captured the imaginations and hearts of men for two thousand years."

Harker frowned. "I don't quite see—"

He stopped. Abruptly the deeper meaning of the priest's words was borne in on him, and he stared at Carteret aghast, wondering. "Would *you* do something like that?" he asked.

"If I had faith in my cause," Carteret said. "Do you have faith in yours?"

Hesitantly Harker said, "I—think so."

"Therein lies the answer, Jim. Think about it a while. Don't rush yourself. I'll leave you now, and let you get used to the idea."

Alone, Harker stared through the office window at the dark, rain-streaked sky outside. Summer lightning crackled suddenly across the darkness; moments later thunder came rolling down from the hills.

A cold sweat came over him as he revolved Carteret's words in his mind: *Our Savior went meekly to the Cross, and on the third day he rose.*

Do I dare, he wondered?

It was, he knew without doubt, the act that would settle the fate of reanimation for good. With success would come triumph; failure for him unquestionably meant the downfall of the project.

Shall I risk it?

Do I dare?

He thought back over a life that had lasted forty-three years, a comfortable life, most of it spent in easy circumstances as he rose through law school to political prominence, then down the other side of the curvex into a short-lived obscurity. He had never known real danger in his life. There had been enemies, of course—political ones, who had worked his downfall. But that was a gentle kind of strife, a chess-game more than a pitched war.

This was different.

This was life or death, on the line—and for what? For a cause. He had never known a cause he might be willing to risk death for. Now that the risk presented itself, he wondered if he had the courage to submit to it.

Harker sat quietly for perhaps half an hour, thinking. Then he reached for the phone and dialed his home number. Lois answered. In a calm, level voice, he told her exactly what he was going to do.

She was silent for a moment; then she said simply, "Jim, why do you have to do this thing?"

How can I explain? he wondered. *How can I show her that a moment can come when you stand between life and death, and* the choice is entirely yours?

He said, "I think it's the only way, Lois. It'll prove to the world that reanimation can be trusted."

"But the awful risk, Jim—"

One chance out of six for idiocy, he thought bleakly. "I wouldn't do it if I thought it was risky, Lois. The whole point is that it *isn't* risky. You think I want to be a goddam martyr?"

"Sometimes I think you do, Jim," she said very quietly.

He chuckled harshly. "Well, maybe. But I know what I'm doing. It'll hammer home reanimation the way no amount of talking ever could."

After a long pause she said, "When—when would you do this thing?"

"I don't know. I'd have to discuss it with the others here first. And we'd need to arrange for proper publicity. Unless the whole world finds out about it, there's no sense doing it."

Forty-three years of life converging toward one moment of decision in a bare little room on a rain-soaked New Jersey hill, Harker thought. *And this is probably the weirdest motive for suicide in the history of the human species.*

Lois said, "Do you have that much faith in those men?"

"Yes. How can we expect the people to trust us, if we don't trust ourselves?"

"All right," she said. Her voice held undertones of quiet resignation. "I guess I ought to fight and cry and tell you not to do it, but I know you too well, Jim. Go ahead, if you think you have to do this thing. I—I guess you might as well have my permission, because I know you'll go ahead and do it anyway."

There was the hint of a crack in her voice. Harker smiled palely, thankful that the roughly-furnished office he had here did not have a visual pickup on the phone. He did not want her to see his face now, for he knew his face was that of a frightened man.

"Everything's going to be okay," he told her, and broke the contact.

It was still raining. He pulled a waterproof from the closet, slung it over his shoulders, and dashed across the clearing to Mart Raymond's office. The sky was dark, gray, bleak.

Raymond was working on records when Harker entered— proceeding mechanically, with the air of a man marking time. They were all marking time, waiting for the Congressional decision.

Harker said, "Mart, tell me something."

"Go ahead."

"How close are you to ironing out the business of loss of mind?"

Raymond shrugged. "I told you. A month's more work, maybe. A little less, if we're lucky."

Nodding, Harker said quietly, "Look here, Mart: I'm going to pull a Mitchison."

"Huh?"

"I mean, I'm going to jump the gun and announce that you've *already* straightened things up, and that from now on reanimation will work every time, provided no vital organs are damaged and that decay hasn't begun."

"What's the point of doing that? It isn't so."

"It *will* be so, sooner or later. Sooner, I hope. But I have an idea for a sort of publicity stunt, a grandstand play that should clinch the idea of reanimation's safety. Or else finish us altogether."

Harker walked to the window and stared out. Raymond said, "Jim, what the dickens are you talking about?"

Harker turned sharply. "Very simple. We're going to give a public demonstration of reanimation, sometime in the next couple of days. In order to prove the absolute safety of the process, I'm going to allow you to kill me under laboratory conditions and bring me back to life."

"Are you crazy?"

"Desperate. It's not quite the same thing."

"But suppose it doesn't work? What if—you remember how Thurman looked?"

"I do. I'll take my chances. If it doesn't work, then we're not much worse off than we are now." Harker turned again and stared out the window.

The rain had stopped; the sun was out. A rainbow arched proudly across the low hills, a many-colored ribbon stretching out to the horizon.

Harker drafted two press releases during the afternoon, and by nightfall they had reached print in the newspapers. Both caused sensations.

At seven that evening he tuned in the video at one of the laboratory dorm lounges, and heard a news commentator say, *"Exciting news from the Beller Research Laboratories of New Jersey today. The last technical flaw in the reanimation process has been licked, according to lab director Martin Raymond. The Beller Lab statement declared that from now on reanimation will be virtually foolproof, with no risk of possible insanity as before.*

"As if to drive home the importance of this new development, a simultaneous statement comes from James Harker, who of course is closely affiliated with the reanimation researchers. Harker let it be known this afternoon that he is suffering from a rare heart ailment, one which has been hitherto impossible to correct because the necessary surgery cannot be performed on a living man.

"Harker declared that he is so confident of the Beller technique's results that he will submit to the operation, necessitating temporary 'death,' and then will be reanimated at the conclusion of the operation."

Harker listened soberly to this largely fictitious news broadcast. He *had* no heart ailment; the last technical flaw had *not* been eliminated.

But never mind, he thought. The essential fact was the last—the reanimation. The rest was camouflage.

One chance out of six. He felt oddly calm about his decision. At last he had found a cause in which he had faith, and he did not expect to be let down.

CHAPTER TWENTY

THERE SEEMED to be a sheath of fog wrapped around him, or perhaps it was a section of cloud. White, soft, without substance, it buoyed him up. He did not open his eyes. He did not need to; the images he saw against the inner surfaces of his eyelids far eclipsed any the mundane world might hold.

Harker saw glowing masses of color, a sky of red bordered with turquoise, clouds of gold, smaller flecks of chocolate and ultramarine. He heard the distant rumble of voices, or was it thunder?

He remembered things.

He remembered someone (Mart Raymond?) looking down at him, lips drawn, eyes ringed with shadows, saying, "Jim, do you really want to go through with this thing?"

He remembered Lurie, looking awkward and ungainly. Poor Lurie. Lurie had got him into this whole mess in the beginning, hadn't he?

Lois had been there too, her face a blank emotionless mask. And there had been others—the four senators, Vorys, Brewster, Dixon, Westmore. The four horsemen of the Apocalypse. The ghostly riders of death.

Reporters? Video men? Yes, there had been quite a crowd. Harker stirred gently in the cradling mass of fog that held him. He had never been so comfortable in his life as now, lying in what seemed to be free fall, no weight on him, no conflicts meshing in his tired brain, nothing to do but relax and dream of yesterday.

There's Vogel, he thought. The surgeon, wielding his tools. Complex dark many-tendrilled machine looming up over me. Yes.

Vogel is whispering something to someone now; I can't catch it.

They lower something over my face. Sweet, too sweet; I breathe deeply.

I sleep. Time passes.

Harker floated gently, guiding himself with his arms, travelling lightly down a river of radiant brightness. No weight. No sensations. Only the endless lovely bath of color, and the distant rumble of thunder.

This is heaven, he thought, pleasantly. Not a bad place at all.

Timeless, voiceless, airless, lifeless. A kaleidoscope of blues and violets overhead. I am pure energy, he thought, unfettered by the ties of flesh.

This is the kingdom of death. There was the odor of lilies somewhere, a cool sweet white smell. I, James Harker being of sound mind—

A golden flame, child-sized, soared near him in the nothingless. It's Eva, he thought. Hello, Eva. Don't you remember your dad?

The golden flame swooped laughingly past him and was gone. Harker felt a momentary pang, but it too passed on; this was heaven, where there was no sadness.

The rumble of thunder grew louder.

(Voices?)

(Here, Harker thought?)

I have given myself voluntarily into the hands of death, he announced silently. Of my own free will did I consent to have the sanctity of my body violated and the free passage of air through my nostrils interfered with. And with the stoppage of the heart came death.

Frowning, he tried to remember more. Recollection grew dim, though, as if he were glimpsing the world he had left behind through a series of warped mirrors. He could see faintly into the world of living people, but the surface was oddly glazed, unreal.

Again came thunder, louder, closer.

Someone said, "I think he's waking up."

Harker remained perfectly still, struggling to penetrate the meaning of those words. *I think he's waking up.*

Waking up? From death?

"He's definitely coming out of it."

Yes, Harker thought, I'm waking up. Returning to the blurred world I left behind so long ago.

He was still bound to that world. It would not release its grip on him. It wanted him, was calling him.

Recalled to life!

With a sudden convulsive moan and whimper, Harker woke.

His mouth tasted cottony, and at first his eyes would not focus. Gradually the world took shape about him. He saw three faces hovering above the bed in which he lay; behind them were green electroluminescent hospital walls, broken by a window through which warm summer sunshine streamed in. Yes, he thought. Recalled to life. *Yea, though I walk through the valley of the shadow of death, I will fear no evil...*

He matched faces with identities. The squarish face badly in need of a shave—which belonged to Mart Raymond. The oval one, ringed by blonde hair shading into gray—that face belonged to Lois. And the other, the lean ascetic rectangle of a face, that was owned by Father Carteret.

Harker said, "I guess it worked. Where am I?" His voice was hoarse and rusty-sounding, like a musical instrument long neglected.

Mart Raymond said, "It worked beautifully. You're in Newark General Hospital. You've been here in anesthetic coma for two weeks. Ever since the operation."

Two weeks, Harker thought. It seemed like two minutes ago that Vogel had lowered the anesthesia cone over his face.

"How—did things work out?" he asked.

It was the priest who spoke. "Perfectly, Jim. You're a national hero."

He glanced at Lois, who bent over Harker and clutched his hand. Hers seemed cold, Harker thought.

They left him after a while, and he lay back in the bed, thinking that it was good to be alive again. The sunlight was bright and warm in the room; it should be nearly August, he thought.

Some time later he was fed, and some time after that a nurse appeared bearing a thick stack of newspapers. "The *Times* since your operation, Mr. Harker. Your wife thought you'd like to see them."

He thanked her and reached hungrily for the topmost paper. It was today's, the latest edition. The banner headline was, HARKER OUT OF COMA, and they had the picture of him that had been used for his campaign posters back in 2028.

He leafed back...July 30, July 29, July 28...

At the bottom of the heap was the July 16 paper, with the account of his sensational submission to death. They described the event in detail: how, cheerful to the last, he had been wheeled into the operating room, anesthetized, killed. The operating room had then been cleared of all but the surgeons, who proceeded with the cardiac operation according to the papers. When the "operation" had been "successfully concluded," an hour later, the observers were called back. Thirty-eight people had watched his untroubled return to life.

He thumbed on through the papers. The suit of Klaus and Mitchison against Beller Laboratories had been thrown out of court on the 18th. The next day, the F.B.I. had repeated its earlier statement exonerating the labs of any guilt in the matter of the death of Wayne Janson, and this time there was no further statement from Jonathan Bryant.

There were statements from various ranking government officials, though. They unanimously favored setting up a federal research grant project for studying further applications of reanimation.

The nurse appeared and said, "Mr. Raymond would like to see you, sir."

"Send him in."

Raymond grinned and remarked, "You look like you've been getting up to date."

"I have been. Things look pretty good, don't they?"

"They look tremendous," Raymond said. "Dixon phoned from Washington to say that Vorys and Brewster have been won over. The Committee's recommending a multi-million dollar federal grant to us for continuing research."

"Great! Now I suppose you can lick the business of insanity, Mart."

Raymond grinned cheerfully again. "Didn't I tell you? We broke through that wall about four days ago. It's a matter of insulating the hormone feed lines. Yours was the last risky reanimation."

Before Harker could reply, the phone by the side of his bed chimed briefly. He picked it up and heard a voice say, "Albany calling for Mr. James Harker."

"That's me," Harker said.

"Go ahead, Albany."

There was a pause; then a new voice said, "Jim? Leo Winstead here. Just heard the news. Everything all right?"

"Couldn't be okayer, Leo."

Winstead coughed. "Jim, maybe this is too soon to ask you to think about returning to work, but I want to put a proposition to you."

"What kind?"

"New York State is short one senator right now. I have to appoint somebody to replace Thurman, I guess. And it seemed to me that *you*— "

Harker nearly let the phone drop. When he had recovered his poise he said, "I'm still a sick man, Leo. Don't shock me like that."

"Sorry if I did. But it's a job I think you're equipped to handle. Interested?"

"I sort of think I am," Harker said wryly.

When he had finished talking to Winstead, he hung up the phone and looked at Mart Raymond. "That was Governor Winstead. He's naming me to the Senate to fill the rest of Thurman's term."

"Wonderful!"

"I suppose it is," Harker admitted.

He sent for Lois and told her about it, and she wept a little, partly for joy and partly, he suspected, because she did not want him to take on any new responsibilities.

Harker flicked the tears away. He stretched gently, mindful of his sutures.

Lois said, "It's all finished, isn't it? The struggling and the conniving, the plotting and scheming? Everything's going to be all right now."

He smiled at her. He was thinking that the stream of events could have come out much worse. He had taken a desperate gamble, and he and humanity both were that much the richer for it.

But the world as he had known it for forty-odd years was dead, and would not return to life. This was a new era—an era in which the darkest fact of existence, death, no longer loomed high over man.

Staggering tasks awaited mankind now. A new code of laws was needed, a new ethical system. The first chapter had closed, but the rest of the book remained to be written.

He squeezed her hand tightly. "No, Lois. It *isn't* all finished. The hardest part of the job is just beginning. But everything's going to be all right, now. Yes. Everything's going to be all right."

THE END

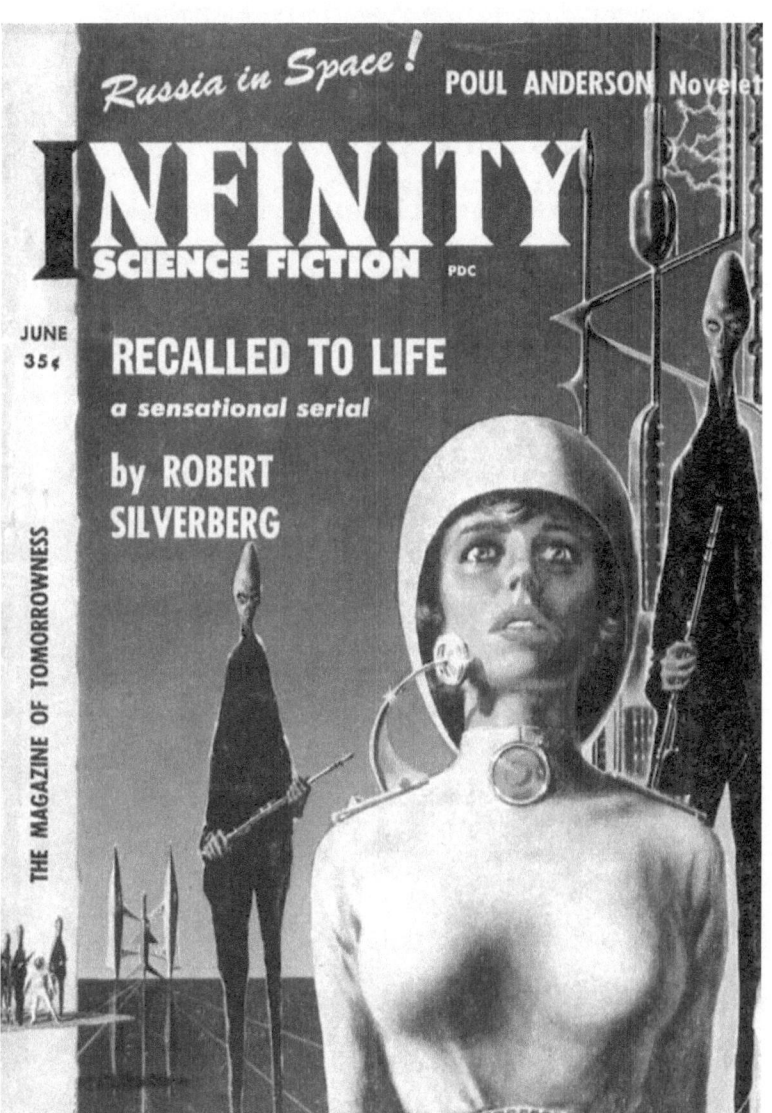

"Recalled to Life," Original Infinity Science Fiction *Cover*

If you've enjoyed this book, you will not want to miss these terrific titles...

ARMCHAIR SCI-FI & HORROR DOUBLE NOVELS, $12.95 each

D-1   **THE GALAXY RAIDERS** by William P. McGivern
         SPACE STATION #1 by Frank Belknap Long

D-2   **THE PROGRAMMED PEOPLE** by Jack Sharkey
         SLAVES OF THE CRYSTAL BRAIN by William Carter Sawtelle

D-3   **YOU'RE ALL ALONE** by Fritz Leiber
         THE LIQUID MAN by Bernard C. Gilford

D-4   **CITADEL OF THE STAR LORDS** by Edmond Hamilton
         VOYAGE TO ETERNITY by Milton Lesser

D-5   **IRON MEN OF VENUS** by Don Wilcox
         THE MAN WITH ABSOLUTE MOTION by Noel Loomis

D-6   **WHO SOWS THE WIND...** by Rog Phillips
         THE PUZZLE PLANET by Robert A. W. Lowndes

D-7   **PLANET OF DREAD** by Murray Leinster
         TWICE UPON A TIME by Charles L. Fontenay

D-8   **THE TERROR OUT OF SPACE** by Dwight V. Swain
         QUEST OF THE GOLDEN APE by Ivar Jorgensen and Adam Chase

D-9   **SECRET OF MARRACOTT DEEP** by Henry Slesar
         PAWN OF THE BLACK FLEET by Mark Clifton.

D-10 **BEYOND THE RINGS OF SATURN** by Robert Moore Williams
         A MAN OBSESSED by Alan E. Nourse

ARMCHAIR SCIENCE FICTION CLASSICS, $12.95 each

C-1   **THE GREEN MAN**
         by Harold M. Sherman

C-2   **A TRACE OF MEMORY**
         By Keith Laumer

C-3   **INTO PLUTONIAN DEPTHS**
         by Stanton A. Coblentz

ARMCHAIR MASTERS OF SCIENCE FICTION SERIES, $16.95 each

M-1   **MASTERS OF SCIENCE FICTION, Vol. One**
         Bryce Walton: "Dark of the Moon" and other tales

M-2   **MASTERS OF SCIENCE FICTION, Vol. Two**
         Jerome Bixby: "One Way Street" and other tales